GAYLE WILSON

In Plain Sight

HARLEQUIN®

TORONTO • NEW YORK • LONDON
AMSTERDAM • PARIS • SYDNEY • HAMBURG
STOCKHOLM • ATHENS • TOKYO • MILAN • MADRID
PRAGUE • WARSAW • BUDAPEST • AUCKLAND

HARLEQUIN BOOKS
225 Duncan Mill Road, Don Mills,
Ontario, Canada M3B 3K9

ISBN 0-373-83620-1

IN PLAIN SIGHT

"I lied to Lisa."

It was so unexpected that Robin wasn't sure what to ask her son next. She glanced questioningly at Matt, and he took up the challenge.

"You lied about something in the woods?"

"I told her I had to pee, but I didn't."

Robin's apprehension that Taylor might somehow know more about his baby-sitter's disappearance was beginning to fade. Apparently this was something that had happened earlier.

In his mind, the two events had gotten tangled together. He had lied to Lisa, and then she'd disappeared. With a seven-year-old's sense of morality, he believed that the wrong he'd done had been responsible for the girl's disappearance. Cause and effect.

"You told her you had to pee," Matt said, "and then what happened?"

"She let me go."

"Into the woods," Matt said, his voice very soft. "And you saw something there, didn't you? You saw something in those woods...."

Also by Gayle Wilson

Single Titles

Keeping Watch
"Heart of the Night"

The Wedding Chase
"Prisoner of the Tower"

Men of Mystery

Where Memories Lie
"Echoes in the Dark"

And recent Harlequin Intrigue titles

Under Surveillance

Rocky Mountain Maverick

Don't miss *Sight Unseen,*
coming in July 2004.

To Katelyn, the other writer in our family.
I can't wait to read your first book!

PROLOGUE

"I HAVE to pee."

He didn't. Not really. At least not bad enough that he couldn't wait, but since they had changed the clocks, it was dark when his mother got home. Too late to go outside, she always said. It was almost dark now, with the clouds and the rain.

"When we get to your house."

Lisa walked him to and from school everyday and then stayed until his mom got home. Sometimes she was impatient, like today. Most of the time she was okay. She didn't ask him a million questions like grown-ups did.

Where did he go to school? What grade was he in? How did he get so tall? They didn't even listen to the answers. They just asked that stuff because they didn't know what to say to kids. Lisa didn't try to talk to him at all.

"I have to go *now*."

Once, when he really did have to pee, Lisa had let him run into the woods that bordered the path everybody used as a shortcut between the school and their neighborhood. He wasn't sure Lisa would let him do that now because so many of the leaves were off the trees and bushes, but he figured it was worth a try.

"I can't wait," he added, clutching the front of his jeans with both hands and hunching his shoulders. He could tell by her face that she was thinking about it.

"You sure?" she asked, her eyes jumping to the end of the path. They had to walk three more blocks after they came out of the woods.

He nodded real quick as soon as she looked back at him. Her mouth was tight, like when she got mad. He was afraid she was going to say no, and now, maybe because he'd been thinking about it, he really did have to pee.

"Okay. Okay." Her voice was as impatient as her face.

She put her fingers over his shoulder, pinching so tight he squirmed under the pressure. She used it to turn him in the direction of the trees.

"Two minutes," she ordered, "and then I'm gonna come in there and get you. It's Tuesday. I've got piano tonight and a ton of homework."

Taylor didn't give her time to change her mind. He pulled away from her hold and ducked between two of the nearly naked trees. He ran across blackened leaves, feeling them shift, slick and wet, under his sneakers.

As he went farther into the woods, he kept looking back, trying to decide how far he had to go before he would be hidden from anyone on the path. Farther than last time, when everything was thick and green.

As he ran, the urge to pee grew stronger. He could still see Lisa's red jacket when he glanced back, so he hurried on, going deeper and deeper into the darkness beneath the dripping trees.

Finally, unable to wait any longer even if someone might see him, he skidded to a stop. He looked back again toward the path. The splash of red was almost hidden by the trunks of the trees between them. He stepped behind the largest of them, fingers fumbling with the zipper of his jeans.

His hands shook with cold and anticipation. Suddenly the metal teeth of the zipper grabbed fabric, refusing to move up or down. Desperate now, he jerked the tab as hard as he could, pulling the teeth free of the denim, and then sliding it down.

His relief was so great he was barely able to keep from peeing until he could get his penis out of his briefs. He held its soft, limp warmth in his cold hand. So cold that, despite his sense of urgency, nothing happened.

He waited, eyes watering from the wind and his need. Then a small stream splattered onto the carpet of dead leaves, steaming as it hit the ground.

He took a breath, relieved. Even, for some strange reason, relieved he hadn't lied to Lisa. He really *had* had to pee, and he was now sure that he wouldn't have made it home.

As he finished, he looked up, still facing away from the path where she waited. And realized only then that he wasn't alone.

Three men were standing with their backs to him. They weren't talking. As quiet as it was out here in the woods he would have heard, even if they had been whispering.

They were looking at something on the ground. All of them were wearing coats. Not jackets, but the long, dark kind old men wore, so that he couldn't see what they were looking at. Not with the coats and the trees between them.

As he watched, one of them kicked at whatever was on the ground. A ball, he thought, before he realized how dumb that was. Whatever those men were doing out here, they weren't playing a game. The way they were standing was all wrong for that.

One of them stooped, dropping out of sight, although Taylor stretched upward, trying to follow the movement. After a few seconds, the man stood up again, holding something out to one of the others. It was almost as red as Lisa's jacket, the color bright between the gray trees and the black coats.

Taylor swallowed, afraid to even think what it might be. Something dead. An animal they'd killed. Or one they'd found. Maybe they were out here looking for their cat, and the dogs had killed it. Maybe—

"Hey!"

Lisa. He'd almost forgotten her. Forgotten that she was back on the path waiting for him. In a hurry to get home because she had piano tonight.

At the sound of her voice, the three men had turned, looking toward him. Except they weren't, he realized. Maybe they couldn't see him because he had chosen a spot where the bushes were thick so that nobody from school would see him standing out here in the woods peeing.

"What are you doing in there?" Lisa called again.

He could hear her coming toward him now. Crackling sounds. Like she was pushing branches aside or stepping on twigs. Or walking across leaves that hadn't been on the ground long enough to get rotten and soft.

He was terrified to move. Afraid to draw the men's attention to him. He wasn't sure why he was so afraid, but he was. He wanted to squat on the ground and pull the sides of his jacket over his head so they wouldn't find him.

Now they were moving too. He could hear them, making more noise than Lisa. Maybe because there were more of them. Maybe because they were beginning to run.

"You better come out of there right now," Lisa demanded, her voice shrill with anger, "or you're going to be in big trouble."

The words made him think about his mom. He wanted to see her. To be with her. To run into her arms and burrow his face against the warmth of her stomach.

In a second or two, the men would be here. And if they found him—

He didn't *know* what would happen if they found him, but suddenly he was even more frightened than he had been before. He turned and began to run toward Lisa, pushing his way through the underbrush. Something, a branch or a vine, hit him in the face, stinging across his cheek and one eye. He was too scared to worry about being careful, in spite of how bad that had hurt.

He was making too much noise, but he didn't care about that either now. He just wanted out of these woods. He wanted to be home. He wanted his mother.

"Taylor," Lisa yelled, drawing the first part of his name out like his mother sometimes did when he didn't answer her.

He cut toward the sound, breath wheezing in and out of his aching lungs. He could still hear the men crashing through the woods behind him.

Suddenly he could see Lisa, the red jacket bright against the growing darkness. He headed toward that spot of color, running as if his life depended on it.

Lisa had been coming toward him, easing her way through the tangled undergrowth. When she saw him, she stopped. Her lips pressed together, straight and hard and ugly.

"I swear I'm gonna tell your mother," she began, but he didn't give her a chance to finish.

"Run," he said, gasping the word.

He grabbed her hand, trying to drag her toward the path. She didn't budge, pulling her fingers from his instead.

"Zip your pants," she ordered. "You're such a baby." And then, almost in the same breath, "What were you doing in there so long? Number two?"

"There were some men," he said, pulling at her jacket as his eyes searched the darkness in the heart of the woods.

"What kind of men?"

"I don't know. They were doing something. Something bad."

He couldn't tell her any more than that about what he'd seen. He didn't know any more. Just that it was something bad. He didn't even want to think about the red thing.

Her eyes left his face, focusing on the direction from which he'd come. "Bad?" she repeated. Some of the disbelief he'd heard in her tone before had disappeared.

"Come on," he begged, tugging at her coat.

He could hear them. At least he thought he could. They had been near enough when he'd started to run that it seemed they should be here by now.

"You're making that up," Lisa accused, her eyes narrowed as she turned to face him again. "You're trying to scare me so I won't tell your mom you ran off."

"No, I'm not. Honest I'm not," he pleaded. "Come on."

This was all his fault. If he hadn't told Lisa he had to pee...

"Please, Lisa," he begged. "Let's go home. You've got piano. Remember?"

Something—his panic or the reminder of her lesson—moved her. She took one last look toward the woods. His eyes followed, sweeping the darkening spaces between the trees where he had last seen the three men.

There was nothing there now.

"Come on," Lisa said, putting her hand on his shoulder again. She turned him back toward the path. Impatient once more, like she had been the one who was in a hurry to leave.

Without arguing, he ran ahead of her. The woods were

less dense here, so that he didn't have to push through vines and bushes.

After only a couple of minutes, he reached the path. It was as deserted as it had been when he'd left Lisa waiting here for him. As soon as he'd reached it, he wheeled to watch her come out of the woods.

"You made all of that up, didn't you?" she demanded.

The fear had not completely disappeared from her face, but out here in the open, the terror he had felt had begun to fade—like a nightmare that doesn't seem so scary when you turn on the light.

"No, I didn't. I promise they were there. Cross my heart."

Even as he denied her accusation, he was beginning to wonder if he *had* imagined it. At least the red part. The part that had really scared him.

They had probably been looking for their pet, he told himself again. Maybe they hadn't understood what Lisa was shouting. Maybe they had thought she needed help. Just because they'd begun to run toward her didn't mean anything bad was going to happen.

He didn't let himself think about why they had disappeared. He was just glad they were gone. Glad to be heading toward home and his mom.

He glanced up at the lowering skies, trying to figure out what time it was so he would know how long until she'd be home. And only when he reached the end of the path and saw the first house did the ache in his chest begin to go away.

CHAPTER ONE

"I DECIDED it didn't make much sense going in for only a couple of hours on Friday. So I'm going to take the rest of the day off and make it a long weekend. Any excuse, you know."

Robin Holt pressed her cell phone between her ear and shoulder as she retrieved the lasagna from the microwave. Her friend and co-worker Alexandra Fisher unerringly timed her calls at the most inopportune moments. It was a gift.

"I don't blame you," she said. "Enjoy. Hate to rush, but we're just about to sit down to dinner here."

As she talked, she carried the lasagna to the table, leaning across to slide the plastic container into its center. A familiar twinge of guilt reared its ugly head, but she ignored it. Cooking from scratch was reserved for weekends and holidays. During the work-week, there were already too few hours in the day.

"I won't keep you then," Alex said. "Just check with Carl about the stuff for Hamilton. See if it's still a go."

Robin shifted the phone to her other shoulder, at the same time opening the refrigerator and visually searching the bottles of dressing lined up on the bottom shelf of the door. She got the phone back to her ear in time to hear part of Alex's next sentence.

"...a necessary evil these days."

Robin had no idea what she was talking about. Maybe the yearly gynecological exam Alex had scheduled for tomorrow.

"I guess," she said.

She reached down and selected a bottle of blue cheese and one of ranch, shifting the first to her right hand before she picked up the second. As she closed the door with her hip, she realized Taylor was standing in the doorway.

"Have to go," she said to Alex. "The food's getting cold."

She crossed to the table and set down the bottles of dressing. When she turned around, she motioned Taylor to take his place.

"Don't forget to ask," Alex prodded. "I'll call you tomorrow night for an update."

"I won't forget," Robin promised.

She turned toward the counter, intending to retrieve the two bowls of pre-mixed salad she'd fixed while the lasagna was heating. As she passed by the oven she stooped to peer inside at the rolls.

"Have a good weekend," Alex commanded.

"See you Monday."

Without giving her friend a chance to respond and prolong the conversation, Robin punched the off button, cutting the connection. She laid the phone on the counter before she picked up the salad. She would come back for the freezer rolls, still unappetizingly pale, after she'd spooned up the lasagna. You would think that after years of doing this she could manage to get everything ready at the same time.

"Alex?" Taylor asked, taking a sip of his milk.

"Who else?"

She set one salad bowl to his right and the other at her

place setting. Still standing, she dipped a spoonful of lasagna onto his plate and then went back to look through the glass of the oven door again. The rolls were finally beginning to brown on top.

"You have a good day?" she asked as she waited.

The delay before he answered was long enough that she turned her head, considering her son. Despite the fact that she hadn't sat down yet, he had already dug his fork into the lasagna on his plate. As she watched, he raised it, still empty, and then poked the tines into the noodles again.

"It was okay," he said.

Mother instinct kicked in, responding to his tone or maybe to the lack of information. "Just okay?"

"Uh-huh."

"Anything happen I should know about?"

"Uh-uh."

"You sure?"

"I'm *sure.*" Slightly defensive.

Filing her unease under unfinished business, she turned off the oven and used a pot holder to remove the baking sheet. She set it on the top of the stove and gingerly lifted a couple of the hot rolls off, dropping them onto the saucer she'd set out earlier.

"What did Alex want?" Taylor asked.

"She's taking tomorrow off," Robin said. "She wanted me to check on one of her accounts."

He poked at the noodles again as she laid a roll on the side of his plate. He didn't look up, not even when she took her place across the table. She had already opened her mouth, deciding that something was definitely going on, when the phone rang again.

Taylor's eyes lifted to hers. Neither of them said anything, nor did they move until the phone rang a second time. Putting her napkin beside her plate, Robin rose to answer it.

Damn it, Alex, she thought as she crossed to the counter where she'd laid the cell.

"Hello."

"Hi, Robin," said the voice at the other end. It was familiar, but she couldn't quite place it. Not until the caller added a couple of identifiers. "Pam Evans. Lisa's mom. I was wondering if she's still there."

"Lisa? No, she's not, Pam. Sorry."

The teenager usually had her coat on by the time Robin got the front door unlocked. She never hung around longer than she was paid to. And of course, Robin didn't expect her to.

She knew the girl had an active social life from the busy signals she'd gotten the few times she'd tried to call home during the hours Lisa watched Taylor. As active a social life as a fourteen-year-old girl could manage in this small, conservative community, she amended.

"Well, she's not home yet," Pam explained, "and we're about to start dinner. It's not like her to be late."

Robin glanced at the clock, trying to control her own sense of alarm. She had been held up at work today, but Lisa had left as soon as she'd arrived. And that had been at least forty-five minutes ago. Certainly long enough for Lisa to walk the short distance to her house, only a few streets over.

"I don't know what to tell you, Pam," she said carefully. "Except that she isn't here. She left maybe…thirty minutes ago."

A small fudge factor. After all, she couldn't be positive of the time. Maybe Lisa had stopped by a friend's house. Or maybe her mom had gotten confused about the day of one of her many extracurricular activities. Robin had trouble keeping them straight. She always had to ask Taylor for the days Lisa had to be out of the house by five.

With that thought, she half turned so that she could see the table. Taylor was making no pretense of eating. Instead, he was openly listening to her conversation. When she realized that, she turned her back to him, unconsciously shielding him, although he could hear only one side of it.

"I can't understand why she's late," Mrs. Evans said again.

The anxiety was clearer now than it had been in the almost cheery question with which the other woman had begun the call. Of course, there was nothing more terrifying than realizing you don't know where your child is. Robin had had that sick, sinking feeling on occasion, if only for a second or two.

Every mother has. Losing sight of your child in a crowded store or in a park. At the ball field. Until your searching eyes have located the familiar shape of his head, every horror story of abduction or accident races through your brain.

"I'm sure she'll be there soon," Robin said comfortingly. "Maybe she had a music lesson. A change in the days or something."

She didn't say "something you've forgotten," but it was implied. Easy enough to do with all the things kids were involved in these days.

"No, there was nothing like that. We have a calendar. I would have put it down. Or Lisa would have," Pam Evans said, her voiced becoming slightly strident. "She's very good about that. Very organized."

"I'm sure there's nothing to worry about," Robin said

again. She wasn't sure, of course, but what else could she say?

"Would you ask Taylor if Lisa said anything about an errand? Anything at all about not coming straight home today?"

"Of course."

She put her hand over the mouthpiece and turned to face her son. His eyes were fastened on her face. The pupils seemed dilated, but maybe that was because she hadn't turned on the light over the table, and it was already pitch-black outside. Or maybe...

"This is Lisa's mom," Robin said, trying to figure out how to word the question to elicit the information she needed and yet not alarm Taylor. "Did Lisa say anything to you about not going straight home?"

For a couple of seconds there was no response, and then Taylor shook his head, his eyes holding hers.

"Nothing, Taylor? Are you sure? Maybe she said something about some kind of lesson or going to visit a friend?"

Again the only answer was a small negative movement of his head. She debated rephrasing the question, but decided that wouldn't really serve any purpose. She had already removed her hand from the mouthpiece in preparation for relaying his lack of information, when Taylor spoke.

"Lisa's not home?"

"Not yet. Can you think of *any* reason she might be late? Her mom's a little worried."

Despite the dimness on that side of the room, she could see him swallow, the movement strong enough to be visible down the length of his throat. His only response was again a side-to-side motion of his head. She waited a moment, but this time Taylor's eyes fell, his fork digging into the cooling mound of lasagna on his plate.

"Taylor can't remember Lisa saying anything about being late. If he thinks of something later on, I'll call you."

"And she left there thirty minutes ago, you say?"

Robin could hear another voice in the background. Clearly masculine. Probably Lisa's dad.

"Maybe a little longer than that now," Robin said.

It was time for the absolute truth. She was sorry she had tried to protect Lisa. After all, it could easily be as much as an hour since the teenager had said goodbye, going out the front door almost as Robin entered.

"Longer?" Pam's anxiety was beginning to be edged with panic.

"I'm trying to think when I got home. Lisa left as soon as I arrived. Probably around...five-twenty or so."

It was a quarter after six according to the clock on the stove. Fifty-five minutes to travel a couple of blocks. Robin's stomach had begun to knot.

"Oh, God," Pam said, giving up any pretense of calmness. "Something's happened to her. I know it has."

"I know that seems like a long time, but—"

The click of the connection being broken put an end to her meaningless platitude. Just as well, Robin decided, punching the off button and laying the phone down on the counter.

An hour was a damned long time for a teenage girl without a car to be late getting home. She would be just as concerned as the Evans were.

She turned and realized Taylor was watching her again. And she didn't have a clue what to say to him.

"You think something bad happened to Lisa?" he asked.

"I think Lisa had something to do this afternoon that she

forgot to tell her mom about,'' Robin said. ''A piano lesson or something.''

''That's Tuesday,'' Taylor said. ''Piano's on Tuesday.''

''Then skating or gymnastics. Lisa's always got something going on. You know that.''

''What if something's happened to her?''

''What's going to happen to Lisa between here and her house?'' she asked.

Taylor had always had an overactive imagination. She had to be careful what he watched on television and which movies she took him to see. Things other kids ate up could give him nightmares.

Too sensitive for his own good, she acknowledged, pushing from her mind Alex's unwanted advice that a masculine presence in his life might toughen her son up.

She didn't want him tough. There was nothing wrong with a little boy who was both emotional and creative.

''But if her mom can't find her—''

Taylor's voice was touched with the same panic she had heard in Pam's. Robin broke in before it could build.

''I told you. This is just a lack of communications. Lisa forgot to let her mom know about something she had to do this afternoon.''

As she talked, Robin crossed the room to take her place once more at the table. She put her napkin in her lap and looked down on the lump of cold, unappetizing pasta and meat sauce on her plate.

''You promise?'' Taylor said.

She looked up and realized that in spite of her attempts to reassure him, something of her own unease must have communicated itself to him. His eyes were wide and dark in a too-pale face.

''Nothing bad has happened to Lisa,'' she said, forcing

her voice to a calm confidence. ''I'll bet we won't even finish supper before her mom calls back to say she's home.''

There was no visible lessening of his anxiety. She supposed the days were gone when she could say, ''Everything will be all right,'' and have Taylor accept it as true simply because she'd said it.

Never again would she have the power to completely allay his fears about the world, possibly because they echoed her own. All of which were based on an unwanted knowledge of its evil.

''So as far as you know, this...'' Matt Ridge looked down at the spiral notebook he held in his hands, searching for the name of the woman for whom Lisa Evans babysat. ''This Mrs. Holt was the last person who saw Lisa today?''

''*Ms.* Holt,'' Pam Evans corrected, her reddened eyes on his penciled notes. She sniffed, holding her husband's handkerchief to her nose as she did. ''Between you and me, I don't think there ever was a Mr. Holt.''

Maybe she was trying to make some kind of moral judgment, but the only thing that information meant to Matt was that there was one less person to question. One less story to check out.

And one less suspect, he supposed, if Lisa Evans didn't turn up safe and sound pretty soon. Of course, calling Robin Holt a suspect was a stretch, especially at this point. He had heard of fathers who molested their kids' babysitters, but never of a mother.

''And according to Ms. Holt, that was around five-twenty.'' As he said it, he glanced at his watch. Quarter of seven. Less than two hours.

Lisa Evans's mother nodded, sniffing again. At least the

quiet, subdued crying was an improvement over the near hysteria he'd faced when he'd arrived.

The decision to call the police in situations like this was always difficult. It required an admission on the part of parents that their child was not just late, but missing. And then, no matter how long it had taken them to reach that decision, they wanted you to do something immediately. Call out the feds and the state troopers. Call out the National Guard and the army. *Find my kid, you bastards.*

No one could understand that feeling better than he could.

"You and Lisa on good terms?" he asked. "No argument or disagreement before she left this morning?"

He anticipated a reaction, but that was a question that had to be asked. Given her age and the crime rate around here, it was a far more likely scenario that the girl had run away than that something had happened to her.

"Her mother is Lisa's best friend," Dwight Evans said emphatically. "There was no argument between them this morning. If you're trying to imply that Lisa hasn't come home because she doesn't want to—"

"I'm just trying to cover all the bases, Mr. Evans. That's something we have to do."

"There was…" Pam Evans began and then stopped. "It wasn't really anything. Not an argument, certainly."

"A disagreement?" Matt was careful to keep his tone neutral.

The mother nodded, looking relieved at his choice of words. His own tension eased a little with the acknowledgement. At Lisa's age, runaways were far more common than abductees.

"It was very minor. She wanted to wear a skirt she'd picked up at the mall this past weekend. I thought it was…inappropriate for school. People—teachers—can be so judgmental. And Lisa will need lots of good recommendations for scholarships. The cost of college these days… But it wasn't in any way an argument," Pam finished, wiping her nose again.

There would be little profit in carrying that line of questioning any further. He'd secured the critical admission.

"You've called her friends, I suppose?"

"Everybody we can think of," the father said. "Nobody's seen her. Nobody's heard from her. And while you're wasting time asking all these ridiculous questions, anything could be happening to her."

Intended to spur Matt to action, the comment provoked a fresh burst of sobbing from Mrs. Evans.

"All the city cars are out searching for your daughter, Mr. Evans. We've notified the sheriff's department as well. And we've put out a statewide alert with her description and what she was wearing today. Until we have more specific information, that's about all we can do. Put people out there, looking and asking questions, and hope that somebody—law enforcement or a private citizen—spots her. Or that they saw something that will give us a lead as to where she is. In the meantime, we need to try to reconstruct exactly where she went after she left school this afternoon."

He didn't know how the hell they were going to do that if none of the girl's friends had seen her. There had been no report of anyone seeing a child approached, much less abducted. No report of anything at all to disturb the tranquil quiet of the fall afternoon.

According to what they knew right now, no one but the Holt woman and her son had seen Lisa Evans after school today. And they had only her word as to what time the girl had headed home. The logical place to start the search for Lisa Evans was with Robin Holt.

CHAPTER TWO

WHEN THE DOORBELL rang, Robin hit the off button on the remote. Between the phone calls and trying to get Taylor to eat something, she had missed the local news. Not that she expected anything about Lisa to be included in the broadcast.

Pam Evans hadn't called back, however, and she was getting anxious to hear something. Maybe Lisa or her mother would be standing outside, she thought as she hurried to the door.

Maybe they had come to offer an explanation for the girl's delay in getting home. Something silly. A forgotten appointment or some prior arrangement that had slipped a busy mother's mind. Miscommunication, just as she'd suggested to Taylor.

Anticipating that scenario, she didn't bother to ask who was outside. She slipped the chain out of its slot, turning the dead bolt at the same time. The door opened to reveal a man she didn't recognize standing at the top of the steps.

As he'd waited for her to answer the bell, he had obviously been looking out at the street. He turned at the sound of the door, reaching toward the inside breast pocket of his sports coat. Her pulse accelerated as if he had pulled a gun and pointed it at her.

It took only a moment for him to retrieve and open the leather case holding his badge. During those seconds a sickening flood of adrenaline roared through Robin's body. When she saw what he was holding out to her, her knees literally went weak with relief.

"Ms. Holt?" he asked.

A small furrow had formed between his brows. The brown eyes beneath them seemed concerned. And curious.

She nodded, fighting for control.

"You okay?"

"Lisa?" she asked, realizing only now how strongly she had bought into the fear she'd heard in Pam Evans's voice. "Something's happened to Lisa?"

"We don't know that, ma'am. All we know is that she hasn't made it home yet," he said after a small hesitation. His eyes were still evaluating her face. "We've got patrol cars out combing the area. I was hoping you could tell me something more than what we know now about what happened this afternoon. May I come in?"

She didn't want him in her house. She didn't want *this* inside. Touching her family. Touching Taylor.

Like a child, she wanted to hide from the possibility that something might have happened to her babysitter. And yet she knew she couldn't do that. She *wasn't* a child. She was a mother. Just like Pam Evans. If it were Taylor who was missing…

"Of course," Robin said, acknowledging that she had no choice. She stepped back, holding the door open for the policeman to enter.

MATT WASN'T SURE what he'd been expecting when he rang the Holts's doorbell. Someone like Pam Evans, perhaps, a veneer of sophistication overlying the reality of a small-town upbringing. Lisa Evans's mother had been fully made-up, every hair sprayed into place, despite the genuine terror in her eyes.

This woman was different. Younger, of course, her face devoid of makeup, other than mascara. Her lashes were probably as pale as the straight, shoulder-length blond hair.

She seemed more vulnerable somehow than the Evans woman. Robin Holt's child wasn't in danger, yet when she had opened the door there had been a matching terror in the clear blue eyes.

"You told Mrs. Evans that Lisa left here around five-twenty."

They had stopped in the middle of the living room, comfortably cluttered with books, magazines and toys. Despite its informality, the room was pleasant, the blend of colors warm and inviting. A throw was draped over the arm of the couch, as if someone curled up there to read or watch television.

"Give or take five minutes," Robin Holt agreed.

"Notice anything different about her today?"

"Different?"

"A sense of anticipation, maybe. As if she had plans to do something other than go home and start her homework."

Robin Holt shook her head. "Actually, I didn't pay all that much attention. She was in such a hurry to be off."

"In a hurry?"

There must have been a thread of excitement in his repetition, because she quickly corrected his impression that what she'd said might be significant.

"That wasn't anything out of the ordinary, believe me. Lisa always had half a dozen things to do after she left here. If I was late, there was this unspoken annoyance that I'd put her off schedule."

Matt examined the words, searching for any lingering

irritation with the teenager. What he'd heard in that quiet declaration, however, had sounded more like guilt.

"If you were late getting home from work, you mean?"

She nodded. "Sometimes it's hard to get away."

"Away from…?"

"Anderson Graphics."

"You do design?"

She nodded again. "The firm is so small that we all do a bit of everything from making coffee to answering the phone. Sometimes our hours extend past the official closing time."

"As they did today."

"Yes, but only briefly."

"And when you got here, Lisa didn't say anything that might lead you to believe that she had something more important than going home on her agenda?"

"Actually, I don't think Lisa said anything at all. I spoke to her, of course, but…" She shook her head as she thought back over those few minutes. "It was just another day. Like every day. I came home and Lisa left as soon as she could."

"I'd like to speak with your son, if you don't mind," Matt said. "He may remember something Lisa said before you arrived. Something she said on the way home, maybe."

"He doesn't. I asked him that when Pam called."

"I'll still need to talk to him, I'm afraid."

There was a slight hesitation.

"He's upstairs."

"You think he'd be more comfortable answering questions up there?"

It was obvious she didn't like the idea. The blue eyes clouded briefly before she made the offer he'd expected before.

"I'll bring him down, but he's getting ready for bed. He probably already has his pajamas on."

"That's fine."

Her reluctance to get her son was almost palpable. Either she was worried about the effect his questioning would have on the kid or she didn't want to leave Matt alone down here. Of course, she had seemed equally reluctant to invite him upstairs.

Left without any option she liked, Robin Holt crossed the room and disappeared into the hall. Matt listened to her footsteps fade as she climbed the stairs.

He used the opportunity to look around. Probably exactly what she'd feared.

On closer inspection, nothing about his initial impressions changed. The room was homey and comfortable. Unlike the house he'd just left, this one actually looked lived in.

There was a grouping of black-and-white photographs on the mantel, all of them in silver frames. All of them of the boy.

There were probably seven or eight, each taken at a different age. They weren't studio shots, at least he didn't think they were, although the quality of light and shadow and the composition seemed exceptional for an amateur.

He made a quick survey of the rest of the room. There were no other photographs. No diplomas or certificates. Nothing personal. Not even a bowling trophy.

Pam Evans might well be right about the absence of a father and husband. There was no evidence in this room of any masculine presence.

There were also a couple of framed watercolors, beach scenes, which to his uninformed eyes also seemed particularly well done. He was trying to decipher the scrawling signature at the bottom when he heard footsteps on the stairs.

Not bothering to move away from the paintings, he turned, watching Taylor Holt and his mother descend the last three or four steps, all he could see from his vantage point. She had her hand on the boy's back as if she were having to urge him on.

As he stepped off the bottom riser, the kid glanced toward the living room, meeting Matt's eyes before he quickly looked down. There had been time to verify what the photographs had already told him.

He looked like his mother. The same fine blond hair, although several shades lighter. Blue eyes. Just as there had been no visible evidence of his father in the house, there seemed to be none in those small, delicate features.

Robin led her son into the room, her arm around his shoulders, fingers smoothing up and down the sleeve of the plaid flannel bathrobe he wore. In comparison to the legs of the much-washed knit pajamas visible below its hem, the robe appeared new. Or, if not new, seldom worn.

"Taylor, this is—"

She stopped when she realized he hadn't told her his name.

"Detective Ridge," he supplied. "Matthew Ridge. Mallory Police Department."

The boy seemed to shrink back, his body pressed tightly against his mother's side.

"He needs to ask you some questions about what Lisa said on the way home today," Robin explained. Her hand had closed around his shoulder, clearly comforting.

Matt took a couple of steps forward so that he was standing directly in front of the boy. The blue eyes, more obviously a reflection of his mother's up close, rose as Matt approached. They were filled with the same apprehension he had already encountered twice tonight.

He wasn't going to get far with a kid who was this nervous. The reaction seemed out of proportion to what his mom claimed he knew about the babysitter's disappearance.

Matt stooped, balancing on the balls of his feet in front of the boy. The position put them eye-to-eye, evoking an unwanted sense of déjà vu.

It had been a long time since he had talked face-to-face to a child, he realized. An accident of circumstance? Or had he deliberately avoided putting himself into this position?

The youngster looked to be about seven. The realization that Josh would have been just about this same age surprised him. His son was forever frozen in his memory as a toddler, bright and inquisitive and outgoing. He wondered if he would have been as reticent at this age as this child appeared to be.

"You aren't in any trouble, Taylor. I want you to understand that up-front." As an added reassurance, he smiled, resisting the urge to touch the small hands that worried the knot on the belt of the robe. "I just need to find out if Lisa said anything that might help us figure out where she was going or what she was planning to do this afternoon before she went home."

The boy studied his face a moment as if trying to assess the truth of his statement. He glanced up at his mother, who nodded encouragingly, her hand again caressing up and down the flannel sleeve.

"Did Lisa mention somewhere she was going after she left here?" Matt prompted.

The question drew the child's gaze back to his face. He shook his head from side-to-side.

"I understand she went to music lessons and gymnastics practice and all kinds of things after she left your house every day. You know what was on tap for today?"

He mentally questioned the phraseology, wondering if the boy would know what was being asked. Before he could clarify what he wanted, however, the small blond head repeated the motion it had made before.

"Piano, maybe?"

"That's Tuesdays."

The response was soft, but it was vocal. A step in the right direction.

"Not today?"

Taylor shook his head again.

"So what's on Thursdays?"

"I don't think that was a regular day for anything."

"So she might have stopped off on the way home to visit a friend or something? If she didn't have anything else to do."

"Maybe," Taylor said.

"She say anything like that to you? Anything about going to see a friend?"

"No, sir."

"So what did the two of you talk about on the way home?"

The breath the boy took was deep enough to be audible. "Nothing."

"You didn't say one word to one another all the way home?" Matt deliberately let his amused skepticism show.

Another shake of the head.

"How about once you got here?"

A hesitation before the head moved back and forth again.

"She fix you something to eat?"

"I don't eat before supper."

"No snacks in the afternoon?"

"No, sir."

"How about Lisa?"

Head shake.

"And she didn't say one single word to you?"

"I think she told me to get started on my homework. She pretty much says that every day."

"You have a lot of homework today?"

"No, sir."

"Did Lisa?"

"I don't know."

"Did she call anybody?"

As hopeless as this seemed, his gut told him the kid knew something. He didn't feel as if the boy were lying. There was just this nagging sense that Taylor Holt wasn't telling him everything. That's why he kept asking questions, hoping he might hit on the one that would elicit that information.

"I don't think so. She could have."

"She do that a lot? Call friends from here?"

"Sometimes."

Robin Holt moved. It was subtle, no more than a shift of weight from one foot to the other perhaps, but it brought Matt's eyes up to her face.

"Several times when I've tried to call home to tell Lisa I was running late or to ask her to take something out of the freezer and defrost it in the microwave, the line would be busy. I think she talked on the phone a *lot*."

"Boyfriend?" he asked, getting to his feet.

"I don't know. I guess it's possible, but...she seems young for that."

Something else they'd have to verify, Matt thought. Fourteen certainly wasn't too young these days for an interest in the opposite sex.

"We'll probably need to check on who she talked to this afternoon," he warned.

"Check my phone records, you mean?"

"If you don't have any objection."

The pause before her agreement was infinitesimal, but it was definitely there. Maybe it would have been with anyone, faced with that loss of privacy, but Matt filed the information away.

"Of course not," she said.

"Good." He looked back down at the boy, whose eyes were still locked on his face. "If you think of anything that Lisa said, let your mom know, and she'll call me. Okay?"

"Okay."

Matt knew there was something else he ought to ask, but for the life of him he couldn't think what it might be.

"We'll need to search your yard, the garage and any outbuildings on your property. The officers will probably ask to look inside as well. We're going to be doing that all along the route Lisa would normally take home."

"Of course," Robin Holt said. She seemed faintly surprised by the request. "I'll be glad to do anything I can to help."

"Is Lisa all right?" the boy asked.

The caressing hand had stilled. Both of them were looking at Matt, two pair of identical eyes waiting for his assurance. He wished he could give it to them.

"We're all hoping that she is," he said. He extracted a card from the pocket of his jacket, holding it out to Robin. "If either of you thinks of anything else Lisa might have said or done this afternoon that was unusual—no matter how trivial it seems—give me a call.''

Robin nodded, reaching over her son's head to take the card. Her face reflected her relief that this was over.

''Thank you. I will.''

''Take care,'' he said. ''I can find my way out,'' he added, stepping around them and moving toward the door that led into the hall.

After he had closed the outside door behind him, Matt stood on the small front porch a moment, breathing in the freshness of the cold night air and thinking about the interview. The feeling that one of them knew something they hadn't told him was so strong he fought the urge to go back inside and demand an explanation.

He couldn't believe Robin Holt was involved in her babysitter's disappearance, but there had been enough wrong with the atmosphere in that house that he knew he was going to have to check her out. And those phone records she'd given him permission to look at would be a good place to begin.

CHAPTER THREE

"SLEEP TIGHT," Robin said, tucking the covers around Taylor's shoulders.

She bent, sweeping the hair off his forehead with her hand to drop a kiss in the center of it. As she straightened, the light from the bedside lamp illuminated the faint scratch she'd noticed on his temple a couple of nights ago. She touched it, feeling the slight roughness beneath the sensitive tips of her fingers. She bent again, placing another kiss on the injury.

As her lips made contact, Taylor turned his head, as if to avoid the gesture. Maybe he thought he was too old for her to kiss things and make them well. He hadn't been last summer, she remembered. Every bump and scrape had required her examination and the obligatory get-well kiss.

"You really think Lisa's okay?"

As it had revealed the scratch, the nearby light illuminated the faint furrowing of his brow. It reminded her of the detective's look of concern when she'd asked him the same thing.

In the familiar ritual of bedtime, she had almost managed to lose the sense of disaster she'd felt at seeing a policeman in her home. Now, with Taylor's question, the anxiety again began to churn in her stomach. If Lisa had turned up safe and sound at home, surely someone would have called her. They must know how anxious she was.

"I think Lisa and her mom got their wires crossed," she said, reaching over to turn off the bedside lamp. The fixture in the hall provided enough light that she could see Taylor's face, but not his expression. She couldn't be sure whether or not he believed her. "We'll probably laugh about it tomorrow."

Tomorrow. She realized that she would have to make some arrangements for getting Taylor to and from school.

She could always drop him off early. There was a breakfast program with an aide assigned to the lunchroom to watch the kids who turned up to eat. As for the afternoon…

As she thought about taking off work to pick him up, she remembered that tomorrow was Alex's appointment. As small as the staff at Anderson's was, they couldn't both take off.

Even if Alex wasn't willing to come in to the office, maybe she would pick Taylor up from school and stay with him until Robin could get here. She would feel more comfortable with that than with trying to arrange for someone else to walk with Taylor. She needed to know that her son wasn't going to disappear on the way home from school.

"Mom?"

"Uh-huh."

"What if…" The question trailed, but his eyes, lit by the faint glow from the light in the hall, again seemed too wide in the darkness.

"What if what?"

Her emotional exhaustion was evident in the impatient tone. And she hated hearing it. He'd been through a lot tonight. Even if he didn't understand everything that was going on, he had sense enough to be worried.

"What's wrong, baby?" This time, carefully, the tenor of the question reflected only concern for his anxiety.

"I just don't want anything to happen to Lisa."

Her throat ached in response to that tearfully expressed hope.

"I know," she whispered, leaning down to touch her lips to his forehead again. "I know you don't."

Small arms closed around her neck, almost throwing her off balance with the fierceness of their hold.

"Lie down with me," he pleaded. "Stay here until I go to sleep."

He was just a little boy. A little boy who had been questioned by the police about the disappearance of one of the few people in his small world.

Without breaking his hold, Robin eased down on top of the covers beside him, putting her arms around him and pulling him to her. He smelled of soap and baby shampoo. Toothpaste. The reassuringly normal scents of bedtime.

She felt the depth of his sigh as he snuggled as close against her as he could manage. They lay in the stillness, listening to the faint, familiar noises of the house and the neighborhood.

A car sped by on the street outside, its headlights reflecting on the ceiling as it passed. Far away a dog barked. And for the first time she became aware that at some point after she had opened the door to Detective Ridge, it had begun to rain. The sound was subtle, but soothing.

As she listened to it, she could feel the tension melt out of the small, fragrant body she held. She put her lips against Taylor's hair, and then rested her chin on top of his head.

She knew that if she closed her eyes, she would probably be asleep before he was. And that was something she couldn't afford.

There were things she needed to do to get them ready for tomorrow. A load of clothes to wash. The supper dishes were still on the table. And more importantly, she needed to call Alex to see if she would pick Taylor up.

Another car went by, traveling in the opposite direction from the first. Patrol cars? she wondered. Looking for Lisa? Searching the neighborhood for any sign of the girl who had disappeared practically from this house?

She took a breath, fighting the sting of tears. She closed her eyes against them, breathing a silent prayer for Lisa's safety.

And for theirs.

ROBIN WOKE with a start, unsure what had awakened her. Eyes wide in the darkness, she realized the rain that had lulled her to sleep had become a storm. Wind-driven sleet battered the house, clicking noisily against the windows.

She glanced to her right, trying to read the display on her bedside clock. Only when she realized it wasn't there did she remember that she was in Taylor's bed.

The reason she was took another few seconds to swim to the surface of her sleep-fogged brain. The remembrance of last evening's events rushed into her consciousness, causing a reactive tightening of her stomach muscles.

She eased her numbed arm from under Taylor's head, being careful not to wake him. She sat up on the side of the bed, waiting for the pins-and-needles sensation in her arm to fade. After a moment, she raised her other hand, using its spread fingers to tiredly push her hair away from her face.

Whatever time it was, she had slept long enough to be groggy and disoriented. And long enough that she probably wouldn't be able to fall asleep again when she reached her own room.

She stood, shivering and then crossing her arms over her

chest against the cold that seemed to have seeped into the house as they'd slept. She couldn't remember turning the thermostat down before she'd come upstairs. After all, she hadn't planned on falling asleep. There were too many things she had intended to take care of before she went to bed. And no matter how late it was, a couple of those still needed to be done.

Before she left his bedroom, she tucked the covers more closely around Taylor's shoulders, bending to touch her lips to his hair. Despite her inability to resist that kiss, her son didn't stir. At least one of them would get a good night's sleep.

She tiptoed out of the bedroom, feeling her way down the hall, her hand on the wall as guidance. The load of clothes and the dishes could wait, she decided as she started down the staircase, but she really needed to get in touch with Alex. She usually sat up pretty late, so if it wasn't after midnight, she would still be awake.

Robin's steps slowed as she approached the bottom of the staircase. It was definitely colder down here. Almost as if someone had left a door or a window open.

She mentally retraced her actions before she'd gone upstairs to tuck Taylor in. She was sure she hadn't touched the thermostat. Maybe Lisa had forgotten to turn up the heat when she and Taylor had arrived home from school today. But if that were the case, surely she would have noticed the bone-chilling cold before now.

Or maybe the house wasn't really all that cold. Maybe it only felt that way because she had just climbed out of a warm bed. Taylor generated his own sweet heat. Sleeping beside him was like being wrapped in an electric blanket.

As she stepped off the bottom step, she glanced to her right. The dining room was dark, as was the narrow utility pantry that ran between it and the kitchen. She could have sworn she'd left the light on back there. After all, she'd been planning to come back downstairs and put the dishes in the dishwasher.

She hesitated at the threshold of the dining room, reaching around the door frame for the switch. When her searching fingers found it, she felt a sense of relief out of proportion to the accomplishment. At least until she pushed it upward and nothing happened.

She flicked the switch down and then back up a couple of times before she admitted defeat. The power was out, obviously the result of the storm. That explained not only the unexpected darkness of the kitchen but also the cold.

She must have slept longer than she'd thought. Long enough for the house to become completely chilled?

She crossed her arms over her chest again, rubbing her hands up and down them. There were a few utility candles in the pantry, and there was supposed to be a box of matches in one of the drawers. Being able to put her hands on either of them in the dark might be another story. She wondered if other people really kept everything in its place, ready for any emergency.

She had already stepped forward when a flash of lightning illuminated the dining room. Her eyes automatically jumped to the double windows. Between the glass and the flare of light that lit the night sky loomed a shape.

Almost before the impression could register on her mind's eye, the lightning flickered away. Instinctively she retreated, her back pressed against the dining-room wall as she tried to rationalize what she'd seen.

Her eyes strained to find it again in the storm-shrouded darkness. When she couldn't, she tried to visualize the location of each foundation planting as well as the normal view through those windows.

Both confirmed what she had known in that first split second. None of the shrubs was tall enough to be visible through those windows. There was nothing out there to explain what she'd seen. A distinct solidness where there shouldn't be anything.

The rush of adrenaline sent her heart rate soaring. Not daring to breathe, she listened for any sound from outside those windows. The rain pounded steadily against the roof. Other than that, she heard nothing.

Pressed into the shadows, she waited a long time, hoping for another flash of lightning to confirm what she'd seen during the first. She didn't want to move, although her rational mind told her that whoever was out there couldn't possibly see inside.

Whoever was out there...

That was exactly what the silhouette she had seen in that flashbulb instant had looked like. Someone. Someone moving around outside her house in the middle of a thunderstorm.

The police?

She rejected the comforting explanation as soon as she thought of it. The cops wouldn't be wandering around out there in the dark. Not without notifying her first. Besides, they had already searched exhaustively before she and Taylor had gone to bed.

Then who the hell was outside? And why?

The obvious answer to the last was one she didn't want to think about. Whoever was outside her house was trying to find a way to get in.

That thought triggered another. A terrifying one.

She couldn't remember locking the front door. They seldom used the back entrance, so the night latch was always on. Detective Ridge had let himself out the front when he'd left, however. Concerned about the effect of his questioning on Taylor, Robin couldn't remember replacing the chain in its slot or turning the dead bolt before she'd taken her son up to bed.

The regular lock was the kind that could supposedly be opened with a credit card. That was why she had had the others installed.

As the possibilities ricocheted through her head, she began to ease toward the opening into the hall. Keeping her back against the wall, she slipped around the door frame. As soon as she was in the hallway itself, away from the dining-room windows, she ran to the front door.

Her fingers trembled so violently that she missed the slot on her first try. As soon as she managed to get the end of the chain into place, she slid her fingers down the smooth surface of the door, finding the dead bolt and turning it.

Mouth open, her breathing harsh enough to be audible, she sagged against the door, leaning her forehead against the coolness of its wood. As she did, she realized that no matter what she believed, she had to go and check the back.

If there really *was* someone outside, she couldn't afford to assume that the door was locked. Given Lisa's disappearance, she couldn't afford to make any assumptions at all about what was going on. Not when it came to Taylor's safety.

Taylor. Who was upstairs alone.

The thought took her fear to a whole new dimension. She wanted him beside her. Not separated like this so that she didn't know what was happening to him.

Nothing's happening to him. Taylor's sleeping. Just like you left him.

There was no way someone could be inside the house, she reasoned, fighting a growing sense of horror that threatened to paralyze her. She couldn't let it. She had to take care of Taylor.

Check the back door. Make sure it's still locked. Then call the cops.

Even if she was wrong about what she'd seen, even if it turned out to be something like a limb blown down against the house, she didn't care. She was willing make a fool of herself to keep Taylor safe. More than willing.

She didn't even have to call from down here, she realized. There was a phone in her bedroom. She could go upstairs and look in on Taylor on the way. Just to make sure he was okay.

Please, God, let him be okay, she prayed, tiptoeing across the hall. When she reached the double doorway into the dining room, her eyes searched the windows on the opposite side, looking for any sign of what she had seen before.

There was no revealing flash of lightning. Nothing but darkness and the sound of the rain, heavy enough that it would mask any movement out there.

As well as any in here.

She closed her eyes, gathering her courage. She had to force them open to blink rapidly against the unexpected burn of tears. Then, without allowing herself to think about what she might encounter in the darkened passage, she ran across the dining room.

The narrow pantry was lined on either side with cabinets, glass-fronted above and enclosed below. There was a workspace above the bottom cabinets. As soon as she entered the room, she put out her hand, finding the top of the right-hand-side counter to use as a guide.

As she approached the kitchen, she realized it was lighter

back here than in the rest of the house. Despite the rain, a faint glow from the halogen lamp on the street behind shone in through the windows above the café curtains.

Her eyes scanned the familiar room where she had prepared dinner tonight. It seemed as if that safe, secure world she had been living in had suddenly been snatched away, replaced by one that was filled with shadows and unknown terrors.

Her gaze focused on the back door. There wasn't enough light to tell whether the night latch was turned. She hurried across the room, feeling for it in the darkness.

On. It was still on.

The overwhelming sense of relief made her knees weak. Before she could turn away, however, the door moved.

Maybe it was nothing more than a gust of wind, blowing with enough force to cause the small vibration she felt, but instinct now and not logic directed her action. She took a step backwards, eyes riveted on the knob. Waiting for it to turn. Expecting it to.

Endless seconds passed as she watched. And nothing happened.

Wind. Just the wind. Call the cops.

It was what she had intended to do as soon as she'd checked the doors. She needed to get somebody out here to take a look around. She didn't care if all they found was a storm and a spooked woman.

Go upstairs. Check on Taylor and then make the call.

She was halfway through the pantry before she remembered that with the power out, the cordless phone wouldn't work.

Cell phone. All she had to do was find it and make the call.

She took a deep breath, willing herself to think about

where she'd put her purse down when she'd gotten home today. She had stopped by the store to pick up the lasagna, which meant she wouldn't have gone into the den. She would have gone straight through to the kitchen as soon as she saw Lisa out the door.

And Alex had called her on the cell. She remembered digging the phone out of her purse and walking around with it while she fixed dinner. Definitely in the kitchen.

She didn't want to go back there. No matter what her rational mind told her, she was convinced someone had been standing on the other side of the back door only seconds ago.

The cell phone was her only access to the outside world, however, so reluctantly she retraced her steps, her eyes focusing on the back door as soon as she reentered the room. At least she wouldn't have to go near it.

She started her search on the cabinets beside the refrigerator because she remembered looking for the dressing with the phone in her hand. Working almost totally by feel, she finally located it.

She punched in the numbers, praying that she had hit the right ones. And then she waited. One ring. Two. Surely they couldn't have so many calls tonight that—

"Mallory 911. What's your emergency?"

The voice was calm. Almost bored. Totally removed from the world created by her own terror.

"There's someone outside my house," she said.

"Ma'am, you'll have to speak up, please."

Unconsciously she had whispered, hiding the call she was making from whoever was outside.

"There's someone outside my house," she said again, pitching the words a little louder this time. "It's 1478

Arundel Lane. Could you send a police car? And tell them to hurry.''

''Your name, ma'am.''

''Holt. Robin Holt. The police were here this afternoon. Detective Ridge. About Lisa Evans's disappearance.''

She wasn't sure why she had added that. Maybe as an incentive to get them here faster. *Anything to get them here.*

''Detective Ridge was there this afternoon?''

Robin could hear the puzzlement in the dispatcher's question, so she attempted to clarify. She realized as she did that it had probably been a mistake to mention Lisa.

''The girl who went missing this afternoon is my baby-sitter.''

''And you want to speak to Detective Ridge again? If so, you'll need to go through the regular—''

''No. What I *want* is a patrol car sent to my house, damn it. Someone's outside, and they're trying to get in.''

As she made her demand, her eyes examined the windows. Only a small portion of glass was exposed between the valance and the curtains. She could see nothing moving beyond it.

''And you say this is connected to the disappearance of the Evans girl.''

''*I'm* connected,'' Robin said, growing increasingly frustrated. When she realized how incriminating that sounded, she wished she had been more careful in her choice of words. ''Look, all I know is that someone is trying to get into my house. If you aren't going to send a car—''

''Calm down, ma'am. The officers are on the way. They're going to come to the front door. When you hear someone ring the bell, it will be them. Okay?''

That sounded as if the woman were talking to a not-quite-bright child. Or to someone too terrified to think clearly.

Not far from reality, Robin conceded.

"Thank you," she said, forcing a matching calmness.

"It's okay now, you hear?" The voice was fractionally friendlier. "You just stay on the line with me, honey, until you hear the front bell. Just hang on."

"I need to go upstairs and check on my son. He's up there alone."

"Can you take the phone with you?"

She could, of course. And she had discovered that she didn't really want to hang up. Despite the condescending tone and the endearment, the dispatcher was a living, breathing fellow creature. One who wanted to help rather than harm.

Before she could respond to the question, Robin heard a siren wailing faintly in the distance. It took only a second to confirm that it was approaching the house.

"I can hear them," Robin said into the phone, her sense of relief growing as the siren became louder.

"Are they breaking in?" For the first time there was anxiety in the dispatcher's voice.

"No, I mean the patrol car. I can hear the siren."

"I thought for a minute there you meant whoever was outside. They're coming to the front door, remember."

"Okay," Robin agreed, heading across the kitchen to the pantry.

"You hang on with me until they're in the house."

"Thank you," Robin said again, her gratitude deep and genuine. Before she reached the dining room, the doorbell rang.

CHAPTER FOUR

"SHE CALLED the emergency dispatcher to report that someone was trying to break into her house."

"Find any sign of forced entry?" Matt asked, considering the apparently undamaged front door by the light of his flashlight.

"Not here. Not around back. According to the dispatcher, she mentioned your name and the Evans girl's disappearance. Figured we'd better let you know."

"Thanks," Matt said. "If there's no damage, what made her think someone was breaking in?"

"Said she was upstairs for a while and when she came back down, she headed toward the kitchen. As she entered the dining room, there was a flash of lightning. According to her, that's when she saw someone standing outside the house."

Matt could hear the disbelief in the patrolman's voice. Not that he blamed him. The situation Robin Holt had described was not conducive to the positive identification of anything. Not on a night like this.

"You check the area for footprints?"

If someone *had* been outside, as wet as the ground was, there should be some evidence of their presence. Of course, that was assuming the police search of the Holt property had been completed before the rain started. Otherwise,

there were going to be footprints everywhere. Cop footprints.

"Concrete driveway on that side. Come morning we can
check the flower beds, but…"

The patrolman's tone was skeptical. He had already put
Robin Holt's call down to hysteria. In his place, Matt might
have done the same thing. Unfortunately, given Lisa
Evans's disappearance, he didn't have that luxury.

"She inside?" he asked.

"In the den. Bert's taking the report."

Matt nodded.

"You dust the doors?" The thought had occurred as he'd
reached out to grasp the knob. He could tell by the officer's
face that they hadn't.

"She let us in this way," the kid admitted. "If there
were prints, we may have screwed them up."

"Check it. Then see what you find on the back."

With the kind of blowing rain they'd had tonight, the
surfaces had probably been too wet to get a usable print,
but it was worth a try. At this point, anything was worth a
try. Which was exactly why he was here in the middle of
the night.

Robin Holt or her son knew more than they had shared
with him. His gut had told him that the first time he'd been
here. Now that she thought there had been an attempt to
break into her house, maybe she'd be more willing to level
with him.

He went through the door the patrolman held open for
him and discovered that inside the house wasn't much
warmer than outside. He wondered if the lack of heat was
an income issue. He had no idea how much money Robin
Holt made, but if she were a single mother, as he'd been
told, maybe she was struggling to make ends meet.

. He could hear voices coming from the room into which she'd directed him earlier tonight. Bert Conroy, the officer in charge, had been with the department for years, which was probably how he'd gotten stuck with the rookie outside.

Matt hesitated in the front hall, deliberately eavesdropping, but all he could hear were the questions. Robin's answers were pitched low enough to be an indistinguishable murmur.

"And that's when you felt somebody push against the back door?" Bert asked.

That hadn't been in the information the kid had supplied. It lent some weight to the nebulous sighting of someone out in the driveway.

Interested in hearing Robin's answer, Matt stepped into the doorway. Although the room was dimly lit by candles that had been set on the coffee and the end tables of the couch, Robin Holt's eyes came up immediately.

There was something in her expression that made him know she was glad he was here. Probably nothing more than seeing a familiar face in a trying situation, he acknowledged, but for some reason, what he saw in her eyes had caused a jolt of reaction in the bottom of his stomach.

"Somebody tried to force the back door?" he asked, picking up the thread of inquiry the patrolman had been pursuing.

"Not force it. It felt as if maybe they leaned against it." She hesitated, and then added, "It could have been the wind. It was pretty strong."

He gave her points for trying to be objective, which was hard when you were scared. She had been. That was obvious by the slight tremor in her voice.

Her arms were crossed over her chest, her shoulders

hunched forward. Maybe that was a reaction to the cold. It was clear now that the electricity had been knocked out by the storm.

"How long's your power been out?"

She seemed confused by the non sequitur.

"I don't know. I lay down with Taylor. He was upset about Lisa and asked me to stay with him until he went to sleep. But I must have dozed off. When I woke up, the house was like ice, so…maybe a couple of hours. Maybe longer."

It was after midnight. If she'd put the kid to bed at eight-thirty or nine, that was possible.

"Have you found her? Lisa, I mean."

He had known what she meant. And what he was about to say wasn't going to make the events of tonight less traumatic. Each passing hour made it less likely they would find Lisa Evans unharmed. Especially if her parents, who were still adamant that she hadn't run away, were right.

"Not yet," he said. "Actually, I was hoping you might have thought of something else that could help us. After all, there may be some connection between this and Lisa's disappearance."

Playing on her fear wasn't something he was proud of doing, but they had a missing teenager on their hands. He needed to know everything Robin Holt could tell him, and he felt there was something she hadn't confided yet.

"Could it have been Lisa you saw outside?"

He could tell the thought had not occurred to her, which surprised him. Lisa worked here. She knew the house. Knew the family's routine. If she had been looking for a place to hide from her parents for some silly teenage reason—

"It wasn't Lisa," she said decisively. "The size was wrong. *Everything* was wrong."

Considering the conditions in which she claimed to have seen whoever was outside, she seemed more sure than the circumstances probably warranted.

"Your babysitter's missing, Ms. Holt. Now someone may have tried to break into your house. Are you sure there isn't anything else you want to tell me?"

She shook her head, her arms still crossed protectively over her chest. She left him no option but to push harder.

"You *do* understand that I'll need to talk to your son again."

That brought her head up, eyes widened. "Taylor didn't see anything. He was asleep when I came downstairs. He's *still* asleep."

"I don't mean tonight. We can do it tomorrow."

"But he's told you everything he knows about Lisa."

"Maybe there's something he doesn't *know* he knows. Something he's discounted as being unimportant. Or, given his age, something that he doesn't realize could be related to Lisa's disappearance."

Who could know how the mind of a seven-year-old would process the kind of information Matt was looking for? All he knew was that all other avenues had proven to be dead ends.

"At the police station?" Robin asked.

"We'll be interviewing Lisa's friends and classmates as soon as possible. We'll probably go to the school complex for that. We'll need to have a presence there in any case to ease the community's fears. Why don't we do it at school?"

"I want to be present when you talk to him."

It was not an unreasonable request, considering the boy's age, but she looked as if she expected to be turned down.

"You name the time," he agreed.

"Early. Eight, if possible. I'll need to get to work. We're going to be shorthanded."

"Bring him to the elementary school office. Ask them to send for me. It shouldn't take long. In the meantime, try to get some sleep," he advised. "The officers will patrol the street every fifteen minutes or so, just as a precaution. Whoever you saw outside isn't going to come back tonight. And tomorrow's going to be a long day."

Understatement. At least as far as the department was concerned. Their resources were strained to the limits, even with the county's help. The chief of police had put in a call to the Georgia Bureau of Investigation, but most of the grunt work, like questioning the kids and tracking down any leads that might garner, would undoubtedly fall to the two local departments.

"Just like today has been," she said, getting to her feet.

For Matt, today wasn't over yet, despite the clock. It wouldn't be any time soon unless something broke very quickly.

"Try not to worry," he said.

There was a flash of emotion in her eyes. He was unable to identify what it was before she hid it with a downward glance at her hands, clasped together at her waist. When she looked up again, whatever had been there was gone.

"Thank you."

"I'll see you tomorrow around eight."

He had already started toward the door, Conroy trailing in his wake, when he remembered the other thing he needed to caution her about.

"It might be better if you don't talk to your son about

Lisa's disappearance or about what happened tonight before our interview tomorrow.''

Better for a lot of reasons, including the possibility of something she'd say inadvertently contaminating his recollection of yesterday afternoon's events. And with his babysitter missing, learning someone had been outside his home tonight could be emotionally devastating for the kid.

''What if he asks about her?''

Matt hesitated, trying to walk that fine line between morality and expediency.

''Tell him she's still missing. You know him better than anyone else, of course, but…'' Matt hesitated, but knew he had no choice but to tell her the truth. ''Whether we find Lisa Evans might very well depend on what your son can tell us about the events of yesterday afternoon. You might want to find some way to convey that to him.''

ROBIN CAME AWAKE gradually this time, without any sense of alarm. She could hear someone talking, but the voices were faint, seeming to come from a great distance.

Trying not to disturb Taylor, she pushed onto her elbow. By that time she had realized that what she was hearing was the clock radio in her bedroom.

It kicked on every morning at six o'clock, when her day normally began. Of course, given what had gone on during the last twenty-four hours, this one would be anything but normal.

Satisfied that she had identified the noise, she eased down again, snuggling close to her son. It was already starting to grow light outside. With the dawn, the fears that had been so real last night seemed almost surreal now. Whatever she thought she had seen or heard had probably only been the effects of the storm, magnified by the stress of Lisa's disappearance.

The early-morning stillness of the neighborhood settled around her. She tried to relax into it. They had made it through the night. Nothing bad had happened. And by now, Lisa was probably back home with her mother and father.

She closed her eyes, which felt gritty with exhaustion. She doubted she'd gotten two uninterrupted hours of sleep. She had lain awake after the police left, listening to every creak of the house and each gust of wind that pushed branches against it. She listened now for the sound of rain, but apparently the storm had passed.

The voice from the radio changed, becoming louder and clearer. Obviously a different announcer with a different cadence to his delivery. It took a few seconds to realize that what she was hearing was the beginning of the six o'clock news.

She eased up, trying to get out of bed without waking Taylor. He was no longer sleeping as soundly as he had been before midnight, however.

"What's the matter?" he asked, blinking at her like an owl. "What are you doing here?"

"You asked me to stay. Remember?"

"Because of Lisa."

It hadn't been a question, but she nodded, watching the memory of yesterday's events seep into his eyes.

"Did she go home yet?"

"I don't know. Maybe we'll hear something today."

"Are you going to take me to school?"

"Nobody else," she promised. "I'm going downstairs to start the coffee. You stay in bed until I come back upstairs."

Usually he was still asleep while she took her shower.

As soon as she was dressed, she would come to his room to wake him. Then she'd lay out his clothes while he washed his face and brushed his teeth. She would do those same things this morning. There was security in routine, and that was something they both needed very much right now.

WHILE SHE WAITED for the coffee to brew, Robin walked into the living room and turned on the TV, although she was almost afraid of what she might see. There were a couple of early-morning shows out of Rome that carried some area news along with the weather and farm reports.

She didn't bother to sit down as she clicked through the channels. If she'd missed the local stories, she'd go upstairs and listen to the radio. Surely there would be something about Lisa—

Then, a sickness forming in the bottom of her stomach, she realized she hadn't missed it. She didn't recognize the reporter, but she knew the building behind him. And the face of the man at his side.

Mallory's chief of police was being interviewed in front of City Hall. His round, florid face was grave, his eyes red-rimmed from a lack of sleep. In the glaring light from the cameras, Robin could see a trickle of sweat on his temple despite the cold.

"Search teams were out all night. They'll be out today as well. Volunteers can sign up inside." Police Chief Henry Dawkins gestured toward the municipal buildings behind him. "We need all the help we can get."

"What does the department believe happened to Lisa Evans?"

The negative motion of Dawkins's head began before his answer. "We're not going to get into that kind of speculation. All I can tell you is that we're doing everything we can to find the girl. I know the community of Mallory is keeping both her and her family in their prayers.''

As he turned to go back inside the building that housed not only the police department but also all the other municipal administration offices as well, a dozen questions were shouted at him, most of them intelligible.

''...suggestions of foul play?''

''How are Lisa Evans's parents dealing with the disappearance?''

''Is it true that the mother of the child Lisa babysat for was the last person...?''

In response to the barrage, the chief turned back, raising both hands, beefy palms held out toward the reporters. Clearly a gesture of appeasement.

''We'll have a statement for you later on today. We're going to be conducting interviews at the school complex this morning. We're hoping to find that one of the other children can shed some light on where Lisa was heading when she left the Holt home yesterday. Now if y'all will excuse me, I really do have to get back to work.''

Although the shouting started again as soon as the last word came out of his mouth, this time the chief managed to make good his retreat. Stunned, Robin sank down on the edge of the couch, watching the anchor's mouth move without comprehending a word she was saying.

In her mind other words reverberated more strongly. *Interviews at the school this morning.*

If City Hall was a madhouse at six, she could imagine what the school complex would be like at eight. All she knew was that it was not somewhere she wanted to be.

She and Taylor had told them everything they knew. They couldn't possibly help locate Lisa, she reassured herself. There was too much at stake to show up simply to go through the motions.

Despite her attempt to rationalize her decision not to keep the appointment she'd made with Detective Ridge, it was becoming increasingly difficult to believe that something *hadn't* happened to the teenager.

In Mallory? she challenged her guilt. *What could possibly have happened to her in Mallory?*

Even if the unthinkable had occurred, she and Taylor had given the cops all the information they had. She couldn't help Lisa, but she could protect her son. As a mother, that was her primary responsibility. One that far outweighed any other.

"WHAT DO YOU THINK about playing hooky today?"

She laid the pair of jeans she'd selected from the bottom drawer beside the small gray sweatshirt on the bed.

"What's hooky?" Taylor asked.

"Not doing what you're supposed to do. Not going to school or work or wherever you're supposed to go."

"Me and you?"

"Me and you," Robin said as she helped him pull his pajama top off over his head.

"Are we going to look for Lisa?" he asked as soon as his face emerged. The eagerness of the question broke her heart.

"We have to let the police do that. They're better at it than we would be. We'd just get in the way. I thought we'd go somewhere, just the two of us, and take it easy. Does that sound good to you?"

"Are we taking our stuff?" Taylor's voice was flat, the previous excitement wiped clean.

"A few things. In case we want to stay a couple of days."

His face didn't change, but a too-adult knowledge was in his eyes. "What about Lisa? If we leave, how will we find out about Lisa?"

"We'll listen to the news," she promised.

She would do that in any case. Her father used to talk about the foolishness of the quail he hunted. If only they'd stay hidden in the tall grass instead of allowing themselves to be flushed...

She had made her decision in the shower, the cascade of hot water hiding the noise her crying had made. Unlike the birds her dad had told her about, she wasn't about to do anything rash. And she had also decided where she was going to hide while she figured out what to do next.

CHAPTER FIVE

"At least it ain't the girl," Ephraim Stokes said as he led the way to the scene. "That's the good news."

Although he appreciated the sentiment, Matt wasn't sure there was anything about this that would qualify as "good" news. Not even to Lisa Evans's parents.

"Who found the body?"

"One of the volunteer search teams. They been out since dawn." The patrolman tilted his head in the direction of the knot of people on the other side of the small clearing. "Carlisle is taking the guy's statement, but what we got on this is pretty much what you see."

"Cause of death?" Matt asked, stooping beside the corpse on the ground.

It was lying prone, the head turned to one side. The eyes were open, as was the mouth. Blood had pooled on the ground beneath, trailing from the corner of the parted lips.

"Take your pick," Stokes said. "Some of the stuff may be postmortem, but for starters, he's got a fractured skull."

Which would explain the blood from the mouth, Matt supposed. He leaned far enough forward over the body to verify the information Stokes had provided. Despite the cold, the sickly-sweet miasma of death surrounded the corpse. He swallowed hard, fighting the urge to gag.

The implications of this find were just beginning to register. They had a body, obviously a homicide victim, and they also had a missing fourteen-year-old girl. Put them together in a town like Mallory, Georgia, and it was enough to panic everybody within a fifty-mile radius.

Including me.

"Coroner seen him?" Matt asked.

"He's been sent for. The photographer's already here."

Matt nodded, his eyes still examining the body. Besides the quantity of congealed blood on the carpet of leaves under the victim's mouth, the thing that struck Matt most forcibly was the way the man was dressed.

The weather had been unseasonably cold for the last couple of days, yet this guy wasn't wearing a jacket. Not even a sweater. Just a thin, dark shirt, whose fabric maintained a slight sheen despite its exposure to the elements, gray slacks, and black dress shoes. Not exactly the attire of a hiker or a nature lover. Not in late November.

"How far would you say we are from Handy's?" Matt asked. He got to his feet, stepping back to allow the photographer to continue recording the crime scene.

The local truck stop cum greasy spoon wasn't frequented by many of the locals because of its reputation, but it got a lot of traffic from the interstate. It was the first place you came to after the exit. The body lay in the heavily wooded acreage behind it.

"Mile. Mile and a half, maybe," Stokes said.

It had seemed longer to Matt as they'd worked their way in through the scrub.

"What about the other way?"

He turned to face the opposite direction, away from the truck stop where he'd left his car. If anything, the woods seemed denser there. Darker and more threatening.

Stokes's eyes followed. They were bloodshot from fatigue and a lack of sleep. With the grisly discovery at their feet, there probably wasn't much chance he'd get an opportunity to play catch-up. As Matt watched, waiting for an answer, the veteran cop's expression altered.

"Shit," he said softly.

"What?"

"The school. There's a short cut. Hell, we used to take it when we were kids. Runs along the back edge of these woods, all the way from the complex to Morningside."

Morningside. Morningside Meadows. The subdivision where Lisa Evans lived.

"SHE SAID to tell you that Taylor's sick," the elementary school secretary said. "He's running a fever, and she's going to take him to the pediatrician. She'll call you as soon as they get back to reschedule the interview."

There was always the possibility that the kid really was feverish. It had been obvious last night that he was pretty upset. It had been just as obvious, however, that Robin Holt was reluctant to let him talk to the boy again. Maybe this was a ploy to delay the interview. With the body in the woods, that was no longer an option.

"What time did she call?" Matt asked.

He had phoned the school to have the secretary tell Robin he was running late, but that he was on his way. Instead, he'd been given the message that she wasn't coming.

"By the time I got through that mob out front, it was nearly seven-thirty. She called maybe…fifteen minutes later. Quarter of eight, I guess."

Matt glanced at his watch. It was almost nine, and he still hadn't gotten a chance to talk to the guy who'd discovered the body. Nor was the coroner through with his preliminary observations at the scene.

"You have a number for the kid's doctor on file?" he asked, waiting while she pulled up the information on her computer.

"No number. Just a name. A Dr. Robert Phillips. That's not one I know, and I know most of them around here. Must not be in Mallory. Maybe she's taking him into Gainesville."

He hadn't told Robin Holt not to leave town, Matt realized. Of course, he'd had no reason at the time to think she would. The uneasiness she'd engendered had more to do with the woman herself than with any suspicion that she might have had something to do with her babysitter's disappearance.

The corpse in the woods changed the dynamics of everything. He would definitely have told her not to leave town had he known then what he knew now. Actually, given the attempted break-in she had reported last night, he would have insisted the Holts be placed under protection.

"I *do* have an emergency contact," the secretary offered, interrupting his train of thought.

"Could you give it to me, please?" Matt asked, holding the phone against his ear with his shoulder as he fumbled a notepad out of his pocket.

"Chuck Parnell at 887-6549." Before Matt could finish jotting the number down, she said, "Wait a minute. I just realized that's the same as her work number. Anderson Graphics. Not much help, I guess."

"I'll give it a shot," Matt said. "Thanks for the information. Oh, and if she brings the kid back to school, give me a call, will you."

"You think she had something to do with Lisa's disappearance?" the secretary asked.

The excitement in her voice set Matt's teeth on edge.

Maybe it was nothing more than small-town curiosity, but he had a feeling that whatever he told her would be whispered across the office counter to anyone who mentioned the case today.

Robin Holt had lost whatever privacy she'd had in this town by virtue of having the missing teenager work for her on the day she'd disappeared. Even if she were simply an innocent bystander, there would always be those who would believe she had somehow been involved. An unwanted notoriety that would linger as long as she lived here.

"We have no reason to think anything like that," Matt said. "We just need to confirm some times with her and the boy."

He took advantage of the disappointed silence that followed to push the off button on his phone. Despite his disclaimer that the department had nothing beyond a routine police interest in Robin Holt, the feeling that there was something about her that he should know—something important—stirred again. And he'd been in this business too long to ignore his instincts, especially when they were this persistent.

"WHEN YOU'RE LUCKY enough that somebody with that kind of talent walks into a place like this looking for a job, trust me, you don't ask questions," Charles Parnell said. "Ability is about the only criteria for employment in a company this size. Along with a willingness to do a lot of hard work for not much money, of course."

"And she was willing?"

"She didn't ask half the questions I usually get when I offer somebody a position. I'm pretty open about the prospects. I don't like turnover. It leaves a gap in our ability to function. Like today. I have to tell you I was fit to be tied when Robin called in to say her kid was sick.''

''How many people do you employ, Mr. Parnell?''

''Robin, Alex, Russell and me. Some weeks that's more than enough. Some weeks we have more work than the four of us can possibly handle.''

''And Ms. Holt does design?''

''Russ does the web stuff. Robin and Alex do everything else. I sell, keep the books, do the invoicing and take care of the occasional advertising.''

''Could I have their full names, please,'' Matt asked.

Maybe Robin Holt's co-workers knew more about her than her employer seemed to. There was so little information on the application she'd filled out that Matt couldn't see how it would be of any use. After all, he already knew her address.

''Alexandra Fisher and Russell Stern.''

''She close to either of them?''

''Alex, I guess. Maybe because they're women. Totally different types.''

''Do you have Ms. Fisher's address?''

''Is Robin in trouble?''

''We just need to talk to her. The Evans girl was her babysitter.''

''I *knew* I'd heard that kid's name before.'' Parnell looked up from sorting through the folders in the file drawer of his desk. ''I told my wife that last night. You don't think something's happened to Robin, do you?''

Despite his previous concern about the attempted break-in, that was something Matt hadn't even considered. According to the school secretary, she'd left on her own.

Of course, someone could have forced her to leave that message...

All the more reason to locate her as quickly as possible, he decided, denying the knife edge of worry Parnell's question had slipped into his mind. Robin Holt was, at the very least, a material witness in the Evans girl's disappearance. Whether she herself was in danger was something he didn't have an answer for right now. One of many things he didn't have an answer for.

"We don't have any reason to believe that. We just have some additional questions to ask her about yesterday afternoon. As far as we know, she was the last person to see the Evans girl...before her disappearance."

He had stopped himself in time, but the word *alive* had been on the tip of his tongue. The longer the girl was missing the more likely it was that Robin had, in fact, been the last person to see her alive.

Parnell's hand hesitated in the act of removing one of the folders from the drawer. His eyes lifted to Matt's, an unspoken understanding in them. He didn't ask any further questions.

"Alexandra Fisher," he said, handing over the file he'd selected. "Her contact information is on the form."

"HAVE YOU DECIDED if we're going to spend the night?"

Taylor's question pulled her back to the present. Apparently Alex had meant it when she'd said she intended to make a day of it. It was almost noon and she still hadn't returned home.

Despite her intentions, Robin had gone over to the front windows again, peering out between the draperies and the frame. The street outside was devoid of traffic.

"Don't you want to?" Alex wouldn't mind, and her couch made out into a bed.

Robin had been given the spare key to the duplex early

in their friendship. She fed Alex's cat whenever she was out of town, which was fairly often. Lisa's disappearance and the attempted break-in would provide all the excuse she needed to broach to Alex the idea of their sleeping over.

"I don't know," Taylor said without looking up.

He was sitting at the small dining table that took up one end of the living room, drawing on the notepad Robin had found by the phone. The cat was an interested bystander.

She was concerned about how quiet he'd gotten as the morning wore on, but there was no news with which she could reassure him. She had checked Alex's kitchen radio, which was tuned to the same station as the one beside her own bed, on the hour. The hourly news would give her any major developments. The rest of what was going on—organizing the search teams and the endless speculation—she didn't need to hear. She wanted to shield Taylor from as much of that as she could.

"Mama?"

He hardly ever called her that. Not since he'd started school. Another sign that despite her efforts to be positive, Lisa's disappearance was having a detrimental effect.

"What is it, baby?"

"What if you do something wrong, but you didn't mean to?"

"Something like what?"

"Tell somebody something that isn't true."

"Did you tell *me* something that wasn't true?"

His eyes came up at that. He shook his head, the vigorous "I'm not lying" motion.

"Detective Ridge?"

Her pulse quickened at the thought. Maybe Ridge was right. Maybe Taylor *did* know more than he had told them.

"It wasn't *nothing* like that."

"Are you sure?"

He nodded, but his eyes didn't hold hers, returning instead to whatever he was drawing.

She let the curtain fall and crossed the room to look down on his picture. Tall trees, branches spiking in every direction loomed over small stick figures. One of them was larger than the others and appeared to be carrying something in its hand.

"What are you drawing?" she asked, reaching down to push the too-fine hair off his forehead.

Despite the fact that he had reverted to calling her "Mama," he ducked away from her hand, putting his palm protectively over his forehead. He lowered the elbow of that arm to the table, propping his head on it as if he were tired.

"You need a nap?" she asked.

"I'm not a baby."

"I didn't say you were. I asked if you needed a nap. Neither one of us got as much sleep as we should have last night."

There was no response.

"Is there something you want to tell me, Taylor?"

The words seemed eerily familiar, but it took her a moment to remember that she had asked him that yesterday afternoon. He had been just this non-responsive to her question about his day at school. And that had been *before* they'd known about Lisa.

"Did something happen at school yesterday?"

He hadn't protested not going this morning. It hadn't struck her as strange at the time because she had been more concerned about everything else that was going on, but Taylor loved school. He had a crush on his teacher. Normally he would have objected to missing a day.

Normally. That was the key. This was anything but normal. She was expecting too much to think it wouldn't have some effect.

He shook his head, eyes still lowered. His right hand moved back and forth, pulling the pen over and over across the middle of the trees. She was about to ask him what the dark spot he was making was supposed to be, when the doorbell rang.

Her heart literally froze at the sound and then began to race as she considered the possibilities. Alex wouldn't ring the bell. Someone from work? Russ or Chuck Parnell? Maybe bringing something they needed Alex to do tonight because she hadn't gone in this morning?

"Mama?" Taylor said. He was looking up at her, his eyes wide and dark.

She put her finger over her lips, urging him to silence. Staying close to the wall, she tiptoed back to the spot from where she'd been observing the street. Moving carefully, she edged the curtain aside a fraction of an inch.

Nothing had changed on the street outside. At least nothing she could see from this angle. Nor could she see whoever was standing at the front door.

As she tried to decide what to do, the bell rang again, the tone seeming more demanding than it had the first time. Only a second or two later the knocking started.

"Ms. Holt?"

She recognized the voice immediately. And tracking her to Alex's would have been simple, of course. After all, she had told him where she worked. She just hadn't expected him to be this persistent.

"Ms. Holt, I know you're in there. Your car's in the garage."

She should have found a way to let him ask Taylor his

questions. *Just do it. Just get it the hell over with.* Instead, she'd panicked like those damn quail.

Now that he was here, there was only one thing to do. She walked across to the door, turned the dead bolt, and opened it. For maybe ten seconds neither of them said anything.

"May I come in?" Matt Ridge asked finally.

"Do I have a choice?"

"Actually, you have a couple of them. You can start telling me the truth, or I can take you with me down to City Hall. There are a lot of people down there, including a couple of GBI agents, who'll be very interested in learning why the last person to see Lisa Evans has been lying to the police."

CHAPTER SIX

DAMN HIM. And damn her stupidity for underestimating him.

"Look," she said, trying for a reasoned tone, "there's obviously been some kind of mistake—"

"If there has been, you're the one who made it," Matt Ridge broke in. "We had an appointment this morning."

"Taylor was sick, and I needed to take him to the doctor. I called the school. I asked the secretary to tell you that I'd reschedule."

"This doesn't look like a doctor's office to me."

"We've already seen him. We got in early, before the office got too crowded. I knew that Alex—Alexandra Fischer, who works with me—is off today. I brought Taylor over here to ask her if she'd keep him while I go to work, but...she hasn't gotten home yet."

It sounded plausible enough. There was no reason for him to doubt any of it. Alex could show up at any moment to bolster her claim.

"What was wrong with him?"

Matt Ridge tilted his chin in the direction of the table where Taylor was sitting. She didn't dare look at her son. It was bad enough having to tell lies in front of him. She couldn't face him while she did.

"Mostly anxiety, compounded by a loss of sleep."

"That's what the doctor said?"

She nodded, despite the mockery in his tone.

"And this would be Doctor...?"

He wanted a name. And judging by what was in his eyes, he would go to the trouble of checking it out.

"I don't remember. It's a group practice. We saw the first doctor who became available."

"Not your regular doctor? According to the school secretary, he isn't local."

On the school forms she had put down the doctor who'd given Taylor the last of his boosters because his name was on the vaccination record required for registration. She couldn't even remember what it was now.

"I couldn't get an appointment with him."

"So you went to someone local instead?"

She nodded, feeling trapped.

"Then we can probably find them in the phone book. There aren't that many group practices in Mallory. Especially not in pediatrics."

The sarcasm was more open this time. He knew she was lying, and she knew he wasn't the kind who would let it alone. If Taylor's scheduled interview hadn't been with him, he might not have taken this so personally.

"Look," she said, giving in, "I just didn't want him any more upset than he already is."

She had lowered her voice so Taylor wouldn't hear. She held Matt Ridge's eyes, trying to convey to him that she was telling the truth. She had noticed their color last night—deep brown surrounded by thick, dark lashes. They had seemed warm and concerned then; now they were hard, almost cynical.

"Trying to take care of your child isn't a crime," she said, attempting to penetrate that cynicism.

"Kidnapping is. A federal crime, by the way."

There was a jolt of fear in her stomach, before she realized what he meant.

"*Lisa?* You think I had something to do with Lisa?"

"I think you were the last person to see her—"

The sentence cut off abruptly. His gaze lifted to Taylor, who was watching them from across the room. This time she allowed herself to glance back at him, assessing. His blue eyes were haunted with the same anxiety she had seen there all day.

"The last person to see her before her disappearance," Matt Ridge amended.

"I understand that, but I've told you everything—"

"Would you get your coat, please?" The detective had modified his tone, but the anger she'd heard before was undeniably still there.

It was carefully controlled, underlying his surface calmness, but she reacted to it. The sickness in her stomach was more a flutter than a jolt this time.

"Where are we going?"

"To the police station."

Where the mob of reporters she had seen this morning would be waiting. By now there might be feeds to the cable news stations. Maybe even to the networks.

"You have to believe me," she said, willing him to listen to her. "I don't know anything about Lisa's disappearance. Nothing happened yesterday afternoon that was in the least bit out of the ordinary. She left my house exactly the same way she always does. Taylor has told you everything he knows—"

"All of that may be true. But when you don't keep an appointment with the police and then lie about the reason, you're no longer a witness who might have information we can use. You become a suspect, Ms. Holt. I don't have any

choice about taking you in. You might want to start thinking about calling a lawyer.''

The word chilled her. If she really were a suspect…

''I had nothing to do with Lisa's disappearance, I swear
to you. She walked out of my door yesterday afternoon the
same way she always did, and I haven't seen her since. I
don't know what happened to her after that, but whatever
it was, I swear to you I didn't have anything to do with
it.''

''The boy have a jacket?'' he asked, breaking the eye
contact she was trying so hard to maintain.

''You don't understand,'' she said.

Before she'd gotten the words out of her mouth, he was
striding over to the front hall closet. He opened it, roughly
pushing the items hanging inside apart. When he didn't find
what he was looking for, he turned to face her again.

''Jacket.'' Clearly a demand.

''Couldn't you ask Taylor whatever questions you want
to ask him here?''

''Too late, Ms. Holt. You made your choice.''

He crossed the room, heading not toward her, but to the
table where Taylor was sitting. The child's face was tight.
Even if he hadn't followed the entire conversation, he had
picked up on the tension between them. He was on the
verge of tears and trying hard to suppress them.

''You have a coat, son?'' Matt asked, looking down at
him.

His voice had softened, without the anger with which
he'd addressed her. She wondered if he had enough experience with children to realize how near the edge the little
boy was.

''Yes, sir.''

''Do you know where it is?''

"In the bedroom."

"Is your mom's in there, too?"

Taylor nodded, his eyes never leaving the face of the man who must seem to be looming over him.

"You want to go in there and get them both, please?"

"Okay."

The boy slid off the chair, sidling uneasily along the narrow space between the table and the detective. He had reached the hall before he turned to ask, "You want me to bring our suitcase, too?"

Matt Ridge's eyes touched on Robin's before he answered. "Yeah, why don't you bring that, too."

He waited until Taylor had disappeared into the hall. "Going somewhere?"

"Here," Robin said. "After what happened last night, I didn't want to stay at the house. I wasn't sure it was safe."

Just for a moment she caught a glimpse of something, regret or maybe even sympathy, in his eyes. At least he didn't seem to think she was lying about that.

Whatever she had seen was quickly masked, however, as he glanced down at the table where Taylor's drawings were lying. The pen was still resting on top of the last one he'd done. The detective pushed it aside to look at the sketch beneath.

Then, his hand still touching the ballpoint, he hesitated, his attention caught by Taylor's scribblings. After a few seconds he tore that sheet of paper off the notebook, holding it out before him. The intensity of his interest was communicated by his absolute stillness.

"How did Lisa and your son get home from school?"

He hadn't looked at her as he posed the question. When she didn't answer immediately, his eyes came up, fastening on hers.

"They walked," she said, wondering where this could possibly be leading.

"You know the route they took?"

"What?"

"Where they walked? Which streets?"

She tried to remember the names on the signs she passed on her way to and from the school. Since she'd found Lisa to walk with Taylor, she hadn't traveled those streets with any regularity.

"Montfort and then Pine into the subdivision. Take the first left onto...Heather. I think that's the name. Two blocks and then right onto our street. Arundel."

"Not the shortcut? You're sure?"

"What shortcut?" she asked, bewildered.

"Behind the school. There's a path that skirts the woods."

She shook her head. "I don't know about any shortcut. I just assumed—"

She broke off as Taylor came back into the room. He had put on his jacket. He had hers draped over his arm, and he was carrying the small overnight bag she had packed for the two of them earlier this morning.

Matt turned his head, following the direction of her gaze. He glanced back at her, one brow raised. It took her too long to understand that he was seeking permission. By the time she'd figured that out, he had already made his decision.

He walked over to Taylor. The boy's eyes widened at his approach. At the last minute the detective seemed to realize the child now saw him as a threat.

He stopped a couple of feet away, smiling down at the boy. The wary blue gaze didn't change. After a second or two, Matt stooped, balancing on the balls of his feet to put himself at eye level with the boy, just as he had last night.

"I've been looking at your drawings."

Taylor said nothing, but something in his face altered. It wasn't the same look she had seen there before. His expression was not tearful, but closed. Opaque.

"Would you tell me about this one?"

Matt held the picture he'd taken from the table out to the side, but Taylor never even looked at it. His eyes held on the big man's face a long time.

"Taylor?"

"It's trees," the boy said finally.

"Some particular trees? Somewhere around here?"

"Not here."

"Near your school?" Matt pressed.

Taylor nodded. The admission had been reluctant, it seemed to Robin, but it had definitely been an affirmative.

"The woods behind the school, maybe? The ones near the path?"

Another nod, the movement smaller this time.

"Is that the way you and Lisa came home from school?"

No response, although Matt waited far past the point where Robin would have been forced to prompt the child for an answer.

"Did you come home that way yesterday, Taylor?"

Nothing.

"Did you and Lisa walk along the path by the woods the day she disappeared?"

Slowly the boy's eyes filled, the blue glazing with unshed tears.

"It's okay," Matt comforted. "Nobody's mad at you, son. And you aren't in any trouble. We just need to know what happened that day. We need to know that so we can help Lisa.''

"I didn't mean to do it," Taylor said. His chin quivered, and the first of the tears escaped, sliding down the rounded curve of his cheek.

With those words, Robin's heart hesitated. And then, as soon as she remembered that Taylor had been with her when Lisa had walked out their front door, safe and sound yesterday afternoon, it began to beat again.

Whatever her son was talking about, it obviously didn't involve any physical harm he'd done to the teenager. Seeing him standing there, small and defenseless, tears welling in his eyes, her initial thought that it might seemed ridiculous.

"I know you didn't," the detective said, his deep voice kind. Understanding. "I just need you to tell me what happened."

He had probably used the same tone a hundred times in questioning suspects. Making them think that he was on their side. That he understood their anguish or their regret.

Maybe that was fair when you were dealing with someone who was guilty of a criminal act. It seemed a cruel treachery to use that ploy on a seven-year-old child.

"I think that's just about enough," Robin said.

"You *want* to tell me what you did, don't you, Taylor?" Matt went on, ignoring her objection. "I know you want to tell somebody. And you'll feel better when you do, I promise."

"I didn't mean for anything to happen to Lisa."

"I know. Maybe nothing has," Matt added, "but we have to know about yesterday. About the woods."

He moved the paper he was holding, as if to bring it to

the boy's attention. The tear-washed eyes glanced at it and then looked away.

By that time Robin had reached her son. She bent, putting her arm around his shoulders. They were rigid, either with fear or with guilt. She couldn't imagine what he thought he'd done that could have had anything to do with Lisa's disappearance.

"It's okay," she said, pulling him close. After a brief resistance, his eyes still lowered, he melted against her side, turning his face into her shoulder.

"I said that's enough," she said to Matt, the words hissed in fury.

"We have to know."

"He didn't do anything to Lisa. He was with me after she left the house. The very idea that he could have had anything to do with anything like that—"

She stopped, unwilling to speak the unthinkable aloud.

"It wasn't yesterday," Taylor said into the silence, the words muffled by her body. "I didn't do *anything* yesterday."

Robin's eyes met Matt's. Again that dark brow rose, less inquiry this time than demand. As much as she hated what was happening, she knew he was right. Whatever Taylor was talking about, they had to know all of it.

She had only been able to justify not keeping the appointment this morning because she'd truly believed the little boy had told the police everything he knew. Even if whatever this was turned out to have nothing to do with Lisa's disappearance, they had to hear it.

"What did you do that you didn't mean to do, Taylor?" she asked, putting her left hand on his other shoulder to hold him away from her body.

His eyes, still blurred with moisture, studied her face a moment. Then he swallowed.

"It's okay," she said again, her heart breaking at the sight of his fear and unhappiness. "Everything's going to be okay. Nobody's mad at you. We just need to know what you're worried about."

He spent another second or two searching her eyes, perhaps to determine if she'd really meant what she'd just said.

"I lied to Lisa," he whispered.

It was so unexpected, so innocent, that she wasn't sure what to ask next. She glanced questioningly at Matt, and he took up the challenge.

"You lied about something in the woods?"

Taylor shook his head.

"Then...what about?"

"I told her I had to pee, but I didn't. Not then. Not when I first told her."

Again Robin was at a loss, but her apprehension that Taylor might somehow know more about Lisa's disappearance than he'd told them was beginning to fade. Apparently this was something that had happened earlier. *I didn't do anything yesterday.*

In his mind, the two events had somehow gotten tangled together. He had lied to Lisa, and then Lisa had disappeared. With a seven-year-old's sense of morality, he had begun to believe that the wrong he'd done had been responsible for the girl's disappearance. That it was a punishment for his supposed sin, perhaps. Cause and effect.

"You told her you had to pee," Matt said, "and then what happened?"

"She let me go."

The words seemed to trigger another wave of guilt. His eyes filled with tears. He sniffed, trying to contain them.

"Into the woods," Matt said, his voice very soft. "Lisa let you go into the woods beside the path."

The boy nodded. He raised one hand, pushing his knuckle into the moisture under his nose and smearing a glistening trail of it across his cheek.

"And you saw something there, didn't you? You saw something in those woods."

Another nod. The child's eyes were locked on the dark ones of the detective. The tears had stopped, but the rigidity was back in the small, straight shoulders.

"You want to tell me what you saw, Taylor? Is that what your picture is about? What you saw in the woods?"

Another nod.

"There were some people there."

It wasn't a question, but it elicited another nod.

"Did they see you?"

The child hesitated. When he spoke, his voice was more subdued than it had been before.

"Lisa started yelling at me to hurry up, and they turned around. I was hid good because I didn't want anybody from school to see me peeing. But Lisa's jacket was red. You could see it a long way through the trees."

"You think they saw Lisa?"

He nodded. "Because of her jacket. And because she was yelling maybe."

The story was finally beginning to make some kind of sense to Robin. As it did, the implications began to sink in.

Apparently there had been someone in the woods behind the school. Lisa had attracted their attention by yelling at Taylor, and now Lisa was missing. Although there were gaps in the puzzle, there were enough pieces for the picture it presented to be chilling.

"You're sure this wasn't yesterday?" Matt probed.

"It was Tuesday," Taylor said decisively. "That's how I got Lisa to leave before they caught us. She had piano. Piano is on Tuesday."

He would know, Robin thought. He always remembered even when she couldn't.

"They tried to catch you?" Matt asked, picking up on the salient part of Taylor's answer.

"They started running when she was yelling. I ran, too, but when I got to Lisa, they weren't there. I don't know where they went."

"How many people did you see, Taylor?"

"Three. Three old men."

"*Old* men? How did you know they were old?"

"They had on old men's coats. The long kind."

"Overcoats," Robin interpreted.

She couldn't tell from the quick look he directed at her if Matt appreciated her attempt to help or if he was warning her to keep quiet.

"You saw three old men," he repeated, turning his attention back to the child. "And they ran toward Lisa when she started yelling for you to come out of the woods. Did they run like old men?"

Taylor thought about it before he shook his head. "They ran fast. I thought they would get to her before I could."

"You think they were angry that Lisa was there?"

"Maybe. Then I thought maybe they thought she was yelling because she needed help. Maybe they were coming to help her."

Matt nodded as if that were a reasonable assumption. "Anything else you remember? Like what they were doing when you first saw them? Before Lisa attracted their attention?''

The boy swallowed again. Only seconds ago, he had seemed relieved to be able to tell this to someone. Now his face changed, becoming less animated. Whatever he had seen the men doing, it was obvious that was information he didn't want to relay.

''Taylor?'' Robin said, pulling him close against her body again. ''You need to tell us exactly what you saw. It might help us find Lisa.''

He took a deep breath, his shoulders lifting beneath her arm. Finally he turned his head, looking back at Matt.

''I thought maybe they were looking for their cat and something had hurt it.''

A heartbeat of silence as they digested the words. Trying to make sense of them.

''Why did you think that?'' Matt asked carefully.

''They were all standing around looking at something on the ground, so I thought maybe it was a cat or something they'd lost. Maybe a dog or a wolf had killed it and they'd just found it out there. But...I don't think it could have been a cat because whatever it was—''

The sentence broke as the little boy visibly shivered.

''What do *you* think was on the ground that they were looking at, Taylor?''

''I don't know. I couldn't see it. One of the men kicked it, and then he bent down and picked it up. It was red. That's how I could see it so good through the trees. Because it was all red. Just like Lisa's jacket.''

CHAPTER SEVEN

AFTER HEARING her son's story, Robin Holt had apparently accepted the inevitability of more police interviews with the little boy. At least she hadn't bothered to protest when Matt had loaded them into his cruiser to take them to City Hall.

As they'd neared the building, he could sense her tension. The crowd out front was even larger than it had been this morning. He wondered if the news about the body in the woods had been released, or if the people gathered there were waiting for the press conference called to announce that find to begin.

Before he'd left to track down the Holts, the department had made a decision to delay the revelation as long as possible. They wanted time to allow not only a complete examination of the site, but also an opportunity to work on a phrasing of a release that would not panic the town.

Of course, with the number of volunteers who had been in the woods between Handy's and the school this morning, they had all known that the time frame in which they had to make the formal announcement before the news leaked out was very narrow. Matt had argued for releasing the information as soon as the crime scene was secured. After all, there was no way the police could couch this so that it wouldn't send shock waves throughout the community, already reeling from Lisa Evans's disappearance.

He'd been outvoted, and now he was out of the loop as to where that investigation and the public's awareness of it stood. Whatever the case, he needed to get the Holts inside before the media began throwing questions at them. He wanted to protect Taylor's recollection of Tuesday's events, especially from the kind of speculation the reporters' inquiries might present.

Although the parking spaces were farther from the building, he pulled around to the side in an attempt to avoid the media's attention. Before he got out of the car, he instructed Robin to keep the boy inside until he could come around and get them.

She had chosen to ride in back with Taylor, her arm around him the entire trip. During the occasional glances Matt had stolen at them in the rearview mirror, the two fair heads had been very close together.

Her hair, only a few shades darker than the child's, had been highlighted by the sun shining in through the back window. The same physical attraction Matt had felt last night stirred again, warring with the uneasiness her behavior engendered.

When he opened the rear door of the vehicle, two identical pairs of blue eyes stared up at him expectantly. He forced his gaze away to look out over the top of the car, scanning the area around them. He was relieved to find it was still deserted.

"Let's go," he said, extending his hand.

After a brief hesitation Robin put her fingers into his. It had been a long time since he'd held a woman's hand, but the delicacy of its shape and feel was eerily familiar. Her fingers were colder, however, than the relatively warm interior of the car should warrant.

Nerves? Or maybe fear. It must be obvious that whatever

her son had seen in the woods a few days ago had plunged him, as well as Lisa Evans, into danger. It also put the attempted break-in she'd reported last night into a more believable, if a far more terrifying, perspective.

He couldn't argue now with the instinct that had led her to get the boy into a safer place this morning. Not even if it meant she'd lied to him.

"Thank you," she said when she was standing beside the car. She reached inside, grasping her son's arm to urge him out.

"Ms. Holt?"

Startled, Matt looked up to see a couple of reporters with mikes and a video cam descending on the car. Somehow the mob around front had discovered them. The shouted question brought Robin's eyes up, confirming her identity for the reporters.

"Come on." Matt put his hand in the small of her back to direct her toward the door.

"What can you tell us about the afternoon Lisa Evans disappeared?"

The woman posing the question hurried toward them, her microphone held out as if to catch anything Robin might say. Instead, head down, Robin put both hands on her son's shoulders, propelling him along in front of her.

The entrance to the courthouse seemed an inordinate distance away. Matt put himself between the Holts and the reporters, using his body as a physical shield.

That didn't stop the assault of questions, however. He could only hope those seemed as much a jumble to Taylor as they did to him. If so, the damage to the information the child carried in his head should be minimal.

With less than twenty feet to the door, he glanced over his shoulder. The noise the first few reporters were making had attracted the rest. They came streaming around the corner, cutting across the winter-browned Bermuda grass of the courthouse lawn, attempting to reach his witnesses before he could get them inside.

Again he was forced to acknowledge Robin's wisdom in protecting her son from the scene that was unfolding. At the same time he cursed his own lack of foresight in planning for this eventuality. He picked up the pace as much as possible, putting his arm around her shoulders in a gesture that was admittedly protective.

Not only were she and her son witnesses in this case, the fragility of the hand she'd placed in his had made him realize that, despite her air of control, she was out of her depth. Right now, she seemed almost as vulnerable as her son.

And he no longer bothered to deny that she reminded him of Karen. There was little physical resemblance between them, of course. It was more an attitude that he had quickly recognized. A stubborn determination to try to handle everything on her own.

From the first time he'd met Karen, that mind-set had provoked admiration and then, ironically, a protective urge. He was reacting to Robin Holt in the same way.

As they neared the entrance, he stepped ahead of her to open the door on the relative safety of the municipal building. The crowd behind him became even more frenzied, realizing they were about to lose the opportunity to question one of the principals in this case.

Just as Robin, her hands still on her son's shoulders, directed Taylor across the threshold, a man's voice carried above the din of the other questions.

"What did you think when you heard they'd found the body, Ms. Holt?"

It stopped her in her tracks. She turned to look at Matt, who was still holding the door. Her eyes were wide and questioning.

"They found Lisa?"

He shook his head without replying, stepping forward to put his hand against the small of her back again, forcing her to take the final steps that would carry her away from the insatiable curiosity of the media. Then he closed the door, turning the inside lock as the first of the reporters thrust his face against the glass.

Shepherding the Holts away from the entrance, he signaled to one of the uniformed officers standing at the end of the hall. As the cop started toward them, Robin stopped, putting one hand on his arm.

"You swear to me they haven't found Lisa?"

"It's not Lisa. I swear to you."

He looked pointedly down at Taylor and then back up, trying to warn her off. As he watched, comprehension filled her eyes. The fingers of her other hand tightened involuntarily around her son's shoulder.

Taylor squirmed beneath the sudden pressure. "Ouch, Mom."

"Sorry," she said, her eyes holding Matt's. "You think that's why Lisa—?"

Before she could finish the question, he shook his head. Another warning.

"There's a conference room down the hall that's usually empty this time of day. I'm going to take you two there while I get the taping equipment and someone to set it up. We need to get Taylor's story on record before we talk."

He didn't say, "Before we talk about what might have happened to Lisa," but he hoped she'd gotten that message.

A lot of time had passed since the events they needed Taylor to describe. Especially for a child as young he was.

Robin nodded, allowing him to lead the way to the room. As he had suspected, there was no one there.

Several half-empty disposable cups and a plate with a few doughnuts stood on the long conference table, giving testimony that the room had been used earlier, perhaps for the meeting between the local law-enforcement team and the agents from the Georgia Bureau of Investigation, who had arrived this morning.

"You'll be safe in here," Matt assured her. "I can send an officer to sit with you if you want, but I should be back in ten or fifteen minutes."

She looked as if she wanted to take him up on the offer, but she shook her head.

"We'll be all right."

"There's probably some coffee—" he began, but a glance at the glass carafes on the counter at the far end of the room disproved that theory. "I can have somebody make a pot."

"I'm fine, but...Taylor hasn't had any lunch. He's used to eating early at school."

"I'll send out for something. Hamburger okay?"

"Thank you. He'd like that."

The same innate dignity he'd noticed before was in her reply. She was still struggling to come to grips with this, but he had to give her credit for not falling apart. And for making sure that her son was taken care of. Whatever else anyone had to say about her, Robin Holt seemed to be a hell of a mother.

"Sure you'll be all right?" he asked again, realizing as he did that his priorities in this case were becoming dangerously skewed.

She had lied to him in an attempt to avoid questioning. Despite that, the primary feeling she evoked was one of concern. He hadn't even been able to hold on to the anger he'd felt when he'd discovered her hiding at Alexandra Fisher's house. Her instincts had just been better than his. Until he'd seen the boy's drawing, he hadn't even considered that Taylor might need protection.

"We'll be fine, just…don't be long," she added softly, her eyes reinforcing that plea.

"As soon as I can," he promised, feeling that undeniable physical response again.

He had always prided himself on being professional. On maintaining the necessary distance between himself and the cases he worked. With this one, that was becoming increasingly difficult. And he was afraid he knew why.

"I'M JUST CURIOUS why you didn't tell me last night about the men in the woods," Matt asked, careful to keep any trace of condemnation from his tone.

Guided by his questions, the boy had told essentially the same story for the tape. The differences in this version and the earlier one had been minor, primarily in an expansion on the conversations between Taylor and the Evans girl, both before and after he'd gone into the woods. Apparently Lisa had never seen the men and hadn't believed him when he'd told her about them.

It was obvious that the events had been traumatic to the boy, however. Enough so that Matt *did* wonder why Taylor hadn't mentioned them to him last night.

He also wanted to know what, if anything, the kid had told his mother. Robin had appeared to be as surprised at the revelations as he'd been, but it seemed to Matt that the boy would have wanted to tell *someone* what had happened, especially given Lisa's disappearance.

"You didn't ask me," Taylor said. "You just asked me about yesterday."

Logical. And damning, Matt thought. He had felt that the boy was hiding something, but in the press of the frantic search for Lisa, he hadn't paid enough attention to his gut.

"And you didn't think that what happened on Tuesday might have had something to do with Lisa not going home."

"I asked my mom, and she said that Lisa was okay. That her mother had gotten mixed up about something Lisa had to do."

Matt glanced at Robin, who acknowledged the veracity of that statement with a small nod.

"So you thought Lisa was okay?"

"My mom *told* me she was. I prayed for her, but…"

"But what, Taylor?"

"I was afraid God wouldn't answer 'cause I'd done something wrong."

"Lying to Lisa."

"I *did* have to pee. Only not when I told her I did. I didn't know those men were going to be in the woods."

"Of course, you didn't," Matt comforted. "You couldn't have known."

The fair head nodded. The child was eager to accept absolution for that sin.

Matt was more than willing to grant it. No one could have known what the little boy would stumble upon during that trip into the woods. Besides, Taylor Holt's lie had given them far more information than the crime scene had provided. Three men in overcoats. At least they had that much now.

"Can you tell me anything else about the men you saw? Maybe something about how they looked."

The boy took a breath, his eyes flicking up to his mother's. She smiled at him, nodding encouragement.

Taylor shrugged his shoulders, tilting his head to the side. "I don't know. They were just like...men."

"Were they black or white, Taylor?"

"White."

"Dark hair or light like yours and your mom's?"

A moment's hesitation while the boy considered his mother. When he looked back at Matt, he said, "Like yours."

"Brown?"

A nod.

"All of them?"

After a small hesitation, another nod.

"Okay, how about size? Were they tall or short? One taller than the others? One shorter? All the same?"

"Maybe the same."

"My size? Or shorter? Taller?"

As he posed the questions, Matt recognized the futility of this. All adults looked the same to a child this age. All tall. All big.

"Maybe...shorter."

Matt was six foot one, so that gave them a range, although not a very accurate one in his book. It was obvious the kid was giving answers without having any notion of the standards adults would impose on such comparisons.

"Fat or skinny?" he asked. That should be safe. Even kids thought in those terms.

Taylor shook his head, however, looking down at the table. He ran one small, ballpoint-stained finger through the moisture the soda from his lunch had left on the table, drawing it out along a line in the grain of the wood.

"Just average size?"

A nod, but his eyes remained downcast. Matt looked at Robin for help.

"This is important, Taylor," she said. "We need to know about the size of those men and anything else you can think of that will help us identify them."

"Did *they* get Lisa?" he asked, looking up at her. "Is that why she disappeared?"

"I don't know," Robin said, looking over his head to meet Matt's eyes. "Even the police don't know, but they need to ask those men about Lisa."

"It was something bad, wasn't it?" Taylor asked, shifting his attention to Matt. "What was on the ground that they were looking at was something bad."

What did you tell a seven-year-old about that body in the woods? What could you tell him?

"You don't need to worry about that, Taylor," he said. "Or about them."

"But if they got Lisa—"

"Taylor..." Robin broke in.

"They aren't going to get you," Matt said. "If that's what you're worried about, you don't have to be. We're going to take real good care of you and your mom."

"If I had told you about those men, maybe you could have taken care of Lisa."

The near-adult perception in that caught them both off guard. Neither of them said anything for a couple of heartbeats.

"Even if you *had* told us, we couldn't have done anything," Matt said. Not the absolute truth, perhaps, but the boy didn't need to feel any more guilt over what had happened. "You didn't see them do anything that was against the law."

As he said the words, he tried to think if he had asked that question. The reason Taylor hadn't told him all this last night was because he hadn't formulated the right questions. Maybe he still hadn't.

"You *didn't*, did you? You didn't see them do anything wrong in the woods, did you?"

"I didn't like the red thing. That's what scared me the most."

Matt nodded without comment.

"And then they all ran toward Lisa. That scared me, too."

"But you didn't see them hurt Lisa?"

A side-to-side movement of his head.

"Or hurt anyone else?" Matt asked.

The same motion was repeated.

For several seconds, while Matt tried to think if there was anything else he should ask the boy, the only sound in the room was the soft whir of the tape. He looked up at Robin, raising his brows.

During most of the interview she had sat silent, but the occasional promptings she'd given her son had been both timely and helpful. Maybe she had thought of something he'd forgotten.

Before she could respond, the door of the conference room opened behind him. Surprised by the interruption, Matt turned to find Ephraim Stokes peeking in through the narrow opening. Without saying anything, Stokes tilted his head toward the hall, an obvious signal that he wanted Matt to come out.

There seemed to be only one reason anyone in the department would break in on this interrogation. Matt had told his chief and the members of task force the bare bones of the boy's story before he'd brought the tape recorder into the room. They all knew how important this could be.

"Excuse me," Matt said, pushing up from the table and then reaching down to punch off the recorder. "Try to think of anything else that happened that day you haven't told me about, Taylor. We want to make sure we've got everything you can remember on the tape."

The boy didn't even look up, still rubbing that small grubby finger along the pattern in the wood. Robin Holt's eyes, however, left no doubt that she'd come to the same conclusion about this interruption that he had.

Her control didn't break, not even now, but the fear and anguish were clearly there. And there was nothing he could do to relieve them.

CHAPTER EIGHT

"THEY'VE FOUND the girl," Matt guessed as soon as the door to the conference room closed behind him.

"I knew you was gonna think that," Stokes said. He must have somehow managed a few hours of sleep since Matt had seen him. The faded blue eyes didn't appear nearly so bloodshot as they had at dawn. "We ain't that lucky."

"Then… What's the problem?"

Eph was too good a cop to interrupt a witness interview without good reason. Other than news of Lisa, Matt couldn't think of anything that would qualify.

"A couple of things are going on I thought you ought to know about. The first is scuttlebutt, but considering the source, it's probably accurate. According to the coroner's prelim, the guy they found in the woods was missing his tongue. And it wasn't at the scene, by the way."

With the information, another piece of the puzzle Taylor Holt had given them fell sickeningly into place.

…he bent down and picked it up. It was red. That's how I could see it so good through the trees. Because it was all red. Just like Lisa's jacket.

"A pretty goddamn obvious warning to *somebody* not to talk," Stokes added. "Wonder if it worked?"

Or an attempt to make sure everybody knew *why* the guy in the woods had ended up dead, Matt thought.

"Could be," he said, wondering how Robin would react to this information.

The new discovery might even make a difference in the degree of protection the Holts would be afforded. Taylor was now too important to the investigation to compromise on that.

"And the other thing..." the veteran cop began. He glanced almost furtively down the long corridor before he looked back at Matt. "The guys from the GBI are coming to talk to the kid. In the spirit of co-operation," Stokes drew out the word sarcastically, emphasizing the first syllable, "Chief told them some of what the boy's said. I didn't know if you was done questioning him, but if not, I thought you'd want to know they're on their way to take over."

"Close enough to being done," Matt said, thinking about what the Bureau's involvement with the Holts might mean. Maybe he was worrying needlessly, but he didn't want anyone else to be in charge of their safety. "They need to be under protection. Both of them. The men the boy saw in the woods were obviously involved in that homicide."

"You think they took the girl? Whoever the kid saw?"

"It makes sense. The boy thinks they saw her. A couple of days later, she's gone."

"If they're so eager to eliminate witnesses, why delay?"

"Maybe they didn't know who she was. Maybe it took them a while to track her down. Or maybe they had to get permission."

That theory would add another layer of suspects, but it was one that should be considered. The men Taylor saw might be the hired help, and not the decision makers.

"If they thought she saw what they did to that guy..."

Stokes paused, shaking his head. "These are *not* nice people. They'll do anything to keep her quiet."

The pool of congealed blood beneath the open mouth of the corpse was in Matt's head. It wasn't an image he wanted there. Not in connection with Lisa Evans. Especially not in connection to Taylor Holt.

"I know."

He did know. All too well. With every passing hour the likelihood of getting Lisa back to her parents safely diminished. And given the scenario the little boy had just outlined on the tape, the chances of that happening now had dropped a hundredfold. The teenager had probably been dead since shortly after she was taken.

A noise at the end of the hall attracted his attention. The two agents from the Georgia Bureau of Investigation, escorted by the chief of police, were making their way toward the conference room.

Their ties, neatly knotted at the necks of heavily starched dress shirts this morning, had been loosened. The shirts themselves were wilted, just like those of the cops who'd been working this case all night.

"You gonna listen in while they question him?" Stokes asked.

"I doubt I'd be welcome."

"Hell, you're the one who figured out the link between the dead guy and the Evans girl."

"They're probably wondering why I didn't do it last night."

"Screw 'em. They ain't got that much."

"They do now," Matt said, his voice low enough that the approaching trio couldn't hear.

"Detective Ridge, you met Agent Burke this morning, I think," the chief of police said, his tone jovial enough to reveal he was nervous about Matt's acceptance of the agents' interference. "This is his partner, Clint Donovan. They want to talk to the Holt kid."

"He's upset about Lisa's disappearance," Matt warned, despite the fact that he knew they weren't going to listen to him. "As young as he is, he's come to believe that he had something to do with it."

"How's that?" Tom Burke asked, seeming genuinely interested.

"He's the one who went into the woods where we found the body this morning. Told her he had to pee. When he didn't come out, the Evans girl came in to get him. In his mind that makes him responsible for what happened to her."

Both men nodded as if they understood, but Matt's stomach tightened at the possibility of their inadvertently reinforcing that notion in Taylor's head. It seemed as if he were deserting Robin and the boy after promising to take care of them. Of course, even if he were in the room when they questioned him, he couldn't do too much to steer the agents away from anything they deemed a legitimate area of inquiry.

"We'll assure him that isn't the case," Burke promised. "I got kids of my own. I know how screwed up their thinking can get. Got kids, Detective Ridge?"

It was a question he'd been asked a dozen times since the wreck. He thought he'd learned a long time ago how to deal with its emotional reverberation.

The first few times it had happened, he'd tried to explain his situation and had ended up making the questioner feel bad. The last couple of years he'd simply said no without offering an explanation. He didn't know why he hesitated to do that now.

"Matt lost his boy a few years back," Dawkins said into the sudden, uncomfortable silence. "Automobile accident."

"Sorry," the GBI agent said. "I didn't have any way of knowing. Must be hard handling a case involving a child after something like that."

He meant Lisa. As much as Matt cared about the missing girl, however, as hard as he was working to find her, at this point it was the little boy in the room behind him who concerned him the most. And he acknowledged once more that his priorities in this investigation were probably not in order.

Except Taylor Holt is still alive. And you now know what the threat against him is. Instead of saying any of that aloud, he simply nodded.

"You've done good work on this," Burke went on, trying to make up for his faux pas, his tone as falsely jovial as the chief's had been. "Finding the Holt kid. Getting his story. Why don't you relax and let us take it from here?"

It was only what Matt had expected, but still it infuriated him. Before he could lodge an objection, his superior sealed the deal.

"Good idea," the chief said. "You look like you could use some sleep, Matt. We need everybody on this, of course, but we can spare you for a few hours. Go on home. Get some shut-eye and grab a shower before you come back."

"I'm fine," Matt said, fighting the wave of resentment at having the investigation taken away from him, especially when it seemed that things were breaking.

Professional or personal resentment? he wondered, and decided it didn't matter. Whichever it was, he was entitled.

"The Holts trust me," he began. "They might feel better—"

"We got it covered," Donovan interrupted, speaking for the first time. The second agent moved past Matt to put his hand on the knob of the conference room door. "You go on home like the chief said. Get some rest. Burnout's too easy on something like this."

"I'm *not* burned out."

The denial sounded both clipped and defensive. The loss of control that represented was so unusual for him that Matt wondered if they could be right. Maybe he *had* gone too long without sleep. Or maybe he was emotionally vulnerable because the case involved a child.

"Good," Donovan said succinctly. "Let's keep it that way."

He opened the door, holding it until his partner and the chief had entered the conference room. It shut behind them with a finality that left no doubt about who was to remain on the outside.

"Bastards," Eph Stokes said under his breath.

Maybe they were, but they were also very obviously in charge now. And there didn't seem to be a damn thing Matt could do about it.

HE STOPPED at the local diner on the way home, catching the tail end of the lunch buffet. And he took the shower the chief had suggested, letting the hot water stream over the knot of tension where his neck joined his shoulders. Then, feeling the tiredness in every bone of his body, he lay down on his bed and tried to sleep.

He should have known it would be an exercise in futility. Everything that had happened in the past twenty-four hours ran through his consciousness like a tape played at the wrong speed. His questioning of Taylor last night. The scene in the woods this morning. The boy's drawings, colored now by Matt's newly acquired knowledge of the horror their stick figures acted out.

Through it all ran the memory of Robin Holt's eyes, lifted to his. In his head her plea repeated over and over again.

Don't be long.

By the time he got back to City Hall three hours later, the number of reporters out front seemed to have doubled. And this time they weren't taking any chance that they might miss something. The side doors were covered by camera crews as well.

He ignored their shouted questions, single-mindedly making his way into the building. He went straight to the conference room and opened the door without bothering to knock.

The room was empty. Someone had cleaned up the cups and the remains of this morning's donuts.

He walked toward the chief's office at the front of the building. On the way he passed several officers, most of whom spoke, congratulating him on securing the Holt boy's information. Judging by the number of uniforms in the building, the department had pulled some people off the search, apparently content to let the volunteers continue it.

At this point, almost twenty-four hours after the disappearance, that was probably a reasonable decision, he admitted. Especially now that they had a new avenue of investigation open to them.

He knocked on the closed door of Dawkins's office and entered when the chief yelled, "Come in." The two GBI agents were seated on either side of his desk. A red and white striped bucket from the local chicken franchise stood in the center amid a clutter of computer equipment and papers. All three men were partaking of the contents.

Early supper or late lunch? That would probably depend on how busy they'd all been this afternoon.

"Where are the Holts?"

Matt knew his question sounded like a demand, but he was past the point of caring what anyone thought. He needed to know that Robin and the boy were safe.

"We sent 'em on home about twenty, maybe thirty minutes ago."

It took a second to process what Tom Burke had just said. There had been no mention of protection, but Matt couldn't believe anyone would be stupid enough not to provide it. Not after they'd listened to Taylor's story. He assumed they had at least done that.

"Who's watching them?"

"Eph Stokes volunteered," Dawkins offered, wiping grease from his chin with one of the paper napkins that had been provided with the meal. "Said he'd stand first watch since he'd gotten a little sleep this morning."

"You got somebody lined up for the rest of the night?"

"I'm gonna see to that just as soon as we eat," Dawkins said. "You had supper? Plenty of chicken in here." He nudged the bucket toward the front of the desk with his forearm.

"Any news on the Evans girl?" Matt asked, ignoring the gesture. He had addressed the question to Burke, but it was the other agent—Donovan?—who answered.

"Yeah, as a matter of fact. We got a confirmed sighting."

He offered that startling development before he nonchalantly bit into the drumstick he held.

"A *sighting?*"

As Matt repeated the word, he realized that he had long ago given up hope that Lisa could still be alive. He'd done the one thing a cop should never do. He had already decided where this investigation was heading, and it hadn't been where Donovan was indicating.

"An off-duty officer saw her at a fast food place in Marietta. She was with a boy who was acting real suspicious. Got spooked when he realized the guy was watching him. The girl never got out of the car, but the witness got a good look at her. Dark green truck. Couldn't see the tag. The Marietta police are searching for it. We're following up here to see if any of the Evans girl's friends has a vehicle that fits the description."

"And the witness is sure it was Lisa?"

Nothing about that made sense. It didn't fit with her parents' certainty that she hadn't run away. Or with Taylor's story about the men in the woods.

"Identified her from the posters," Donovan said. "Right down to the clothes she was wearing yesterday."

Jeans and a red jacket. Despite the argument about it, her mother hadn't been able to remember what color top she'd finally worn. A sweater, she believed, but she couldn't even be sure about that. Just that it was not one that Pam Evans had thought was too revealing.

"The parents swore she didn't *have* a boyfriend."

"Yeah, well, they've had some second thoughts on that this afternoon. They think maybe this could be somebody she met at camp last summer. That maybe the two of them had been corresponding by e-mail."

"And they didn't think to mention that until now?"

"Could be somebody she met on the Internet," the chief offered. "Hell, these days people don't know who their kids are talking to. Wasn't that way when we was growing up, I can tell you.''

"What about the Holt boy's story?" Matt asked.

"The one about seeing some men in the woods a few days ago?" The tone of Donovan's question was smug. Condescending. He looked as if he were trying not to grin as he asked it.

His partner shrugged. "According to the mother, the kid's got an imagination. A real creative type."

"You think he made it up?" In Matt's opinion that was a patently ridiculous supposition, given the wealth of detail Taylor had provided.

"New kid in town," Burke said. "Maybe he wanted to make an impression. Or maybe he just wanted in on the excitement. His babysitter disappears. Everybody's all concerned about her and asking him questions, so he thinks up something to tell them."

Not *them,* Matt thought. Taylor hadn't told *them.* He had told *him.* And he believed every word the boy had said. He hadn't made the story up to get in on things. Matt had had to drag every last detail of it out of him.

"Except there really was a body in those woods. How do you explain that?"

"That's probably what set him off. He hears about a body in those particular woods—someplace he's familiar with—and he just takes it from there," Burke said. "Like I said, real creative."

"And right away he becomes the center of attention," Donovan added. "Just what he wanted."

"That *isn't* what he wanted."

"First time you questioned him, the night the girl disappeared, he don't mention anything about a body or going into the woods. It isn't until *after* they find the body that the kid becomes this fountain of information. Something about the timing on that didn't seem right to us. Now we know what it was.''

''The Holts didn't know a body had been found until *after* Taylor told me his story. The reporters asked Ms. Holt about the find as I was bringing them into City Hall this morning. She thought they were talking about Lisa.''

''She's admitted she had the radio on most of the morning. The kid could have heard about it even if she didn't.''

''Except he knew a few things that haven't yet been made public,'' Matt reminded them.

The information Stokes had given him hadn't yet been released. There was no way Taylor could have known about the mutilation.

The agents' eyes met across the desk.

''Or maybe you're reading more into his story than you should be,'' Burke suggested, his lips pursed. ''According to the tape, the kid talked about dead cats. People playing kick ball. That *ain't* what happened to that guy in the woods.''

''Besides,'' Donovan added, ''if Lisa Evans is riding around Marietta with her boyfriend, then whatever the kid says he saw don't amount to a hill of beans. It's not relevant. Not to her disappearance.''

''Somebody tried to break into their house last night.''

''Maybe. Maybe not,'' the chief offered. ''There's a storm. Power goes out. Maybe after Lisa's disappearance, Ms. Holt just got spooked. No sign anybody tried to force entry. No sign of an intruder at all. No footprints in the damp soil. And *that's* according to the report *you* filed, Matt.''

''There were so many footprints left by the searchers that a new set would have been hard to spot.''

"Bottom line is that we don't think the kid's story has anything to do with Lisa's disappearance," Dawkins said. At least he had the decency to sound regretful. "We're gonna keep an eye on the Holts, mind you. Leastways until we get the Evans girl home safe and sound, but… The kid's got an active imagination. Even his mama's admitted to that."

Rage, so strong it shocked him, swept through Matt's body. Anger generated by the assumption that he had been taken in by a seven-year-old? Or anger on behalf of Taylor Holt, who had done anything *but* seek the limelight.

"If Lisa Evans *is* safe, then nobody's going to be happier than I am," he said. "That doesn't mean that what the Holt boy said isn't true. And you're dead wrong about the motives you're ascribing to him. This *wasn't* a play for attention."

"You seem to be pretty heavily invested in the kid's story," Donovan said. "Maybe you've gotten too close to the situation."

"According to the chief, he's about the same age your boy would have been," Burke added.

The rage ratcheted up another notch. There were some things that should be off-limits. Even in something like this.

"I think the kid's telling the truth about what he saw. That's my *professional* opinion," Matt said.

It was. He was thankful his voice was steady as he gave it.

"We appreciate that," Tom Burke said.

"We just happen to disagree," Donovan added. The smugness was back.

"You get some sleep when you went home?" Dawkins asked.

"I'm fine," Matt said. It seemed as if he'd been saying that a lot lately.

"Good. 'Cause I need somebody to coordinate things with Marietta. Give them all the information we got on this. Talk to their witness. Make sure his story is as solid as we've been led to believe. You up to that?"

It was a way to determine if the sighting was valid, something he doubted. If the girl the off-duty officer had seen in Marietta *wasn't* Lisa, then the agents would be forced to reconsider their opinion about what Taylor had told him.

"What about continuing the protection for the Holts?"

He didn't care if they thought he was wrong. Or obsessed. He wasn't about to let this slide no matter what the GBI wanted to believe.

"Stokes is probably good until eleven. I'll have someone lined up to take over long before then."

"I want your word on that, Hank."

"We aren't taking any chances. I promise you that. Not with *any* of this. Not until we get to the bottom of it. You can have my word on *that*."

CHAPTER NINE

"I THOUGHT you might like some coffee," Robin said, holding the steaming mug out like an offering.

Despite the assurance from the GBI agents that Lisa had been spotted, she couldn't shake the sense of threat she'd felt since Pam Evans's phone call yesterday evening. She was very grateful Officer Stokes was here. More grateful for his promise that someone would be on guard at the house all night.

More than once in the hours since they'd been home, she had found herself hoping Matt Ridge would come by to check on them. It seemed strange that after the interest he'd shown, he would just disappear. It was always possible his attention had been strictly professional, of course. A good cop doing his job. Just because she had felt there was more to it than that didn't mean she'd been right.

She had already reconciled herself to the probability that he wouldn't be Stokes's replacement. Detectives weren't assigned this kind of duty. Not with everything else that was going on.

"If that's in the way of a bribe, I accept," the older cop said with a smile.

"It's not decaf," she warned as she handed it over.

"Even better." Stokes blew across the top of the mug to cool the liquid it contained before he took a tentative sip. "Your boy asleep?"

She had been surprised at the ease with which she'd gotten Taylor down. She had expected him to beg her to lie down beside him again. Instead, although it was only a little after eight, he'd said his prayers and been asleep before she'd eased out of the room.

Telling Matt Ridge what he'd seen on Tuesday seemed to have relieved his anxiety. It was almost as if he'd given that worry over to the adults and retreated back into the thoughtless innocence of childhood. She wished she could do the same.

"It's been a *very* long day."

It seemed as if it had been a month since she and Taylor had sat down in this same kitchen last night for supper, only to be interrupted by the Evans's phone call. A little more than twenty-four hours ago, she realized. And an eternity.

Officer Stokes nodded agreement. Elbows on the table, he was holding the mug in both hands as if to warm them. The cold that had pervaded the house last night, however, had been replaced by the warmth of her reliable furnace. And light was again available at the flick of a switch.

"You can go on to bed if you want, Ms. Holt. I'm gonna be here until somebody comes to relieve me."

"If you don't mind some company…" Robin ventured hesitantly.

She slipped into the chair across the table without giving him a chance to protest. She didn't want to be alone. That's why she had come back downstairs rather than going to her bedroom.

As exhausted as she was, she doubted she'd be able to sleep. The last twenty-four hours had been an emotional roller coaster. And the ride wasn't over yet.

It couldn't be. Not for her. Not until Lisa was home.

And not until the murder of the man found in the woods today had been solved.

Despite the agents' skeptical questions, she had no doubt Taylor had seen something alarming Tuesday afternoon. Maybe his fear and anxiety about Lisa had caused him to embellish what had happened, but he had always been a truthful child. She had never known him to fabricate something out of whole cloth.

"Company's always welcome on a job like this," Stokes said. He took another sip of coffee, and then looked at her over the rim of the mug, his eyes assessing. "Don't you let them bastards make you start doubting your boy, Ms. Holt. He saw *something* in those woods. Matt Ridge believed him, and Matt's too good a cop to be taken in by a kid's tall tales."

The comment so accurately echoed what she'd been thinking she wondered if she were that transparent. In any case Stokes was right. Matt had spent far more time with Taylor than the agents had. They had come to the interview with a lot of preconceived ideas because it appeared everyone had been wrong about something bad happening to Lisa.

Even if that were true, it didn't mean Taylor was lying about what he'd seen. As Stokes said, Matt had believed him.

"Have you known him long? Detective Ridge, I mean?"

The cardinal rule of her existence had been not to let anyone become too interested in her. The second one should probably be that she not become too interested in anyone either. It was a little late for that now.

She had liked everything about Matt Ridge. The way he looked. The way he carried himself. The way he had made her feel, both fragile and protected.

She had especially appreciated the kindness with which he'd treated Taylor this afternoon. She was unable to resist the opportunity to find out more about him.

"Known him since he was a rookie."

She waited through another, longer swallow of coffee, wondering if that would be the extent of the information the older man was willing to share. She watched as he took a white handkerchief out of the back pocket of his pants and unfolded it to wipe traces of coffee off his mustache. Only then did he add the kind of detail she had been eager to hear.

"First time I met him, Matt was fresh out of college with a brand-new degree in criminal justice. He'd spent some time in the military before he'd gone to school, so he was older than most starting out in this business. I figured he'd stay here six months or so, get something on his résumé, and then move on to greener pastures. Somewhere with higher pay. Better benefits. More opportunity for advancement than Mallory. He had ambition written all over him."

"But he didn't leave," Robin prodded after another pause during which Stokes refolded the handkerchief and laid it beside the mug he again cradled between his palms.

His eyes came up to hers before he answered. "He mighta done that. If it hadn't been for meeting Karen Stoddard."

Something shifted unpleasantly in her stomach, like a cold stone settling into the silt at the bottom of a pond. She acknowledged the ridiculousness of the reaction. Intellectually acknowledged it. Emotionally…

Just because Matt Ridge didn't wear a wedding ring was no reason for her to have assumed he was unattached. A lot of men in the South didn't wear rings.

And if there hadn't *been someone in his life—someone*

named Karen? What possible difference could that make to you?

"Karen was a Mallory girl, born and bred. Her family's been here for a hundred years. Maybe more. She wasn't about to pull up roots and move somewhere else. And I expect she told Matt that in no uncertain terms."

His grin faded, and he took another dab at the mustache with his handkerchief.

"About went under when her and their baby was killed. Six months or more, he walked around looking like Death taking a—" The faded blue eyes widened before Stokes chose a less vulgar comparison. "Like Death eating a cracker. It'd hurt your heart to see *anybody* in that much pain, but especially a man."

"What happened to them?"

Even as she asked the question, Robin admitted she didn't want to hear this. Not a story about the death of a child. Not with Lisa still missing.

"Driver of an eighteen-wheeler went to sleep and crossed the median. Karen had taken Josh in for some kind of booster shots that morning. Doc Jacobs was still doing obstetrics then. He was running late 'cause he'd had an unexpected delivery. If he'd been on time, she woulda been home long before the truck hit that stretch of interstate."

The old man's eyes were no longer focused on the cup he held between his hands. They were seeing the accident. Or the face of the man whose life it had devastated.

"I remember him saying that to me a couple of weeks later. Never been able to get the idea out of my head since then. How big a role chance played in what happened. If she'd been two minutes one way or the other leaving Doc's office…"

Robin let the silence lie between them, respecting the sorrow she heard in his voice.

''Cops are notorious for bad marriages,'' Stokes went on after a moment or two. ''Too much stress. Too many opportunities for extramarital experiments, if you take my meaning. It was a real shame for something like that to have happened to one of the good ones.''

''How long ago?''

How long had that pain been in Matt Ridge's eyes when he looked at a child? She hadn't known until now what it was she had seen in their dark depths.

''Must be...five years. More like six now, I guess,'' Stokes amended. ''I remember it was right before Christmas. Hell of a time to lose somebody. Every carol, every decoration, the whole thing's gonna come back.''

Six years. If Matt Ridge's son had been a baby that Christmas, then had he lived...

''He would have been about Taylor's age,'' she realized softly.

''I thought about that,'' Stokes said. ''That and—'' The words were cut off as the faded eyes considered her face.

''What?'' she asked, uncomfortable with what was in them.

''She was a lot like you. Karen. About the same size. Same...mannerisms. Coloring. I thought that the first time I saw you and the boy. Figured Matt had to have seen it, too.''

If so, that might explain why he had been so determined to follow up on the missed interview this morning. It might also explain his consideration of Taylor. Even his treatment of her.

It had been a long time since a man had touched her. A

longer time since her body had responded to the feel of a man's hand.

She remembered the strength of his long, dark fingers taking hers to help her from the car. The intimacy of his palm fitted against the small of her back.

And she *had* responded. She had been very aware of the sheer masculinity of the man who had sheltered hers and Taylor's bodies with his as he'd hurried them into the courthouse today.

"He didn't tell you," Stokes said, his inflection flat rather than questioning.

"He never mentioned them. I wondered, though, when I saw him with Taylor…"

She was unable to put into words what there had been about Matt's interaction with the little boy that had impressed her. Maybe the same sense of being protected that had enveloped her when he'd put his arm around her shoulders at the courthouse. Whatever she'd felt, it had instilled a deep sense of trust.

"That's the one thing them two bastards said today that I agreed with," Stokes said.

"What's that?"

"How hard it must be for him to work a case involving a child."

Especially a little boy.

Poor Matt, she thought, never realizing that she had long ago stopped thinking of him as Detective Ridge. And never realizing that the fine line of emotional detachment she'd walked for the last four years had now blurred irreparably.

"WELL, SHE'S A RUNAWAY all right," Lieutenant Reynolds said, propping a hip on the battered desk they'd let Matt use. "She just ain't *your* runaway."

"You sure?" Matt asked, feeling the tension that had dissipated as he'd worked with the Marietta police this evening begin to twist his gut again.

"Highway Patrol stopped the two of 'em this side of Cedartown. Two scared kids in his old man's pickup. Which he'd taken without permission, of course." The Marietta detective pulled a spiral notebook out of the breast pocket of his blazer and flipped it open. "Jimmy Purdue and Dana Lynn Bickle. She's got the identification to prove that, by the way, including a state driver's license."

Matt knew the patrolmen who had stopped them would have confirmed its validity before they called this in. He didn't even bother to ask the question.

"It's easy to see why there was some confusion," Reynolds went on. "Same physical description as the Evans girl. They were heading to Alabama to get married. She's got an aunt in Eufala she thought would sign for her. She's four months pregnant and terrified of what her daddy's gonna do when he finds out. That's Dana Lynn that's pregnant, not the aunt," Reynolds added with a grin.

And not Lisa Evans.

It was a good thing the search hadn't been called off, Matt thought. Thanks to the media, however, word of the Marietta sighting had spread through the volunteers like wildfire.

He wondered how many had called it a day earlier than they might have if this story hadn't surfaced. He also wondered how many cops had grabbed a couple of hours of sleep they would have foregone if they hadn't believed the missing girl had been seen, safe and sound, on the other side of the state.

"Sorry to be the bearer of bad news," Reynolds went on when Matt didn't respond to his attempt at humor.

"Witness seemed so damn sure. And everything matched. Even to the clothes your girl was wearing."

"They all seem sure," Matt said with a trace of bitterness.

They had received hundreds of tips throughout the day on the hotline set up for that purpose. None of them had been as credible as this, but the department had checked each of them out. All had been dead ends.

"I'll let the parents know," he said. "Thanks for all your help."

"Wish it *had* been yours. However much trouble Dana Lynn thinks she's in, it pales in comparison. Y'all identified that body yet?"

"We're working on it. His prints don't seem to be in any database. No identifying tags in the clothes. We've put out the guy's picture."

"I saw it. Somebody didn't like him too well."

"You don't know the half of it," Matt said, and then wished he hadn't.

The mutilation was still being kept under wraps. Even though he was talking to a fellow officer, it would have been better not to hint that there was more involved than the obvious injuries the camera had captured.

He could blame that slip on a lack of sleep and disappointment, he supposed, but as far as he was concerned neither was a legitimate excuse.

"At least you got you a witness now."

It took a second for the words to penetrate his tiredness. A few longer for the surge of anxiety for the Holts, engendered by the Marietta cop's bad news, to balloon into full-blown terror.

"What do you mean?" he asked, working to keep that sudden fear out of his voice.

''The kid. The one the Evans girl was babysitting for. They said he was able to give you guys a description of the perpetrators. 'Course, I wondered when I heard that how much help a seven-year-old was gonna be. I guess you never know.''

The last was a subtle play for more information. Matt ignored it.

''You hear that from someone with our department?''

It was always possible. Officers talked, but usually with something like this, it was on a need-to-know basis. Matt couldn't think of any reason Marietta would have been told about what Taylor Holt had seen.

''Saw it on one of the cable news networks. Could have been local, but we usually keep the set tuned to FOX during the day. Whoever it was showed the kid and his mother being escorted into the courthouse. They said something to the effect that y'all were hoping his description of the men he'd seen in the woods would prove helpful in the investigation.''

The silence stretched as Matt fought to contain his anger. There was no legitimate reason for that information to be released. It wouldn't aid in the search for Lisa. All it did—

All it did was put Taylor into greater danger.

''I take it you didn't know that was out there,'' Reynolds said, finally realizing what was going on.

''I can't imagine why it would be,'' Matt said, his voice stiff with fury. ''Seems like sheer stupidity to me.''

It was hard not to rail against whoever had released the information. Harder not to blame himself for bringing the Holts in to the courthouse today.

Of course, it had already been widely reported that Robin was the last person to see Lisa before she'd disappeared. They were witnesses, so no one should have been surprised that they would be interrogated. That should have been explanation enough if their presence there had been questioned.

"Yeah, well…" Reynolds folded the notebook and stuck it back in his pocket before he looked up again. He raised his brows, tilting his head to the side as if embarrassed either by Matt's anger or by his department's screw-up. "I guess I should say sorry for *again* being the bearer of bad news. Things leak out during investigation. It's the nature of the beast. Everybody wants to share whatever insider knowledge they have. Make themselves look important. I'm sure your witnesses are being protected," he added, straightening away from the desk. "No harm, no foul."

No harm, no foul.

God, he hoped that was true, Matt thought, picturing two pairs of blue eyes that had looked trustingly into his.

Don't be long, Robin Holt had urged. Sidetracked by what had turned out to be a wild-goose chase, he had been. Way too long.

He could only hope that whoever the idiot was who had let the news slip about the information Taylor carried in his head was not the same person who had been put in charge of arranging security for Robin and her son.

"NOT OUR GIRL," Matt said, holding his cell phone with his shoulder as he took a sip of the coffee he'd just picked up at the drive-through window.

The entire expedition had been a dead end….in a case that suddenly seemed to be full of them.

Maybe his exhaustion had affected his perspective. Or perhaps it was the officiousness of the two GBI agents in taking control of the only promising angle he'd seen in this mess. Whatever excitement he'd felt listening to Taylor's story this afternoon had faded with tonight's disappointment.

"We know."

There was some nuance in Hank Dawkins's tone he couldn't quite read. Maybe that, too, was a by-product of his tiredness. Dawkins wasn't noted for his subtlety.

"Marietta already call you?"

Reynolds hadn't indicated that he intended to. Maybe word had gotten to the media. They were hungry for any scrap of information, and they'd been playing up the supposed sighting all evening.

"They didn't have to," Dawkins said, sounding as wiped out as Matt felt. "I shoulda called you, Matt. My bad."

It took a few seconds for Matt to reach the only conclusion those two phrases could lead him to. "I shoulda called you" because he was still the lead detective on the Evans case. "They didn't have to" because at some time during the night it had become obvious to the Mallory Police Department that the sighting in Marietta was bogus.

"They found her," Matt said flatly.

Despite his increasing certainty that Lisa was dead, the realization that her body had been found was like a kick in the stomach. And because of the chief's tone, the one he hadn't been able to read, there was no doubt in his mind that what they had found had been the girl's body.

The smell of coffee, which only moments before seemed so appealing, nauseated him. He lowered the cup to the holder, and then straightened, holding the phone to his ear with the hand he'd just freed.

"One of the cadaver dogs. They'd buried her, just not deep enough."

The face in the photo Pam Evans had handed him last

night was in his mind's eye, the smiling features now smudged with the dirt of a hastily dug grave.

"What do we know?" he forced himself to ask.

"Broken neck. No sign of sexual assault. That ain't been ruled out yet, you understand, but nothing about the condition of the body led the coroner to think it had happened."

"How long?"

"The cold last night might be a factor, but his preliminary time of death is between six and midnight yesterday."

He'd be willing to bet that if the ME were able to narrow the range, it would be closer to the lower end of his estimate. Lisa Evans had almost certainly been dead within minutes after she disappeared through Robin Holt's front door.

They'd been lying in wait for her. Certain where they could find her because they had followed the two of them out of the woods that Tuesday afternoon? And if so...

"What about the Holts?"

"I didn't see any point in calling 'em tonight. They've probably gone to bed already."

"I meant what about increased protection for them?"

Why was it that no one seemed to realize that Taylor's story connected all the dots, including the ones that led the killer to Lisa? And to the boy.

"We got it covered," Dawkins assured him. "I told you that this afternoon. We ain't gonna let nothing happen to that boy, I promise you. By the way, you got a couple of calls while you were gone. Sheriff Eagleton wanted to touch base on extending the search parameters. I guess that one can wait. And somebody named Rippetoe called. Wants you to call him back. When you get here, I'll fill you in on everything that's happened. This is still your case.''

Still his case. And it was no longer a kidnapping, but a murder.

CHAPTER TEN

ROBIN WASN'T SURE what had disturbed her sleep this time. Not a drop in temperature like last night. Or a voice on the radio like this morning.

Her awakening had been instantaneous. Her eyes had jerked open as if someone had thrown cold water on the bed.

Instantly awake. Instantly aware that she had to get to Taylor and hide him.

The rational part of her brain spent a few futile seconds arguing against her awareness, but instinct was stronger than logic. She slipped out of her bed and ran on bare feet to drag Taylor from his. By the time she reached his bedroom, she could hear noises from below.

A struggle? Or something falling? There were no voices, but she believed that must have been what awakened her. Voices. The sound of something taking place that shouldn't have.

She bent over Taylor's bed, cupping his cheek with her palm as she whispered to him. "Wake up, baby."

He didn't stir, not even when she put her other hand on his shoulder, shaking him gently. She didn't want to frighten him into crying out, but it was difficult to contain the sense of urgency that had driven her here.

"Taylor, you have to wake up."

She shook him harder this time and was rewarded by the

slow, upward rise of his eyelids. Despite the night-light, she couldn't gauge his degree of alertness. And it didn't matter, she decided. She couldn't wait any longer.

"Come on. Get up," she said, slipping her arm under his shoulders to lift him physically.

His body was unresponsive; his expression unchanged, the slack-mouthed, heavy-lidded appearance of a child who has had too little sleep. He murmured something incoherent, turning his face away from the light as his eyelids began to droop.

"There's someone in the house," she whispered, giving up any pretence that she could protect him from the knowledge of what was happening. "We have to get out of here."

His eyes widened. In anticipation of the noise he might make, she moved the hand that had been cupping his cheek and put it over his mouth.

"Shh…" she cautioned. "Come on."

She helped him climb out of the warm nest of sheets and blankets. Then she used a few precious seconds to rearrange his pillows long-ways in the center of the bed and to throw the covers back over them.

She hadn't thought to do that in her own room, but they weren't looking for her. Maybe that simple deception would give them an extra second or two.

Time. She had no idea how long it had been since she'd been awakened. Three minutes? Five? And no way of knowing what was happening downstairs.

"Where are we going?"

Taylor's whispered question echoed her own. Even as she'd been trying to wake him, she had been considering their options. And discovering they were too few.

When she'd first moved into the rental house, she had thought about getting one of those fire ladders for the upstairs bedrooms. With the steep pitch of the roof, Taylor's age and the fact that most of the windows up here were painted shut, she had settled for multiple smoke alarms instead.

Next year, she'd told herself. *Next year.*

So now there was no exit from this floor except down the staircase. No way to get onto the roof. And that meant…

Even before she had consciously arrived at her conclusion, she'd been guiding Taylor down the hall to the guest room. Once there, she hurried him over to the sliding doors of the double closet. She pushed one of them to the side and stepped inside, pulling Taylor in with her before she slid the door back into place.

In the darkness, she couldn't see the thin rope that pulled down the folding attic stairs. She flailed at the ceiling, trying to find it, and stumbled against the stack of junk—some out-of-season clothing, a few games and toys—that she hadn't found a place for since the move.

Something fell off the top of the pile, landing with a soft plop onto the hardwood floor of the closet. She froze, holding her breath as she listened.

Even if whoever was downstairs had heard the noise, however, there was nowhere else for them to go. No other option.

With that renewed realization, she stood on tiptoe to reach upward again. Moving more carefully this time, she waved her hand back and forth along what she thought was the center of the closet.

Her fingers contacted the rope. Before she could grasp it, it swung away from her. Thankfully, she captured it on the next attempt.

She pulled on it as hard as she could. The attic staircase

descended with an ominous creak of metal that must have been loud enough to be heard below.

Trying not to think about that or about anything other than what she had to do, she felt around in the darkness until she had located the bottom step. She tugged on it, and the lower section of stairs slid downward on its metal rails, separating from the top. It came to a stop about two feet off the floor.

"Climb," she whispered, putting her mouth against Taylor's ear. She held him until his feet had found the bottom rung. "Go on," she urged, pushing him upward with both hands.

As soon as he began his ascent, she grasped the wooden rails and located the bottom step with her bare foot. She pulled herself onto the staircase, then clambered up it and into the attic as quickly as she could.

Whoever had lived in the house before had laid some pieces of plywood over the ceiling joists, making a loose floor that was suitable for storage, if for nothing else. It was rough and cold under her feet.

She knelt at the top of the stairs, trying to figure out how to get them up. She bent forward and grasped the handrails, trying to pull the staircase to her. After a few seconds spent straining against its weight, she knew she didn't have the upper body strength or the leverage to manage that. Not from this angle.

She would have to pull the bottom half up onto the top half first. Maybe then she could lift the staircase back into the opening. She turned, starting to climb back down the steps, when Taylor grabbed the sleeve of her nightshirt.

"Mama? Don't leave me up here."

"It's okay," she whispered, attempting to disengage his fingers from the material. They clung with a desperation born of panic. "I have to lift the stairs back up so they can't find us. I can't do that unless I go partway down them."

"Let me go, too."

"You can't, baby. Turn loose, Taylor," she begged, prying at the fist closed over the fabric of her nightshirt. "I'm just going to climb down a couple of steps. I'm not going to leave you. You wait here. I'll be right back."

With a final jerk she pulled the clutching fingers away. Without giving him time to protest, she stepped back down the stairs, gripping the railings with both hands.

"Mama," he wailed, his voice loud in the confined darkness.

"Shh," she pleaded. "I'm right here. Shh."

She had reached the end of the top half and the end of the rails. She turned and then bent, holding onto the railing with one hand as she grasped the second step of the lower half. She strained as hard as she could, trying to pull it upward and back into position atop the upper section of the stairs.

Finally it began to move, sliding upward along the metal side rails into the closed position. As it did, she was forced to retreat up the stairs toward the opening until she was once more kneeling on the rough plywood.

She leaned forward as far as she could, reaching downward for one of the steps on the lower half, which now lay atop the upper. Again she strained against the deadweight of wood and metal. It wouldn't budge.

One step lower, she thought. If she could reach a few inches farther down, it might give her the leverage she needed.

She lay down on the plywood, draping her upper body along the stairs. She inched forward until the edge of the opening was under her hipbones. The wood cut into her flesh as she stretched down as far as she could, wrapping her fingers around the rim of the lowest stair she could reach.

Gritting her teeth, she pulled, pain screaming through the muscles of her stomach and back. She had to do it now. She knew that she didn't have time or strength for a second try.

With a soft groan, the staircase began to rise, the squeal of metal moving against metal seeming louder now. Magnified, or so she hoped, by the enclosed space of the closet.

Her breath came in ragged gasps as she strained to bring the staircase up to fill the opening. Slowly, requiring every particle of strength she possessed, it began to rise.

With her right hand, she reached back and found one of the rafter supports the previous owner had installed. Trembling with exertion, she pulled her body up, bringing the staircase with her until it was once more in the closed position.

For a moment she couldn't believe she'd done it. She eased her numbed fingers off the step, almost expecting the stairs to unfold again.

When they didn't, she sagged against the wooden beam she still grasped with her right hand, listening for any noise from below. There was nothing now but the sound of her own breathing, her inhalations audible in the stillness.

She closed her mouth, holding her lips tightly together. In the breathless silence, she could hear him. It sounded as if he were pulling things out of closets and turning over furniture, not bothering to be careful about the noise he made.

And she knew what that meant. Whoever had been standing guard over them, Stokes or his replacement, was no longer a threat to the intruder. There were only the three of them inside this house now, and he had all night to find them.

In response to that realization, she pushed up onto her knees. The muscles in her thighs and torso trembled with the recent exertion, but she managed to get to her feet. She had to duck her head a little to avoid the low rafters.

She turned, searching in the darkness for Taylor. He was standing behind her, a small ghostly figure, visible because of the light-colored pajamas he wore.

Far too visible.

Despite the fact that the plywood covered only part of the attic, mostly the area around the trapdoor, she knew that they couldn't stay here. All he would have to do was discover the access staircase—

Another sound. As unidentifiable as the others, but it seemed closer.

Was he already on the second floor? She had known it was only a matter of time, but somehow the thought that he was just below them, in the hall or perhaps in one of their bedrooms, broke through her paralysis of fear and exhaustion.

She tiptoed across the rough flooring to take Taylor's hand. His fingers, ice-cold and shaking, clutched convulsively at hers.

Holding them tightly, she scanned the darkness that surrounded her, trying to orient herself, trying to remember what she had seen when she'd made that one brief visit up here in the daylight.

There were ventilation grilles on both ends of the house. A faint hint of moonlight seeped in between their metal slats. She rejected those locations on that basis, deciding that the narrow space right above the eaves would be safer.

*Safer than what? Than staying here, exposed and vul-
nerable?*

Fighting that renewed sense of terror, she started toward
the side, pulling Taylor with her. She extended one foot
tentatively before her, feeling her way. She didn't dare put
any weight on it until she had assured herself that she was
still on the plywood.

They'd go as far as the flooring went, she told herself.
If she had been alone, she might have tried to crawl along
one of the exposed joists, but Taylor would never be able
to do that. Not in the state he was in.

As she began to move slowly and carefully across the
plywood, her foot encountered something. She put her free
hand out, quickly tracing over the obstacle in her path.

It took only seconds to identify what she'd run into. She
had instructed the movers to place their store of Christmas
decorations in the attic. The boxes were stacked one on top
of the other, the highest at about chest level, far enough
away from the stairs to allow other items to be stored up
here.

She drew Taylor around behind them, realizing as she
did that the boxes were sitting at the edge of the makeshift
flooring. As far as they could safely go. And the stack represented the only cover the open attic could provide.

She eased down behind them. Silently, she urged Taylor
into her lap. Together they listened to the noises filtering
up from downstairs. Louder than before. Definitely closer.

She hugged Taylor tighter, wrapping her arms around his
chest. His body was rigid. As she held him, it was occasionally racked by an uncontrollable tremor.

He didn't make a sound, however. He hadn't. Not since
he'd begged her not to leave him in the attic alone.

She would never have done that. She could never leave

him. She knew, however, even if he didn't, how little protection she could offer him.

All she had was her life—to her last breath—to put between him and the menace that had invaded their home.

CHAPTER ELEVEN

HAVING PUSHED the Crown Vic to over eighty most of the way back, Matt found it difficult to slow the car to a speed appropriate for the narrow streets of the subdivision. He had to force his foot to ease off the accelerator when he neared the end of Heather.

He had come straight here without reporting in at the department. It seemed far more important right now to verify that Robin and the boy were safe than to get to the bottom of the leak Reynolds had mentioned. Or to answer a couple of phone calls. Besides, with the confirmation of Lisa's death, his anger over the release of the information about Taylor would probably cause him to say something that he'd have to apologize for in the morning.

He slowed the car even further to make the last turn. As he started up Arundel he realized there were still lights on in a few of the homes, but not at the Holt house.

It was as dark as it had been during his previous visit. The one he had made sometime around midnight last night in response to Robin's 911 call.

Of course, she had had a sleepless night followed by a long, tension-filled day. It shouldn't be surprising that she and the boy had already gone to bed, he thought as he pulled the car parallel to the curb in front. Especially since she hadn't yet been told about Lisa.

He glanced down at his watch and was surprised to find it was twenty past eleven. Not as early as he'd thought.

He was relieved to see two police cruisers parked in the driveway. Apparently, despite the supposed sighting of the missing girl, the chief wasn't taking any chances.

A dinged fender on the vehicle parked nearest the front door identified it as the one the department had issued to Ephraim Stokes. With that recognition, Matt blew out a breath, releasing with it the tension that had been building since the lieutenant in Marietta had broken the bad news.

Of all the people who might have been given this assignment, the veteran cop would have been his first choice. And he was vastly relieved he was still here. Nothing—and nobody—would get into that house past Eph Stokes. Not without a fight.

The word seemed out of place in the peaceful stillness of the subdivision. Somewhere in the distance a dog barked, the noise muffled by the car windows. Other than that, there was no sound at all on the street.

Maybe Reynolds had been wrong. Maybe he'd gotten mixed up about where he'd heard that Taylor was a witness. Maybe he'd picked up on a department rumor and then seen the clip of the Holts at the courthouse today and juxtaposed the image onto the gossip. Maybe…

Deliberately he dismissed the issue that had occupied his mind during his drive home. As he opened the door and stepped out on the curb, the cold dampness of the November night settled around him like a fog, quickly penetrating the cotton dress shirt he wore. Instead of reaching back inside the car for his jacket, however, he closed the door.

Its small slam seemed to echo in the stillness. There was no reaction. No lights came up in the Holt house. No neighbor peered out a window to identify the cause of the noise.

And despite what the lieutenant had told him had been reported in the media, no reporter jumped out of the shadows to shove a microphone under his nose.

The place seemed as quiet as a tomb. He shivered. A reaction to the cold or the cliché? Or a product of his grotesquely long day?

He started up the sidewalk, his shoe heels loud against the concrete. The dog had quieted, leaving only the sound of his footsteps and the occasional drip of condensation from the bare branches of the trees onto the rotten leaves below.

He hesitated before he stepped onto the Holts' front stoop. If he knew Eph—and he did—the old man would be around back. He would have set up shop near the coffeepot in the kitchen, at least until the family had bedded down for the night.

There was a decidedly physical reaction to the term *bedded down,* which he chose to ignore. Instead of ringing the bell, he cut across the dead grass of the front lawn and through the shadows of the driveway.

As he passed the cruiser pulled in behind Eph's, he put his hand on the hood. In spite of the cold night air, the metal was still warm.

Second shift. Whoever was replacing Stokes must have arrived only minutes ago.

He hoped the few hours of sleep Eph had managed today had been enough to tide him over until his relief had arrived. Those and the endless cups of coffee the veteran cop consumed throughout the day.

As he neared the back of the house, Matt expected to see light streaming out into the yard through the kitchen windows. However, the house seemed as dark as it had from the street. He remembered from his previous visit that the back door opened into a small utility room, which then led directly into the kitchen.

As he rounded the corner, he automatically undid the snap that secured his weapon in its shoulder holster. Despite the reassurance of police cars in the driveway, there was something about this he didn't like.

There were supposedly two cops inside this house. He couldn't come up with any reason why they would be there in the dark.

Shoulders pressed against the cold dampness of the aluminum siding, he sidestepped along the back wall. When he reached the rear door, he stopped, listening for noise from inside. The murmur of conversation, maybe. Or the sound of a television, its volume lowered to keep from disturbing the family sleeping above.

There was only silence. His fingers wrapped around the grip of the Sig Sauer, easing it free of the leather case. The smooth, cool weight of the semi-automatic settled into his palm with the welcome familiarity of a friend's handshake.

With his other hand he grasped the handle of the storm door, and then, stepping to the side, he pulled it open. There was a telltale scrape of metal against metal.

Again he paused. Listening for a reaction. Waiting for one.

When it didn't come, he put his hand around the knob of the inside wooden door. He hesitated before he turned it.

Two cruisers. Two cops. Both armed. He'd be an idiot to walk unannounced into that darkness.

He thought about calling out to Eph. He even briefly considered going back to his car and having the dispatcher try to raise the patrolman on the radio. Or better yet, have her send some backup.

He did none of those things. Something about the quality of the silence inside the house prevented him from taking what should have been normal precautions.

The hair on the back of his neck had begun to lift. Something here was very wrong. He knew it on the same gut-deep, primeval level that was causing the prickling sensation along his spine.

He turned the knob, praying the door would be locked. Secured against an intruder. As it should be in any house that Eph Stokes was guarding.

The comforting thought of Eph's seasoned reliability dissolved as, under the direction of his fingers, the doorknob completed its half circle, releasing the latch that held the door in its frame. Again he waited, expecting—anticipating—a challenge from the two officers inside.

When it didn't come, he put both hands around his gun, the left supporting the right, and pushed the door slowly inward with his foot. The warmed interior air was drawn outward by the contrast to the cold of the exterior. It carried with it the evocatively pleasant scent of coffee.

Underlying that was another smell. One that was not so familiar, but identifiable. He knew it was something he had smelled before. He just couldn't think when or where.

It was darker inside the house than in the yard. The chill that had crawled along his spine shifted to his stomach, turning his guts to water. He ignored it, forcing himself to step across the threshold.

Something isn't right, he thought again, taking another careful step. *Something—*

Whatever his foot encountered was solid. Heavy. Unmoving.

Resisting the urge to look down, he scanned the utility room instead, the muzzle of the semi-automatic tracking across the shadowed patches of black and lesser black as his eyes examined them.

Nothing moved. No threat presented itself.

Having assured himself as much as he could that he was alone in the room, he slowly bent his knees. His left hand released its hold under the right to reach downward.

He knew with the first brush of fabric under his outstretched fingers what it was he had almost stumbled over. Just to be sure, he ran his palm across the shoulders covered by the woolen broadcloth of the department's winter uniform.

Then he traced along the outflung left arm. The man's fingers, when he reached them, were warm. Soft. Pliable.

He made himself feel under the cuff of the shirt for a pulse. Despite the warmth of the body, he couldn't find one.

Eph? There was only one way to know for sure. Hand outstretched again, he searched for the face.

The eyes were closed. Despite tracing along the length of the nose, he found he had no idea what it would look like. Only when his fingers found the stiffness of that meticulously groomed mustache did he know for sure.

Despite his need to find out what was happening in the rest of the house, he also knew that he might represent his friend's last chance for survival. Given the warmth of the body, it was possible that if he went back to the car and placed a call to the dispatcher, the paramedics could do something.

He felt for the carotid artery, hoping against hope that the pulse of blood he'd missed in the wrist might be there. Instead, his fingers found a thick viscosity that he recognized immediately as clotting blood.

Bile rose at the realization that the old man's throat had

been cut. He swallowed against its burn, refusing to let himself think of this as a person. And a friend.

Instead, he wiped his fingers on the uniform shirt, returning his left hand to its steadying position under the right. They must have timed the intrusion for the change of shift, knowing that the cop on duty would have to open the door to let in his replacement. It would be the perfect moment—the only possible moment—to overpower the two of them and gain access to the house. If that was what had happened, then where the hell was that second officer?

After the few seconds he'd spent in the confines of the small room, his eyes had adjusted enough to allow him to see the dark sprawl that was Stokes. He examined the few feet of pale floor tile that lay between Eph's body and the kitchen door, but there was nothing else there. No one there. *Unless...*

He rejected the idea immediately. The town was small enough that he knew every man in the department. There was not one of them who was capable of this.

Or of the violence that had been enacted on the corpse in the woods? Whoever had done that—whoever had broken Lisa Evans's neck—would have no compunction about killing a fellow officer.

He couldn't believe that any of the cops, most of whom he'd known for almost ten years, had had a hand in any of this. *Then where the hell is the second officer?*

A sound almost directly over his head brought him to his feet. The clatter he'd heard was unidentifiable. Something had fallen? Or been knocked over?

His eyes lifted to the ceiling as if he could see what was going on up on the second story. Realizing the futility of that effort, he stepped over Stokes's body, making as little noise as possible as he crossed to the kitchen door.

No experienced cop would go into a situation with as many unknowns as this one without calling for backup. *Not unless two innocent lives were at stake.*

He had no doubt now that they were. And no doubt that whatever was happening on the second story of this house would be over long before anyone else could get here.

CHAPTER TWELVE

ALL ROBIN could do was listen, mouth dry, heart beating so loudly it almost drowned out the noise whoever was in the room directly beneath them was making. She positioned Taylor behind her, intending to use her body as a shield.

His arms wrapped tightly around her waist; his cheek pressed against her spine. She wondered how much he understood about what was happening. She could only hope it was not as much as she did.

By sound, she had followed the intruder's progress through the rooms of the second floor. Now he had reached the last of them. The one with the closet and the descending staircase that would give him access to their hiding place.

And there was nothing she could do to prevent him from searching that bedroom. Nothing she could do to keep him from discovering the rope she'd struggled to locate in the darkness.

After all, he was free to turn on the lights. Or to use the flashlight he would surely have brought with him if he wanted to keep the house shrouded in darkness as he searched.

Either way it was only a matter of time until he would spot the dangling cord and climb the access stairs to investigate. And there was no longer any doubt in her mind, having listened to the systematic havoc he'd wrought as he made his way through the house, that he would.

She wondered if she could ease Taylor farther back toward the place where the rafters joined the wall. Maybe if they lay down flat across the exposed joists…

That's what they *should* have done. She should have taken Taylor there despite the very real danger that one wrong step would send them plunging through the ceiling below. It would have been far better than staying here, with only a few cardboard packing boxes between them and discovery. Anything would have been better than here.

It was too late to move. Too late to do anything but wait. She had made all her choices, right or wrong, and now she would have to live with them.

Live with them…

There was time for the irony of that phrase to echo in her head before she heard the sound she'd been waiting for. And dreading.

The closet door below their hiding place slid open. As it did, coherent thought process screeched to a halt.

She'd been right about the flashlight. She could see its beam filtering through the cracks between the staircase and the plywood. With a light he would be able to spot the rope immediately—

The grating metal-on-metal noise that had accompanied her lowering of the access staircase sounded from the closet below. Then the scattered threads of light became a single powerful beam as the stairs dropped, exposing the opening into the attic.

The bottom half of the stairs was pulled downward, sliding away from the top on its metal rails. Taylor's arms tightened spasmodically around her body as he turned his face back and forth against her shoulders. She squeezed the small, trembling forearms against her ribs, trying to console him.

She prayed he could control his fear enough not to start sobbing. Or to cry out. That was almost too much to ask of any child, especially one who had been through all he had in the last few days, but silence was their only hope now.

The stairs creaked under the weight of whoever was climbing them, which they hadn't done when she and Taylor had scrambled up. A man, she thought. A big man. As he neared the top, she could feel the vibration of his movement carried along the joists under the plywood.

She lowered her head. She had already pulled the sleeves of her dark gray nightshirt over her hands in an effort to hide every bit of skin she could. Its fairness would be as revealing as the pale knit cotton of her son's pajamas.

She knew when the invader had reached the top of the stairs because of the change in the quality of the light. Even with her head lowered, she could tell that he was directing the beam around the attic. Searching what could be seen of it from his position at the top of the stairs.

The Christmas ornaments would afford them cover as long as he stayed in the opening. If he stepped onto the plywood overlay, however, and did a more thorough search of the space, he would find them.

Please, God.

There were so many needs in that prayer she didn't dare enumerate them. Instead she repeated the phrase over and over in her mind like a mantra while the beam of the flashlight made its slow circuit around the attic.

And then it stopped. Again, even with her head down, she could tell that he was playing the light very slowly over the area where they huddled together.

Examining the cartons with her careful, hand-written labeling? Or had he seen something? Something that had given away their hiding place.

What had she missed? Their tracks across the dust that would have accumulated on top of the false flooring, perhaps?

The light went out unexpectedly, plunging the confined space into total darkness. She heard the stairs creak, and her heart hammered in her chest with renewed hope.

Was he going back downstairs? Could this ill-conceived hiding place have worked?

She listened, trying to gauge his progress down the steps, just as she had been able to track him up them. The heavy tread she'd heard before didn't descend, however. Instead, judging by the increased vibrations of the plywood she was sitting on, he had stepped out of the stairwell and onto the attic floor.

Please, God.

She forced herself to keep her head down despite how desperately she needed to know what he was doing. She couldn't afford to make a mistake. Not now. This was a game of cat and mouse, and the only chance they had was to play it out to the end.

He began to cross the plywood, his steps felt rather than heard. Was he moving on tiptoe?

The flashlight was still off. Maybe he was trying to fool them into believing he had gone.

Suddenly, the image of the quail her father had talked about was in her head. In her mind's eye, she watched their panicked flight, flushed from safety to be picked off by the waiting hunters. She used the thought to force herself to complete stillness, controlling even her breathing, as he came nearer to the boxes behind which they were hidden.

Nearer and nearer—

"Robin?"

The sound of her name floated up from the floor below, the voice that had spoken it instantly recognized. By some miracle, maybe the one for which she had just prayed, Matt had come to find them.

The urge to call out to him was so strong she sank her teeth into her bottom lip to keep from responding. The man with the flashlight was between them. If she called out now—

"Robin? Where are you? Talk to me?"

The footsteps in the attic began again, but they were moving away from her now. The man with the flashlight was still making an effort to mask their sound, but he was no longer going slowly.

She waited for the creak as he descended the stairs, but there was nothing. Which meant he was still in the attic. He didn't want to chance going down the staircase, with its telltale sound effects. That would immediately give away his location.

To Matt. Who had come to find them.

Was it possible Matt didn't know there was someone else in the house? She rejected the idea, remembering that he hadn't rung the bell. He wouldn't walk into her house in the middle of the night unannounced.

"Taylor?"

The convulsive tightening of the little boy's arms told her that his desire to answer that trusted voice was as strong as her own. And there was no guarantee he wouldn't. Not if he didn't fully understand what was going on.

"Shh…" she breathed, praying that he could hear her and that the intruder could not. "Shh…"

There was some sound from across the attic. In response to her whisper? Or to Matt's voice?

She could hear Matt moving below now. She followed the sound of his footsteps down the hall, coming nearer to the room where the three of them waited. Unaware of the man waiting in the opening to the attic?

But surely by now Matt must know something was wrong here. *He's too good a cop...*

Officer Stokes's opinion was based on a long acquaintance. Matt wouldn't be taken unaware. He would exercise every precaution. He didn't need her to warn him. Not at the expense of Taylor's safety.

She listened to his footsteps enter the guest bedroom below. She couldn't remember if the man at the top of the stairs had closed the closet door when he'd entered it or not.

If he hadn't, then Matt would come over to investigate. But would he look up at the ceiling to find his enemy?

Would anyone, no matter how experienced, expect an attack to come from the top of a closet? And if something happened to Matt, then what would happen to Taylor?

"He's hiding in the ceiling of the closet."

The words, screamed at the top of her lungs, seemed to have formed in her mouth before she'd had time to frame the warning. Once she'd issued it, however, she let it go, concentrating again on her responsibility.

She threw herself to the side, carrying Taylor, who was clinging to her back, with her. Then she scrambled across the rough plywood, attempting to take them as far from the spot where they'd been as she could.

The sound of the gun was far softer than she'd expected. More of a hollow *phut* than a shot. She knew what it was, however, because one of the boxes holding ornaments was knocked backward. It fell with the tinkle of breaking glass.

The second bullet sent splinters from the plywood floor

beside her up into her arm. By that time she had rolled over on top of Taylor, shielding him as well as she could.

The third shot was different in sound, enough so that she understood it came from another gun. The report was louder, despite the fact that she knew it must have come from the room below.

The bullet ricocheted off something and then whined across the attic. Matt's first shot was immediately followed by a second from his gun, which was answered with one of those pneumatic coughs.

The intruder was no longer firing at them, she thought in relief. Then the memory of Matt's eyes, dark with concern, was in her head. He had distracted the gunman's attention, but in doing so, he had put his own life on the line.

As she huddled over Taylor, Matt fired twice more in rapid succession. There was a sound, almost like a grunt, from the direction of the opening.

And no ricochet. She realized only belatedly what that must mean.

The noise the gunman's body made falling down the stairs was far louder than his ascent had been. The stairs creaked with each bump and thud.

When it was over, the sudden silence was shocking. Holding her breath, she listened as tensely as she had while she'd tracked the invader through the house.

For endless seconds there was nothing. No sound. No movement. Nothing.

"Mama?"

Taylor's whisper was nearly soundless, his breath warm against her cheek.

"Shh…"

Not daring to move, she strained to hear anything from below. If Matt were still down there—

The assorted creaks of the stairs had become so familiar that she identified this one immediately. Someone had stepped onto the bottom step.

Matt?

It had to be. She had heard the other one, the man with the flashlight, fall.

But if Matt *were* on the stairs, why didn't he call out to her as he had done before? Why didn't he identify himself?

Then, as if in answer to that unspoken question, "Robin? It's okay. He's dead."

She finally remembered to breathe, drawing in air that held the acrid odor of gunfire. Somewhere in the middle of the inhalation, the breath turned into a shuddering sob. She closed her mouth, determined not to cry. Not now that it was over.

"Mama?"

Taylor. She pushed her upper body away from his on arms that trembled uncontrollably. Delayed reaction.

Somehow she managed to get to her knees, but she felt light-headed. Disoriented. Almost faint. She sat back on her heels, an admission that she didn't think her shaking legs would support her.

"Can we get down now?"

She nodded before she realized Taylor wouldn't be able to see her. "Detective Ridge is here. It's safe. Everything is okay."

"Robin?"

"We're up here," she called. "We're all right."

Thanks to you.

She didn't say the words, but there was no denying them. They owed their lives to Matt's arrival.

He had promised them protection. And despite his unexplained absence this afternoon, when it had counted the most, he'd provided it.

She listened to the tread of the man climbing the stairs this time without fear. When Matt reached the top, she could see the outline of the white shirt he wore. She wondered, ridiculously, as if it mattered, whether it was the same one he had been wearing the last time she'd seen him. The contrast between the pale material and the darkness behind him made his shoulders seem incredibly broad.

"The light switch is on the support to your right." Her voice sounded far more collected than she felt.

It took him a moment to locate the plate in the darkness. When he did, the sudden brightness of the single overhead bulb was almost painful. She blinked against it, ducking her head to allow her eyes time to adjust.

Taylor didn't need as long to make the transition. He scrambled to his feet, running past her as she tried to marshal the strength to get to hers. The little boy threw himself at Matt, undeterred by the gun he still held.

Matt reacted by wrapping one arm around his bottom, lifting him easily as he stepped up onto the plywood. Taylor's arms were fastened tightly around his neck. As if he had known this man all his life, he hid his face in the space between the detective's neck and shoulder.

Matt continued across the attic toward her, still carrying her son. He shoved the overturned box out of his path with his foot, glass tinkling again as the broken ornaments it contained shifted.

Then, without saying a word, he stood looking down on her. His expression was one she couldn't afford to analyze too closely.

Seeing what was in his dark eyes, she was suddenly envious of her own son. Jealous of the fact that he was sheltered in arms she knew were strong enough to protect him, no matter the threat.

She hadn't even dared to dream about how it would feel to be comforted like that. To let someone take care of her for a change. And take care of Taylor.

His security had been her sole responsibility for so long, she had almost forgotten how to share that burden with someone else. That didn't mean she didn't want to.

Perhaps something of what she was feeling was reflected in her eyes. Matt bent, carefully setting Taylor on his feet. Then his body continued to lower until he was balanced on the balls of his feet in front of her, looking straight into her eyes. Just as he had looked into Taylor's that first night he'd come into their home.

"Are you all right?"

Mutely she nodded, again fighting the urge to cry. This time it had been provoked by the solicitude in his deep voice.

Deliberately she broke the powerful connection that had sparked between them by reaching out to touch Taylor's arm. The little boy appeared almost dazed.

And why wouldn't he be? Someone had just tried to kill them. Someone had stalked them throughout the one place that should always be the safe, secure center of any child's world.

"Hey, baby," she said softly, trying to reassure him. "It's okay now. Everything's okay."

"I know."

The boy's eyes tracked to Matt's face. Taylor's open trust in the detective caused her throat to close.

For so long *she* had been his anchor. Her strength, his security. Now, whether she liked it or not, it was obvious that some of his security had been shifted to Matt Ridge's more than capable shoulders.

Her gaze again focused on his face. He was still looking at her with that unspoken compassion.

She realized that whatever there was about him that had earned Taylor's trust had also earned her own. No matter how much she believed she'd adjusted to having only herself to depend on, what was happening in their lives right now was something she wasn't equipped to handle.

"Are you sure you're okay?" The concern she had seen in Matt's eyes was reflected in his voice.

"I'm just..." She hesitated, uncertain whether to confess to either the absolute terror that had gripped her or to the aftermath of longing.

"Robin?"

As he said her name, he reached out, putting his fingers against her cheek. There was nothing remotely sexual about the gesture. She might have done the same thing to Taylor. Or he might have.

There was nothing childlike, however, about her response. The masculine abrasiveness of his fingers produced a sensual stirring deep within her body. Her lips parted, but still she said nothing.

Their eyes held, the dark pupils in his suddenly dilating at what he saw in hers. In response, his head began to tilt as his mouth slowly lowered.

She should do something to prevent what was about to happen. Put her hand on his chest. Turn her head. Remind him of the watching child.

She did none of those things. She raised her chin instead, waiting for his kiss. Wanting it.

When his lips found hers, their touch was as light as the guiding hand he'd laid against the small of her back today.

There was no demand. There was invitation instead. One she no longer had the will to resist.

Her mouth opened under his as her tongue made the first careful contact. As soon as it had, any trace of tentativeness on his part disappeared.

His hand slipped behind her neck. His fingers moved upward, spreading through her hair, urging her closer.

Despite the awkwardness of their positions, there was nothing awkward about the kiss. It was as natural as if they had done this a hundred times.

His tongue caressed with a confidence that was comforting in the face of her uncertainty. Then he deepened the kiss, taking away the need for her to make any decisions. He was in control, and he left her in no doubt about that.

It wasn't until he pulled her to him, her breasts pressed against his chest, that she remembered how forbidden this was. The cardinal rule of her existence.

In spite of what she felt, a longing to be held that was almost overpowering, she put both palms against the fabric of his shirt. Pushing him away.

His lips lifted a fraction. For a heartbeat hers clung to the moisture on them, as if reluctant to let go. Then he raised his head far enough to look down into her eyes.

''What's wrong?'' he whispered.

''Taylor.''

Once she had hated lies. Now they were second nature.

Without releasing her, he reached to the side, putting his arm around the little boy and pulling him into their embrace. Taylor pushed eagerly into the narrow space between their bodies, unbalancing Matt.

He put his right hand down on the plywood to regain his equilibrium. The move brought the gun he held in his left into the midst of the circle formed by their bodies. It was an unwanted reminder of what had just occurred.

"We have to get out of here," he said.

For an instant, despite his words, she thought he might lean forward again. Then, with a determination that was palpable, he moved back, putting distance between them.

"Let's go, partner," he said to Taylor.

The enthusiasm he'd tried to imbue into his voice seemed out of place. And Taylor was clearly reluctant to move, his face buried against her shoulder. Matt got to his feet, holding out his hand to help her to hers.

"What about Officer Stokes?"

He shook his head, the motion small and tight, but his eyes had already given her the answer. Tears threatened again. She fought them this time for Taylor's sake.

"They came in on him during the change of shift," Matt explained.

Which meant there should have been another officer here. Unless…

She glanced toward the opening as if she could find the answer there to that unspoken question.

"No one I recognized," Matt said.

He put his hand on Taylor's shoulder, turning him toward the stairs.

"Then…where's the officer who was supposed to be Stokes's replacement?"

"I can't imagine. But it's something we have to find out."

CHAPTER THIRTEEN

THE COPS on the response team eventually discovered the body of the second officer. The trail of blood drops showed that he'd been dragged from the back steps into the bushes behind the garage.

When Matt saw the body, he realized it was the rookie who, along with Bert Conroy, had answered the 911 call last night. That was probably why they'd sent him. He was already familiar with the location.

And because of something that simple he was dead. Wrong place. Definitely the wrong time.

The kid's name was Bobby Early, but Matt hadn't remembered until someone else mentioned it. He did remember talk about a bachelor party a couple of guys in the department had thrown for him, complete with a couple of high-priced strippers from Atlanta. Lap dancers. And that couldn't have been more than six months ago.

"Somebody notify his wife?" he asked, watching the EMT pull the blanket over Early's face.

At least his throat hadn't been cut. The tech's guess was a couple of blows to the back of the head by someone who knew what they were doing. Like the guy they'd found in the woods.

"I sent Bert to tell her," Dawkins said. "He'd kind of taken the kid under his wing. I thought he'd be the best person to break the news. He's gonna stop by and pick up their preacher on the way.''

"And Eph?''

Matt forced himself to ask the question, hoping Dawkins wouldn't suggest he undertake that task. He and the old man had been friends since he'd started with the department, but having to tell his wife what had happened to him would be even more difficult than discovering his body had been.

"That one I do myself,'' Dawkins said. "I've known Eph and Margaret more than fifty years. The three of us went to grammar school together. No hurry about getting over there tonight though. She'll be sleeping. Margaret never could abide a scanner in her house. Said she didn't want to know what Eph was up to. This is probably the last good sleep she'll get for a long time, so I'm gonna let her have it. You go to bed at night, you don't expect something like this to happen to your loved ones. Not around here.''

It never had. Not like this. A child disappears and a mutilated body is found in the woods. Now two cops were dead, one of them a veteran with more than thirty-five years on the force.

"Still no ID on that corpse?'' Matt asked, blocking the thought of what had been done to Eph.

"We got nothing. Whoever he was, he's not in any of the databases. Never been in the military. Zilch. It's like he dropped out of the sky.''

"I want charge of the Holts,'' Matt said, turning to face Dawkins.

The chief reacted by tearing his gaze away from the paramedics. "What the hell does that mean?''

"I want to be put in charge of their protection.''

"Why?"

"Because what we've been doing isn't working. That bastard almost got to them tonight."

It made him physically ill to think how close it had been. If the Marietta cops hadn't spotted those runaways when they had... If he hadn't pushed his car beyond the speed limit... If he'd gone by the department to report in as Dawkins had suggested...

"What about the Evans girl?" the chief asked. "You're still the lead on that."

"They grabbed her, Hank, and nobody saw a thing. At that time of day in a neighborhood like this, it would take somebody who knew what they were doing to pull that off. Tonight they catch Eph Stokes unaware and slit his throat. And you and I both know he was nobody's fool."

"He musta heard the squad car. Looked out through the window and knew it was his replacement. Then somebody knocks on the back door..." The chief made a gesture with one finger drawn across his throat. "That's the only way I can figure Eph would have unlocked that door to an intruder."

"That's what I mean. The change of shift was the vulnerable point in the department's arrangements. Whoever this is figured that out and took advantage of it. They overpowered Eph without letting him get off a shot. Or warning the Holts."

"Poor bastard."

The paramedics were wheeling Bobby Early's body down the concrete driveway in front of them, the stretcher bouncing slightly as it rolled over the rough surface. Matt wasn't sure whether the chief meant Eph or the kid. It didn't really matter. The comment was appropriate for either of them.

''Bureau's gonna want to have some say in any arrangements you make for the Holts,'' Dawkins warned.

That didn't sound as if he intended to refuse Matt's request, but he knew that the chief wouldn't defend it if the GBI pushed.

''The Bureau got us where we are tonight. The Holts should have been in a safe house. Not someplace where everybody and his brother knew how to find them. Those bastards probably grabbed Lisa when she walked out of this front door. They came back last night, intending to break in. Robin's 911 call stopped them. So tonight we put the Holts right back in the same place. Hell, it was an open invitation to come after them.''

Dawkins rolled his tongue over his front teeth and then released it with a sucking sound as he watched the body being loaded into the ambulance.

''You got some place else in mind?''

He did, of course. The plan had occurred to him after the impromptu kiss he and Robin had shared.

And that, too, was something that would have to be taken into consideration. It was possible she would refuse to go along with what he wanted. If she did, he could lay the blame on his lack of control.

He could claim it had been nothing but relief at finding they were still alive. A natural desire for human contact after danger. He could claim that, but he, at least, would know the truth. He had wanted to kiss Robin Holt long before somebody had cornered her in an attic and tried to kill her son.

Maybe it was the fact that she reminded him of Karen. He no longer bothered to deny that, not to himself at least, but as he'd held her tonight, he had been forced to acknowledge that there was more going on between them than some kind of loneliness-induced déjà vu. And she had responded as if she'd been aware of the same attraction he had felt since the moment she'd opened her door to him.

"Matt?"

"Trevor's cabin. There aren't half a dozen people in town who even remember that the place exists. The few who do, other than Karen's folks, couldn't find it if their lives depended on it."

Karen's kid brother had turned a cabin on land his grandfather had left them up on Templar Mountain into a hunting lodge. More drinking and more lying *about* hunting had gone on there than actual hunting, but that wasn't all that unusual.

Trevor and a few high-school buddies used to spend the occasional weekend up there, but to Matt's knowledge it hadn't been used in years. Probably not since the accident. Karen's mother had told him that all the wildness seemed to have gone out of Trev with the tragedy that had taken Karen's and Josh's lives. All the wildness *and* the joy.

"You gonna take a woman and a kid up there? Is it even fit for human habitation any more?"

"Knowing Martha it will be."

Karen's mother wasn't the kind to let a house, even one as rustic as the cabin had always been, fall to rack and ruin. There were probably clean sheets on the beds right now, just in case Trev decided to head up there some weekend.

"You got a key?"

"I've still got Karen's."

It was hanging on the key rack by the back door, the word *Cabin* written on the tag in Karen's neat script. He thought it should feel wrong to contemplate taking another woman to the cabin, but it didn't.

He had loved Karen. He still did. And he had been faithful to her memory for a lot of years. This was the first time since her death that he'd been attracted to a woman, although he'd gone through the motions a couple of times.

And besides what he felt for Robin, a child's life was at stake. Karen would be the first to tell him he should do everything he could to protect Taylor Holt. Right now, this seemed the best way.

"And nobody but you is to know where they are," he bargained with the chief. *"Nobody."*

"You know I can't do that," Dawkins said. "Those GBI boys are gonna be all over my ass if I try to pull a stunt like that."

"How are you gonna feel, Hank, if that *kid* ends up with *his* throat cut?"

In the silence that fell after the question, the chief's tongue rolled over his front teeth again, followed by the same sucking noise as it released. He refused to meet Matt's eyes, but he could tell Dawkins was thinking about what he'd said. The suggestion made too much sense for him not to be.

"The next time it could be a fire," Matt went on, pressing the advantage he sensed. "Or a bomb. And the Holts don't live in Atlanta, Hank. They're citizens of Mallory. That means they're our responsibility."

"You can't do it alone. Not 24/7. Who you want to take out there with you?"

Before tonight, Matt wouldn't have had to think twice about that choice. Now, remembering the doubts that had surfaced so quickly when he hadn't been able to locate Stokes's replacement, he couldn't come up with the name of a single person on the force he'd trust with this secret. Not with the leaks that had come out of the department in the last thirty-six hours.

"The fewer people who know what I'm doing, the better."

"You're the one who's been talking about responsibility. You looking to take this on all by yourself?"

"Somebody leaked that the kid was a witness to part of what went on in those woods. One way to shut down that kind of information is to restrict access to it. That's what I plan to do."

"Somebody's gonna have to authorize—"

"That somebody is *you,* Hank. This is *your* town, *your* jurisdiction. *You* make the decisions here. We protect the Holts or we leave them vulnerable to another attack. Just like we did tonight. And if we do, I guarantee you somebody else will end up dead."

"I give 'em to you, and you're gonna guarantee that they won't?"

Matt knew by the chief's phrasing that he had won, so he didn't bother to react. What he wanted to do *did* seem the height of arrogance: To assume full responsibility for Robin and Taylor's protection because he didn't trust anyone else to handle it.

"Nothing we signed on to do comes with a guarantee. Nothing in life does." That was one of the lessons he'd learned from Karen's death. "All I can tell you is that I lost a good friend tonight. I don't intend to let those bastards kill anybody else."

"I DON'T understand."

Robin was sitting on one of the metal equipment boxes the paramedics had taken out of their truck before they began work. At some point she had changed into a pair of jeans and a T-shirt. The fleece jacket she'd been wearing over it was across her lap.

There was a piece of white gauze taped over the upper part of the arm she had wrapped around Taylor's body. The boy was sitting in her lap, his eyes red-rimmed and exhausted. Hauntingly empty.

Matt had overheard one of the paramedics whisper the word *shock*. At the time he hadn't known whether the EMT was referring to Robin or the child. Now he did.

"It's just a way to get you away from the scene without anyone being able to follow," Matt explained patiently. He had stooped, balancing once more on the balls of his feet so that they were eye-to-eye.

"In an *ambulance?*"

"The paramedics' van," he corrected. The terminology didn't matter, but her cooperation did.

"To where?"

There was nothing slow about Robin's mental processes. Not even after all she'd been through.

"Eventually, to a safe house."

Her eyes held his a moment, evaluating. "You're going with us?"

"With the sheriff's escort, the paramedics will drive you to the maternity entrance of the hospital. They'll take you both inside, where you'll wait for me. When I get there, we'll exit through another entrance. Just another family leaving the hospital after a late-night visit."

The hour wouldn't be as noticeable if they left through the emergency entrance, he decided. He hoped that neither she nor Hank Dawkins realized that he was making this up as he went along. All he was sure of was that he wanted Robin and the boy away from Mallory. And that he intended to be with them.

"And after that?"

"We'll travel together to a secure location."

"In Mallory?"

"Somewhere nearby. Somewhere safe."

"And you'll stay there with us?"

He should probably be flattered by her insistence on his presence. Seeing the two of them so physically and emotionally battered, however, brought home to him exactly what he was taking on by asking for this assignment.

Keeping them safe was now his responsibility. His job. One that his growing paranoia wouldn't allow him to share with anyone.

"From the moment you get into my car."

"Until…?"

"Until this is over."

Her eyes considered his. The silence stretched thin and long, edging into discomfort. He was the one who finally broke it.

"What happened between us tonight…" he began and then hesitated, seeking the right words for the reassurance he thought she wanted. "You don't have to worry about it happening again. It was…relief, I guess. A need for human contact."

Said aloud, the reasons didn't sound particularly plausible.

"Human contact," she repeated. It wasn't a question.

"After being in danger, people have a natural tendency to seek out…" He paused again, searching for something other than the phrase he'd just used.

"Human contact," she supplied with a hint of mockery.

"I'm just trying to reassure you that what happened… won't happen again."

Not unless you want it to. He buried that thought, concentrating instead on letting her see his sincerity.

"Of course," she said finally.

With the relaxation of tension that had grown between them during his fumbling explanation, he realized that the boy was watching him. His head lay against his mother's shoulder, but his eyes had never left Matt's face. For some reason, their steady regard made him feel like a liar, even though he had meant every word of what he'd just said.

"It's for your own protection. And Taylor's," he added, pulling his gaze from the boy's face to focus again on hers.

There was no way to protect this child from the reality of their situation. Not after what he'd seen tonight. He had witnessed more depravity in the past few days than most people did in their lifetime.

"I don't suppose we have any choice," Robin said.

"If you'd prefer some other arrangement—"

He broke the sentence, knowing that even if she did, he wasn't going to agree to it. There was no one else he trusted to do this.

"No," Robin said. She reached up and put her palm against the little boy's forehead to brush the fine blond hair away from his eyes. "I'm not suggesting another arrangement. I was simply trying to understand what you planned to do with us."

"Take you to a place no one else knows about."

He became aware only when she looked up that someone was standing beside him. His peripheral vision provided the information that whoever it was, he was wearing uniform pants.

He glanced up to find the paramedic he'd talked to earlier hovering over them. Matt put his hand on the edge of the box Robin was sitting on, using it to help himself to his feet. The effort that required brought home to him how tired he really was.

"Ready when you are," the EMT said. "Don't tell the county about this, okay?"

"Police business. Nobody gets told."

"Ma'am? You folks ready?"

At the hesitation, Matt looked down. Both Robin and her son had been looking at him rather than at the paramedic.

"Whenever you are," she said softly, effectively putting both their lives into his hands.

CHAPTER FOURTEEN

THE HEADLIGHTS reflecting off the trunks of the pines cast eerie shadows on the unpaved road. He had never driven to the cabin at night before, and even at the crawl he'd maintained during the last five miles, it had proved a challenge.

Because of the darkness, however, he could be sure no one was following them up the winding logging road. There had been no lights behind them since they'd left the county two-lane. And no car would have been able to navigate these hairpin turns in the pitch-black, not even trailing the taillights on his SUV.

He had stopped by the house before he'd gone to the hospital, grabbing not only the key to the cabin, but all the portable foodstuffs he had on the shelves of the pantry and a few items of clothing. The armload of quilts and blankets had been an afterthought, but since he had no idea about the wood supply for the fireplace, they were a necessity. By the time he'd stuffed everything into the back of the car, he was beginning to wonder if this whole idea had been as ill-conceived as it now seemed.

Henry Dawkins was right about one thing, at least. The responsibility he'd asked for was overwhelming. When he'd suggested it, he hadn't even thought about the logistics of feeding the three of them at that remote location.

There were probably half a dozen other things he hadn't

thought of, but it was too late to back out now. Not yet, he hedged. They were good for a couple of days, which would give him time to refine his plans.

He glanced across the front seat at Robin. She was still holding the little boy, who had long ago succumbed to exhaustion. Despite her own tiredness, her eyes had remained on the road in front of them. She seemed to be mentally trying to help the four-wheel drive make the switchbacks that made driving up here so treacherous.

"You okay?" he asked, checking the relatively uneventful stretch of road in front of him before he glanced at Robin again.

She turned her head at the question, her eyes meeting his for the first time since he'd helped her into the car in the emergency parking lot of County General.

"How much farther?" she asked.

"We're almost there. A little more than a mile."

There was no response, as her gaze returned to the trail ahead. It had narrowed, still climbing precipitously.

"I overheard one of the cops say something about Lisa. When he saw that I was listening, he stopped talking."

He thought about offering her some platitude, but her life and that of her son might depend on her understanding of the hard reality.

"One of the search teams found her body tonight."

"Whoever took her killed her."

"Shortly after she disappeared."

There was a small silence as she digested the information she must surely have suspected since the conversation she'd overheard.

"How could they have been so wrong about that sighting?" Her voice seemed emotionless.

"It was some other girl. A pregnant runaway and her

boyfriend. They saw a cop and panicked. She had dark hair and was dressed like Lisa, so somebody decided it had to *be* Lisa.''

''What will happen to them? Those kids, I mean.''

''Nothing as far as the state's concerned. I imagine their parents will have a lot to say to them.''

''Were the Evanses informed that Lisa had been seen?''

''I don't know.''

It was as near a lie as he was willing to have between them. As elated as everyone in the department had been at the news of the supposed sighting, he was pretty sure someone would have told Lisa's family.

He knew the media had gotten hold of it. They would have wanted the family's reaction. He wondered who had had to inform the Evanses that what everyone had thought had turned out to be wrong.

Like informing Eph's wife, that was a job he was glad to have escaped. And under normal circumstances, as lead detective, it should have fallen to him.

''It would have been better if they'd never been given that hope,'' Robin said.

''I doubt parents ever give up hope in a situation like this.'' He thought, but didn't add, *Not as long as no body's found.* ''Miracles do happen. Kids have shown up years after they've been abducted.''

He didn't know why he had mentioned those rare cases. Only seconds ago he had been trying to make sure she understood what Lisa's death meant for Taylor.

''Rarely enough that those occasions are still *called* miracles.''

He shouldn't be surprised at her cynicism. Not considering that someone had tried to kill her son tonight. He imagined Robin Holt's view of the world, like his, had changed dramatically in the last forty-eight hours.

The beams of the headlights picked out the squat shape of the cabin from among the vertical lines of the trees that surrounded the clearing where it sat. He couldn't tell anything about its condition, but at least the place was still standing.

"Is that it?" Robin leaned forward, peering through the windshield.

"I warned you it was primitive."

As they rounded the last curve, the headlights illuminating the front door, he also wondered how great an understatement that now was. He pulled around the back and doused the lights.

He sat in the darkness for a moment, just listening. The only sounds were the faint noise made by the cooling engine and the wind moving through the tops of the trees.

There were no lights. No sound of another car. Nothing but the peace and quiet he had always found here.

"I'll go start the generator. That will give us light and eventually some hot water."

He had already put his fingers around the latch of the door when her hand closed over his other wrist.

"Do we have to do that tonight?"

They didn't, of course. Without the headlights, their eyes had adjusted to the darkness enough to allow them to get the little boy inside and into one of the beds. There was really no desperate need for artificial light during the brief hours that remained of the night.

"Are you okay with that?" Only after he'd asked the question did he realize there was more than one interpretation of what he'd asked.

"The darkness feels...safer somehow."

Her instincts throughout this whole thing had been better than his. He wasn't going to argue with them now.

He opened the door, stepping out into the nighttime stillness of the forest. It was late enough in the year that the sounds of crickets and tree frogs, which he always associated with time spent up here, were missing.

Reluctant to break the silence, he eased the door closed, pushing the latch home with his hip. As he walked around the back of the car, he surveyed the area around the cabin.

A tree had come down some time in the five years since he'd been up here. No one had bothered to cut it up for firewood. Other than that, it seemed nothing much had changed.

He opened the passenger door, his eyes still examining the shadows on the mountain side of the cabin. The door he held moved a little under his hand. He looked down to find Robin trying to shift the child into some position that would allow her to climb out of the car while carrying his full weight.

"I'll get him," he offered.

He bent, reaching for the child. As he did, there was another jolt of déjà vu. He and Karen must have made this same transfer a hundred times. Coming back from vacation or from visiting family or after a movie.

There was time for those bittersweet memories to register before the small, warm body of the boy was placed in his arms. The blue eyes opened briefly, gazing up into his face before they closed again with a quick drop that reminded him of the mechanical motion of a doll's eyes.

Apparently the sight of his face looking down on him rather than his mother's hadn't jarred Taylor out of sleep. His head relaxed against Matt's shoulder, his legs dangling bonelessly over the other arm.

Matt straightened, automatically shifting the child's weight into a more secure position, just as Robin had tried to do. His lids remained closed, even when Matt moved back to allow Robin to step out of the car. Only then did he realize that the key to the cabin was not on the ring with his car keys, which he was holding in his hand.

"The front door key's in my jacket pocket," he said, turning to allow her access to it.

"What?"

"The key to the cabin. It's in my pocket. Unless you want to take Taylor…"

She eased the door closed as soundlessly as he had and then stepped toward him. Gingerly she lifted the flap on his blazer pocket and inserted her hand.

He discovered that for some reason he was holding his breath. Her fingers closed around the key almost immediately, but before she could step away, the scent of something floral and very feminine surrounded him.

It was gone as quickly as her nearness, leaving him wondering if the whole thing had been a product of his imagination. He hadn't noticed the fragrance before. Not even in the confines of the car. Of course, they hadn't been in such physical proximity then.

In any case, the elusive aroma wasn't something he could afford to dwell on. Not given the recklessness of the kiss they'd shared tonight.

"This way," he said, starting toward the back of the cabin.

He wanted to take another look down the trail they'd just driven before they moved out into the open. There was a door at the back, but it could only be unlocked from the inside.

He stopped at the corner of the cabin, again surveying

the clearing. No one had followed them. No one knew they were up here, so he couldn't explain the sense of foreboding. Neither could he deny it.

"Can you take him a minute?"

Without answering, she moved around him. She reached for the child, slipping her right hand under Taylor's head and her forearm under his knees. The transfer this time was more practiced, as if this *were* something they'd done a hundred times.

As he shifted the solid warmth of the little boy's body into her arms, the top of her head was just below his nose. What he had smelled before was her shampoo. Something sweetly subtle. Tantalizing.

His groin tightened, responding to the fragrance or to her nearness. Or, he acknowledged, to their isolation.

He ignored his reaction, his fingers closing around the butt of the semi-automatic to lift it out of the holster. "Stay close," he ordered as he stepped in front of her.

To make sure she obeyed, he put his left arm behind him to encircle her body and move it behind his, physically forcing her to obey his directive. He didn't remove it as he started forward. Carrying the boy, she moved in unison with his steps, his body shielding theirs from an assassin's bullet.

It never came, of course, not even when they reached the front door. Standing to one side of it, he turned his hand, palm upward.

Obediently she placed the key on it. In a matter of seconds he had opened the door and ushered them inside. Only a few more passed before it was again locked.

Then he waited, allowing his eyes to adjust to the darkness inside the cabin. The air was rich with the years' accumulation of dust and mildew.

Maybe he'd been wrong about Karen's mother. Maybe she, too, had been unable to come up here without remembering. Maybe she had decided never to put herself into the position where she would be forced to relive the happiest times of their lives.

"Wait here," he whispered.

An oil lamp had always stood on the end of the rough-hewn log that formed the fireplace mantel. He couldn't remember lighting it himself, but he must have watched Martha or Karen do it dozens of times. The process was so simple that he should be able to manage it even in the dark.

He felt his way across the room, unerringly remembering the placement of each piece of furniture. His reaching fingers located the mantel and then traced along it until they encountered the box of matches that was always kept beside the lamp.

The small flare of light from the one he struck revealed that there was still oil in the bottom of the glass globe. He had time to turn up the wick before the heat from the head forced him to shake out the match. With the next one, he succeeded in lighting the lamp, its soft glow spreading through the central room.

Robin was standing exactly where he'd left her, just inside the door. Despite the flare of light, Taylor hadn't stirred, pale lashes unmoving on the fragile skin beneath. Robin looked almost as tired, the fair, transparent skin under her eyes darkened like old bruises.

They needed to be in bed, and the cabin offered several options. There were two small bedrooms, their space almost totally filled by the old-fashioned double beds that occupied them. There was also a sleeping loft, which held a pair of twin beds.

Besides those, the couch in this room, although not a

sleeper, was wide enough to hold one person comfortably. He had slept there a couple of times when he'd joined Trev and his buddies for a weekend.

His inclination was to have Robin and the boy sleep in here so he could keep watch over them. It was always possible, however, that she would prefer privacy to his protection.

Despite his anxiety over their safety, that should be an option. He'd brought her here because he believed it was safe. There was no reason to start second-guessing his own decision now. No reason they couldn't sleep securely in one of the bedrooms if that's what she wanted.

"There are two rooms, a double bed in each. The loft has a pair of twins. You might sleep better if you don't share a bed."

She glanced toward the ladderlike steps to the sleeping loft and visibly shivered.

"No stairs, please."

"I can carry Taylor up for you."

"It isn't that. Just…no stairs."

"There isn't much to choose between the other rooms," he began, walking across the central room and into the short hallway to open the door of the nearest.

The same odor that had assailed them when they entered the cabin wafted out of the bedroom. The sheets would be cold and damp this time of year, no matter how frequently Martha came up here.

"I've got some dry blankets in the trunk," he added.

"Then why don't I just put him down here," she said, tilting her chin in the direction of the couch. Her expression was almost challenging, as if she expected him to refuse.

"What about you?"

"I don't think I'll be able to sleep. If I am, it isn't likely to be in some dark room alone. There's room enough here for both of us.''

It was the first verbal admission of fear he'd heard her make. And considering all she'd been through, it was remarkably low-key.

''Fair enough,'' he said, feeling a sense of relief that was out of proportion to her concession.

He wanted them both where he could see them. The fact that she seemed to want the same thing made his job that much easier.

He watched as she carried Taylor to the couch and laid him down. The boy didn't wake, not even when she lifted the arm that had fallen over the edge of the couch and placed it on his chest.

''Blankets?'' she prompted quietly.

Along with the rest of what he'd crammed into the trunk, he thought. Especially some of the food.

He had to stop and think about the last time he'd eaten. Lunch yesterday, he realized with a sense of surprise. Unless he counted the candy bar he'd grabbed from a vending machine at the Marietta station.

''You'll be okay until I get back,'' he said.

It hadn't been a question, but she nodded. He eased his weapon out of the holster again and started for the door.

''Don't be long,'' she added, echoing the words she'd said to him this afternoon.

Before they'd sent him on that wild-goose chase that had almost gotten her killed.

''Not this time,'' he promised, glancing down at the little boy on the couch. That feeling of déjà vu washed over him again, seeming to transpose the features of the sleeping child into those of the son he had lost.

Not this time.

CHAPTER FIFTEEN

"Is THIS your house?"

The question forced Matt to pry open his eyes. They felt as if they had been filled with a combination of sand and glue.

Despite his intentions, he had drifted off. He was still sitting on the floor, the rough, uneven planks of the front door against his back. He had chosen the position as much for its discomfort as for its strategic possibilities, but obviously it hadn't kept him awake.

In the thin light of dawn Taylor Holt stood looking down on him, blond hair disordered from sleep. He was still wearing the beige knit pajamas he'd been wearing during the siege in the attic.

Befuddled with sleep, Matt thought briefly about trying to explain the ownership of the cabin and then settled on one of those compromises with the truth adults make when talking to children.

"Yeah."

"I can't find your bathroom," Taylor said.

His hand clutched at the drooping material around his crotch. It was a gesture any parent would have recognized, even without the narrative that had accompanied it.

"Okay," Matt said, trying to drag himself back to full consciousness.

That wasn't what he wanted to say, but thankfully he

had presence of mind enough to keep the other words to himself. He put his left hand on the floor to begin the painful process of getting to his feet. As he did, he discovered that his right hand was still encumbered with the semi-automatic he'd held all night. At least the part of the night that had been left after they'd reached the cabin.

He had been so damn sure he could stay awake until dawn, and he'd been wrong. Besides that, the half hour or so of sleep he'd inadvertently gotten had made him feel worse than if he'd had none at all.

He was stiff from sitting on the floor with the cold outside air seeping in under and around the door. He grunted with the surprising effort getting to his feet required.

"Why are you sleeping down there?"

Instead of answering with another half lie, once he was upright, Matt held out his hand. The little boy hesitated a few seconds before he put his into it.

His fingers were cold and very small. Matt resisted the impulse to sandwich them between the warmth of his palms, just as he had once warmed another grubby little hand.

"You sleep good?" he asked as he led the way to the larger of the two bedrooms, which contained the only inside toilet.

The boy nodded, but the hand not holding Matt's still clutched worriedly at his crotch as he walked. As they passed the couch, Matt realized that Robin was now awake, probably disturbed by the sound of their voices.

"I'll take him," she offered. Her hand was on the edge of the blanket that covered her, preparing to throw it back and get up.

"We've got it," Matt said. "You stay warm."

That reminded him that he needed to check on the supply

of firewood. The heat the generator provided wouldn't be enough to keep them comfortable at this time of the year.

He also needed to bring the rest of the food he'd stacked in the back of the SUV inside. And check the perimeter. And call the chief to see if there were any new developments. The list seemed to grow with each step he took.

He had asked for this responsibility, had been eager to accept it, but after only one night without food or sleep, he had begun doubting his ability to carry it off.

He pushed open the door to the bathroom, which seemed ten degrees colder than the rest of the cabin. Taylor physically flinched as his bare feet made contact with the linoleum floor.

Matt released the child's hand and lifted the lid of the commode. The water inside it was a deep blue.

"What's that?" the boy asked suspiciously, staring down into the bowl.

"Antifreeze. It keeps the water from freezing in the winter."

He hadn't been wrong about Martha taking care of the place. Once he had a fire going in the fireplace and had gotten the generator working, he'd pull back the coverlets on the beds and let her clean sheets get warm and dry. They would all sleep more comfortably tonight.

Even as he thought longingly about stretching his aching body out on a bed, he wondered if he'd be confident enough about the security of their location to do that. Of course, he might not have a choice. He'd already demonstrated that he couldn't continue to function without sleep.

"Can't we get some *real* water in there?"

Taylor's question pulled him away from the problem of having someone on guard at all times. Despite the boy's obvious need, he appeared to be stalling.

Maybe it *was* the color of the water. Or maybe he wasn't prepared to use the facility in front of someone.

Matt reached over and pushed down the handle that flushed the commode. Together they watched the dark blue swirl downward to be replaced by a paler hue from the tank.

"That better?"

"I guess."

"Okay, then. Have at it." Matt started to turn, intending to give the child some privacy.

"Are you leaving?" Taylor's fingers clutched at his arm.

"I'll be right outside the door."

There was a long hesitation during which the blue eyes considered his face. Matt could almost read the thoughts warring in the brain behind them. A genuine fear of being alone. An equal fear of being thought a baby. Along with a natural reluctance to perform a bodily function in front of someone who was virtually a stranger.

"You want me to call your mom?"

It had been the wrong thing to say. He realized that when Taylor blinked, fighting a glaze of moisture he couldn't quite hide.

"How about if I wait for you over by the door?" Matt asked, trying to find a compromise that would neither humiliate the boy nor make him more fearful. "*Inside* the door."

"Okay." Taylor's relief was as obvious as his reluctance had been.

Matt had started across the five or six feet that separated the john from the door to the bedroom when Taylor added, "Don't look. Okay?"

"Cross my heart," Matt said, hiding his smile.

"DID YOU get *any* sleep?"

Robin was taking the items he'd grabbed from his pantry out of the garbage bags he'd carried them in and putting them out on the counter. Displayed like this, his selection didn't look very promising. Of course, if it didn't come out of the freezer and go immediately into the microwave, he didn't buy it. That meant some of this stuff must have been on the shelves since—

He destroyed the thought, concentrating on watching Robin while she attempted to put the haphazardly chosen items into some kind of order. As she worked, her hands moved with an unthinking grace and economy of motion.

"Not much," he admitted. "More than I intended to, however. We need to think of some other arrangement for tonight."

She looked up, her eyes questioning. "An arrangement for standing watch?"

"Something like that. I dozed off this morning around dawn without even realizing it. I was lucky it was Taylor who walked up on me."

She studied his face for a moment. "You said we'd be safe here."

"It's as safe a location as we could find. That doesn't mean we can afford not to be vigilant."

"What do you want me to do?"

"You know how to shoot?"

Her eyes fell to the weapon holstered just beneath his arm. "A pistol?"

"Anything."

She shook her head. "Not really. My neighbor had a BB gun when I was a little girl. I fired it a few times."

The words produced an immediate mental image. A female version of Taylor at around the same age. He wondered if she had been a tomboy. If she were shooting her neighbor's gun that was a possibility.

"That's a start."

"You want to teach me how to shoot your gun."

"Point and squeeze. That's all you have to remember."

"Point it at *somebody*. That's a little different."

"If you'd had a gun last night," he interrupted, "would you have fired it? To protect Taylor?"

They both knew she would have. And without a second thought.

"You may be placed in that situation again," he went on. "It isn't a bad idea to prepare for that eventuality."

"Are you suggesting target practice? *Outside?*"

It was deer season. There would be gunfire echoing through the woods all over this state. That would be rifles, however. Anyone familiar with guns would be able to tell the difference between those and the sound of the semi-automatic.

"Maybe," he said, careful not to commit to the idea until he'd had time to think it through. "Maybe just handling the weapon to become familiar with it. Just to see how it works."

Her reluctance was as easy to read as the boy's had been this morning in the bathroom. And it made about as much sense.

She'd already conceded that she'd do anything to protect her son. There was no reason not to make sure she had the skills necessary to do it effectively.

"All right," she said finally.

"We'll start after breakfast."

"Breakfast." Her eyes left his to consider the items on the counter again. "Just add water," she read off the box of pancake batter. "Since that's all we have…"

He hadn't thought about bringing eggs or milk or anything perishable. He hadn't checked to see if the ancient refrigerator was still functioning.

Of course, the root cellar contained a concrete trough through which the clear, cold water of a mountain spring flowed year round. That was one thing they would have plenty of, even if the pipes froze. Martha used to keep soft drinks cold by laying the bottles on their sides in the trough. This time of year, it would probably work for eggs and milk as well.

Taking the mix with her, Robin had walked over to the stove and begun opening drawers and cabinets in its vicinity, obviously searching for a frying pan. He remembered where Martha kept them, but he didn't offer directions. He told himself that she needed to familiarize herself with the kitchen, but there was also a part of him that simply enjoyed watching her.

She was wearing the same pair of ancient jeans and the fleece jacket she'd changed into before they'd left the house last night. Her hair pulled back into a low ponytail and her face devoid of makeup, she looked like a teenager herself.

Again, that graceful economy of motion was apparent in every movement. Finding the measuring cups and spoons. Adding the mix and then the water to a crockery bowl.

"No one's coming up to relieve you?"

She didn't look up as she posed the question, her hands engaged in stirring lumps out of the batter.

"The fewer people who know we're here, the better. The change of shift was the weak link last night."

That was reason enough. He didn't want to confess that he didn't trust anyone in the department enough to let them in on where they were hiding.

"He was your friend, wasn't he?"

She was talking about Eph. And he found that he didn't want to. That loss was too new. The hurt too raw.

"He thought a lot of you," she said, still not looking at him. "He told me that you were too good a cop—"

"Too good a cop to what?"

He knew that whatever Eph had told her would be painful to hear, but he couldn't resist asking. It was important to him what the old man thought. It always had been.

"Too good a cop to be fooled by a kid. He said that if you believed Taylor was telling the truth, then I could."

"You *doubted* him?"

He never had. Everything the boy had told him had fit seamlessly with what they now knew.

"They seemed so sure he'd heard the reports on the radio and made it all up. The story about the men in the woods. About Lisa. They said he was obviously a very creative child. And he *is*."

"He didn't make it up," Matt said, more sure of that than he'd ever been. "And remember that when they told you that they were still operating under the assumption that the girl who'd been spotted in Marietta was Lisa."

"I wish it had been," she said. "I'd give anything if it *had* been Lisa."

She glanced toward the central room of the cabin. Taylor was lying on his stomach before the fire Matt had built, clearly more interested in watching the flames than in listening to their conversation.

"He's stopped asking about her," she said, turning back to meet his eyes. "I think he knows I won't be able to offer him the reassurances I did when she first disappeared. And if he does ask…"

"Maybe he won't. Until he does, don't tell him anything. At least," he amended, realizing that he was giving advice he had no right to give, "if he were *mine,* I wouldn't tell him."

Her lips parted as if she wanted to say something. Then she closed them tightly—deliberately—looking down at the batter again.

"Look, I didn't mean that you shouldn't tell him if you think it's the right thing to do. I don't know anything about kids that age."

"Officer Stokes wouldn't agree." She glanced up at him through her lashes. "He thought you understood Taylor very well."

"Eph might have been a little biased." He smiled, both at her teasing and the thought of Stokes defending him. "He was a good friend."

"And because of us, he's dead."

His smile faded at the regret in her tone.

"Don't you ever think that way. That's who Eph Stokes was. It's what he did. His whole life. He *protected* people. It was his job and his calling."

"His...*calling?*"

He was embarrassed by his own passion. Not because what he had said wasn't the truth, but because he'd given voice to something that cops didn't talk about. Not openly. Now that he had...

"Some people feel they're called to preach or to teach. To be doctors or nurses."

"And some are called to be cops?"

The edge of cynicism he'd noticed before was back in her voice. This time it bothered him.

"Not all of them," he conceded. "But some. Men like Eph, who devote their whole lives to the job. They guard the community at the expense of their health and their families."

"He said cops are notorious for having bad marriages."

"Maybe, but he and Margaret were married more than thirty-five years. I don't think theirs would in any way, shape or form qualify as a 'bad' marriage."

"He didn't think yours and Karen's would either."

Hearing Karen's name on her lips revived his earlier guilt and feelings of disloyalty. He was in Karen's family's house with another woman. A woman he was attracted to.

"I'm sorry," she said quickly. "I thought it was a compliment. I thought you'd want to know what he thought about you. I didn't mean to…" She hesitated, obviously unsure of how to characterize what she'd just done.

He had no idea what his face had revealed. Clearly, enough to make her uncomfortable.

"I *did* want to know. Thank you for telling me," he said evenly.

"He also told me…" Once more she hesitated, finally choosing not to finish the sentence she'd begun. "I can't imagine what it must be like to lose a child."

Her eyes again sought the little boy lying on the rug beside the hearth. When she turned back to Matt, her lips were parted as if she intended to add something else. What was in his eyes must have stopped her.

She looked down and then up quickly, lifting the bowl of batter, the gesture apologetic, obviously intended as an excuse for ending the conversation. She turned toward the pan she'd been heating on the stove, but not before he'd seen the sheen of tears in the clear blue eyes.

CHAPTER SIXTEEN

"DON'T TRY to aim. Hold the weapon out in front of you in both hands and point it at the target, just as if you were pointing your finger."

She held the gun gingerly, but exactly as he'd showed her, her left hand supporting the right. She straightened her arms, bringing the big semi-automatic into firing position, and pulled the trigger. He had removed the clip, so there was no discharge.

She turned her head, arms still extended. Her eyes met his, seeking approval.

"Slow squeeze," he corrected. "If you pull it like that, the weapon will jerk up, taking the next shot out of alignment. Try it again."

She took a deep breath in response, but she didn't argue. She had proven to be a good pupil, following his directions exactly.

He had resisted the temptation to stand behind her during the lesson. To put his arms around hers to offer hands-on guidance.

Of course, that position wasn't necessary. It certainly wasn't the way he'd been trained. And she was smart enough to see through any such ploy if he'd tried it.

"Okay, arms down at your sides," he instructed, making her start at the beginning.

Obediently she released the hold of her supporting hand,

bringing her body out of the slight shooter's crouch. She allowed her right hand to fall, carrying the gun to her side.

She tilted her chin upward and turned her head from side to side, attempting to ease the tension that had built in the muscles of her neck. Then she straightened her shoulders, standing almost at attention. Her lips were parted, the tip of her tongue at the corner of her mouth as she awaited his signal.

"Now," he said, working to ignore that temptation as well.

She assumed the stance he'd shown her, feet apart, knees slightly bent for balance, as both arms came up. The left cupped under the right again, steadying the weapon. This time he couldn't fault her pull of the trigger.

Once more her eyes cut to his face. Awaiting his judgment.

"Better," he conceded.

"Can I try next?"

They turned to find Taylor standing in the bedroom doorway. Obviously he'd been watching them, something Robin had wanted to avoid. Before they'd begun, she had placed him at the kitchen table with Matt's notebook and ballpoint pen and told him to stay there.

Although they had moved to the back bedroom, they'd left the door open. The boy had apparently been drawn by the sound of their voices. Or maybe, to be fair, by the same desire not to be left alone he'd communicated so clearly this morning.

Robin's "No" sounded on top of Matt's "Maybe."

"No," she said again into the sudden silence that fell after their conflicting messages. "He's too young."

The last had clearly been directed at Matt.

"It might not be such a bad idea."

The possibility that Taylor could be forced to have to defend himself was absolutely a worst-case scenario, and one Matt was determined would not come to pass. Any reservations he might have about teaching him to handle the gun were not because of the boy's age, however.

He'd been younger than Taylor the first time his father had taken him hunting. And his instruction in the proper handling of firearms had begun months before that unforgettable morning.

"He's too young," Robin said again.

"A lot of kids his age—"

"No." Unequivocal.

"Robin—"

"Go finish your drawings, Taylor," she ordered, her voice harder than Matt had ever heard it before, especially when she was speaking to her son.

"Are you going to shoot those people if they come here?"

It wasn't clear to which of them Taylor's question had been addressed, and for a long heartbeat neither of them attempted to answer it.

"They aren't coming here," Robin said finally.

"Then why are you learning to shoot his gun?"

Another silence. Then Robin swallowed, the movement visible down the line of her throat. She turned, holding the weapon out to Matt, muzzle down.

"Go on. Take it," she prodded when he didn't move.

Holding her eyes, he took the weapon and slipped it back into the shoulder holster.

"Now you go back and finish your drawings," she said to her son.

"It got lonely in there."

"I'll be there in a minute to start lunch," she said. "Go on, Taylor. *Now.*"

The boy took a deep, sighing breath, but he obeyed. Not before he'd made a show of his reluctance by trudging slowly back across the central room.

"Nothing's changed," Matt warned, hoping she would remember the question he'd asked her in the kitchen this morning.

"I can't do this," she said. "Not in front of him. It will make him think I believe shooting people is right."

"Sometimes it is."

"Maybe. But he isn't capable of distinguishing when it is and when it isn't. Not now."

"*You* are," Matt said, not bothering to hide his irritation over her decision. "*You're* the adult. You *are* capable of making that distinction. As a parent, it's your job to make the hard decisions. And it's also your job to protect your child."

It was clear from the tightening of her lips that she didn't like being lectured, although she didn't deny what he'd said.

"If it ever comes to that, I'll manage. Point and squeeze. I'm a fast learner."

"For Taylor's sake, I hope so."

UNABLE TO RESIST, she tucked the quilt more firmly around Taylor's shoulders. Then she bent, breathing in the sweet, familiar scent of his hair before she pressed a kiss against the strands.

He turned his head restively, but thankfully that unnecessary bit of mothering didn't wake him. After the sleep he'd lost the last two days, probably nothing short of a nuclear blast could have done that.

Still, he had delayed bedtime as long as he possibly could, so she was relieved when he'd finally settled down. Given everything that had happened, plus the fact that he was sleeping in an unfamiliar environment, it actually hadn't been too difficult a process.

She straightened, turning away from the bed, and saw that Matt was standing in the doorway. To offer protection? Or for some other reason?

The same reason, perhaps, that she'd felt his eyes on her a couple of other times today. The first time she'd glanced up and realized he was watching her, he had looked away. The second time he hadn't bothered. He had held her eyes for a moment before he'd turned to answer a question Taylor had posed as if nothing had happened.

Now he was watching her again. The bedroom was dark, the only light in the cabin from the fire in the central room. Although she couldn't see Matt's face, his body was silhouetted against the firelight behind him, his shoulders seeming to fill the narrow doorway. As she walked toward him, he stepped aside to allow her passage.

"I think he's down for the count," she whispered. She reached back for the knob of the door, intending to pull it closed behind her.

"Considering what he went through *last* night..."

"You think I should stay with him?"

His tone hadn't been critical, but maybe he thought it was strange that she hadn't lain down beside Taylor. Or perhaps it was her own guilt over that decision which had caused her hand to hesitate.

She wasn't ready to go to bed. She knew that when she did, all the horrors of the last few days would be there in the darkness with her. And despite her exhaustion, she wouldn't be able to sleep. Not for a while. Until she could, she wanted to be with someone who would keep those terrors at bay.

"I think he'll be fine," Matt said reassuringly. "If you leave the door open, we'll be able to hear him if he wakes up."

With a final glance at the bed, she pulled the door closed only far enough that the low light from the central room wouldn't disturb Taylor. Then she moved past Matt to walk across to the fireplace. She held her hands out to the comforting warmth of the blaze.

"Stop worrying. Nothing's going to happen tonight," he said as he followed her into the room.

He had gotten a few hours sleep on the couch this afternoon while she sat in the armchair, the semi-automatic lying inconspicuously on the table beside her. Taylor had alternately drawn in the notepad or looked at the children's books she'd found in a bookcase in the back bedroom.

Tonight their roles would be reversed, and she was far more comfortable with that. There was no doubt in her mind that she would be able to pull the trigger of Matt's gun if she had to in order to protect Taylor. What she feared was that in her inexperience, she would hesitate too long, making a fatal error of judgment.

"I wish I were as sure of that as you are," she said without turning to look at him.

Since Lisa's disappearance, it seemed that one person after another had told her that everything would be all right. In the beginning she had even tried to make Taylor believe that.

And no matter how many times the platitude had been offered them, it hadn't been "all right." She wondered if anything in her world would ever be again.

"There aren't half a dozen people in this area who know

about this place," Matt said. "And none of them were involved in what Taylor saw in the woods. We're ten miles from the nearest road. You saw that if you didn't know the trail up here, you'd never be able to follow it in the dark. And until you got within a hundred yards or so of this place, you wouldn't have known it was here."

Although she had no way to verify the first of what he'd said, the last was probably true enough. As soon as he'd gotten the generator working, Matt had pulled the drapes and then nailed the blankets and quilts he'd brought up over them.

The extra insulation not only kept the heat inside, but the material acted as a primitive blackout curtain. Now, with only the fire, there was little possibility anyone could see light coming from inside the cabin.

"Relax," he suggested again.

She turned to face him, clasping her hands behind her back. "That's easier said than done. People seemed to have acquired the unfortunate habit of dying around us."

"Well, nobody's going to do that tonight."

"Officer Stokes was probably just as convinced of that *last* night."

"I'm not going to let anything happen to you or to Taylor, I promise you that, Robin."

It was far more personal than anything he'd ever said to her. Almost as personal as that impulsive kiss.

That's all it had been, she'd decided. An impulse. Relief. Elation that they'd escaped unscathed.

She'd had no illusions that it had meant anything other than that. If she had, the carefully professional distance he had maintained today would have disabused her of the notion.

Of course, she had been just as careful. Just as distanced.

That hadn't prevented her from remembering what leaning her head against his shoulder felt like.

Even now, the memory produced a small, shivering reaction. To hide it, she crossed her arms over her chest, rubbing her hands up and down them as if she were cold.

"Thank you," she said softly. "And despite what I said about last night, I *do* mean that. I'm very grateful for what you're doing."

"You don't have to thank me. It's my job. The job of the Mallory Police Department. It's about time we started doing it."

Although she knew his comment was intended to be comforting, it brought back her sense of guilt about the deaths of those two officers. There was no rational reason to blame herself for that. She and Taylor hadn't asked for this. Still, she couldn't help but think about the families of those two men.

"It seems to me that job has been pretty well performed. At a terrible cost. I can't help but feel…" She shook her head, unsure how to express what she felt.

"That's not *your* fault," he said, seeming to understand intuitively. "That's not the fault of anyone but whoever killed that man in the woods."

"I know, but I'd feel better if I knew something to do to bring an end to this. I really do think Taylor has told you everything he remembers."

She waited, hoping for his agreement. She didn't want her son to be questioned again, but it would probably be necessary if something didn't turn up soon.

"The forensics examination may give us something new."

It took her a moment to realize he meant the examination

of Lisa's body. Of her clothing. Even of the area around that shallow hole they'd buried her in.

She shivered again, trying to imagine the depth of terror the girl must have felt. Thinking, too, that it could just as easily have been Taylor in that makeshift grave.

"Cold?"

Matt's question brought her eyes up. He was holding out the fleece jacket she'd discarded this afternoon after the generator and the fire had begun to heat the cabin. Mutely she shook her head.

"I can't get it out of my head. What Lisa must have been thinking and feeling. How afraid she would have been."

He nodded, lowering his eyes to the jacket dangling from his hand. He looked big and dark and very competent holding the lightweight garment. After a moment he tossed it onto the couch behind him.

"I don't know if this will be any comfort, but according to the coroner, it was very quick." His voice was low, filled with a compassion she could feel. "They don't think she was assaulted."

"Assaulted?" She was dead. How much more assaulted could she have been?

"Sexually." He added the word of explanation she'd sought.

"They weren't interested in that," she said bitterly. "All they were interested in was making sure she couldn't describe them. And what they didn't realize—"

What they didn't realize was that the only person who could do that was Taylor.

They could have taken both of them that first afternoon. He and Lisa had walked home from school together, apparently following the same route they had always used.

Why had the killers waited until Lisa left the house before they snatched her?

The only explanation was that they didn't know Taylor had been in the woods that afternoon. His story had been consistent from the first. The men had run toward Lisa. If they hadn't seen Taylor...

"How did they find out about him?" she asked. "How did they find out he'd seen them?"

"Maybe because he was with her the afternoon they waited for her outside your house. They may have had to get permission from someone higher up before they took Lisa. Otherwise—"

"Otherwise they would have grabbed her the afternoon Taylor saw them in the woods."

"That's the only thing that seems to make sense of the delay."

"Then later that night they came back for Taylor."

The pause before he responded was long enough to be noticeable.

"Maybe. Or maybe whoever—or whatever—you saw that night had nothing to do with Lisa's disappearance."

"You don't believe that."

"I think it's possible. The presence of two policemen wasn't a deterrent last night. I'm not sure why the sound of a siren would have been the night before."

"That's just a little too coincidental for me to swallow. That on two consecutive nights there would be two unrelated incidents in which someone would try to break into my house—"

She stopped in midsentence, wondering if that was what had happened. Now that he'd introduced the idea, she would be forced to consider it. And she didn't like thinking about who else might have been lurking outside her house.

"What is it?" he asked.

She closed her mouth and shook her head. "Nothing. Just... That seems a ridiculous supposition."

"No one knew Taylor was a witness until yesterday. They knew he was one of the last two people to see Lisa alive, but not that he was connected to the murder in the woods."

"Until *yesterday?* What happened yesterday that would let them know he'd seen them that day?"

His lips pursed, as if he were trying to decide what to tell her. *Don't blow it now,* she thought. *Don't start equivocating or keeping things from me for my own good.*

"Someone leaked the information to the media."

She didn't know why she was surprised. She hadn't thought she could be shocked any longer at people's capacity for duplicity. Not even when a child's safety was involved.

"Are you saying...someone in the *police* department?"

She knew she should be outraged by that. And on some level she was. There were other considerations, however, that seemed far more important at the moment.

"That seems the most likely place for the information to come from."

"They leaked to the local media?"

"According to the people I was with in Marietta last night, it appeared on one of the cable news networks. They used the film someone had shot of you and Taylor being brought to the courthouse as background for the story."

"Film." Her voice sounded strange.

"That may be why they came for Taylor last night."

"You're saying that because someone in your department leaked information, the men who were in the woods now *know* that Taylor can identify them."

"*If* they didn't before. It's always been a possibility—"

"You just said you didn't think they saw him. That whoever was outside my house the night Lisa disappeared wasn't connected to this."

"I said that was a possibility."

"This is what you meant when you said it was about time the department started doing its job. And here I was feeling guilty because those two officers died protecting us last night. But I really can't take the blame for that, can I? Their blood is on the hands of whoever released that information."

"People talk. They don't think about the consequences."

"I wonder if they're thinking about them tonight."

She didn't bother to hide her anger. People *did* talk, but law-enforcement officers should know better.

"If we're passing around blame, part of it should probably be mine."

She didn't believe he'd given information to the media, so whatever he was talking about, it wasn't that. And she couldn't think of anything else he'd done that would have led to the carnage that had occurred at her house last night.

"*Yours?*"

"If I hadn't taken you back to the courthouse that day, they wouldn't have had tape to run with the story."

She had tried to avoid the kind of scene they'd run into that morning by lying to him about the visit to the doctor's office. Maybe if she hadn't lied, he wouldn't have been so insistent that she come with him. Maybe if she'd just gone to the school at the same time as all the other mothers…

Maybe, maybe, maybe. The same game he was playing. And it would get neither of them any closer to an end to all this.

"You couldn't have known what was going to happen. Not any of it."

"It's my job to figure those things out."

"It's my job to protect my son. But I'm not omniscient. I couldn't imagine what might result from letting him walk home from school. We never know what's going to happen as a result of our most ordinary actions."

She hadn't been thinking about his wife and son when she'd stated that, but it seemed eerily parallel to what he'd told Eph Stokes. *If she'd been two minutes one way or the other leaving the doctor's office…*

"There'll be other leaks," he said. "I can virtually guarantee it."

She nodded, grateful he didn't seem to have associated what she'd just said with his family. He had already beaten himself up enough about that decision to run the gamut of reporters at the courthouse. He didn't need to be reminded of that other guilt.

They were a fine pair, she thought, too ready to accept responsibility for things that were beyond their control. She had done that for years until somehow she'd found the courage to stop being a victim.

"I think I *would* like my jacket, please," she said, determined that was one thing she wasn't going to dwell on tonight. *Sufficient unto the day…* "The temperature must be dropping outside."

He turned and retrieved the jacket from the couch, but instead of holding it out to her in one hand as he had before, he held it up by the shoulders, inviting her to put her arms into the sleeves. For a moment she hesitated, and then, afraid that he might think she was reading more into the gesture than he'd intended, she took the few steps that separated them and turned her back to him.

She slipped her arm into the right sleeve and the other into the left. He pulled the jacket up over her shoulders. Then, unnecessarily, he turned the collar down, taking care to straighten it. As he did, his fingers brushed her neck, sending a shiver through her frame.

His hands settled around her upper arms. She was conscious of their size and their strength and their warmth.

She closed her eyes, savoring the feeling. She wanted nothing more than to lean back against his chest and have him wrap his arms around her as he had done last night.

Maybe in trying to muster the resolve to resist, she stiffened her shoulders. He released her immediately, his hands moving away from her body and out to the side.

Which was *not* what she wanted. If she didn't act quickly, he would once again adopt that air of professional distance he'd maintained all day.

She turned around, moving so quickly that he was forced to lean back to avoid a collision. She looked up at him, her lips parted as she tried to formulate what she wanted to say. When she couldn't find the combination of words she wanted, a small furrow formed between his brows.

"What's wrong?"

There were a dozen ways to answer that, none of them easy. Being a coward, she chose the one that required no further search for words.

She put her hand on the back of his neck, stretching upward on tiptoe. He made no attempt to meet her halfway, his eyes looking into hers until her lips reached a point just below his.

And then his eyelids fell, their thick lashes veiling his eyes as his arms closed around her, gathering her to him. His head tilted, seeking the proper alignment, before his lips closed over hers.

CHAPTER SEVENTEEN

WHATEVER REASONS he'd offered for last night's kiss, there was no doubt why he was kissing her now. Perhaps she had been the instigator this time, but his response had been immediate. And unmistakable.

His tongue demanded entrance, pushing into her mouth ruthlessly. Hungrily.

A hunger he'd denied all day by keeping his distance?

His hand slipped under the bottom of the ancient T-shirt she wore. His palm, callused, sensually abrasive, slid over her stomach. At the same time his little finger edged under the waistband of her jeans, searching until it found the indention of her navel.

A flood of hot moisture released within her. It had been so long since someone had made love to her. Too long. Her body was as eager for his touch as her heart had been for his concern.

When she didn't protest what he was doing, his hand continued to explore. His fingers trailed across her ribs, skimming them until they had rounded her side. Then his hand moved up her spine to spread between her shoulder blades, supporting her as he deepened the kiss.

She responded, fingernails digging into the ridge of muscle that lay across the tops of his shoulders. With a quick expertise he unfastened the hooks of her bra, easing his hand under the material as it parted.

Then his fingers began to move again, tracing under the now loosened undergarment across her back and around her side. There was no time to think. No time to remember any of the rules she had created for her lonely existence.

The same callused palm that had weakened her knees by brushing over her stomach destroyed her last reservations by sliding under the weight of her breast. Cupping it. Claiming it.

Claiming her.

She drew a shuddering breath, unintentionally pushing the softness of her breast against the unyielding masculinity of his hand. It tightened, a pleasure so exquisite it bordered on pain.

Her gasp caused him to loosen his hold. His thumb found her nipple instead. He moved the edge of his finger down and then up again, over and over until the sensitive skin began to tauten and grow hard.

Her breasts felt exactly as they had when she'd nursed Taylor. Aching for relief. Except this time...

As if he'd read her mind, he reached down with his other hand to grasp the bottom of her T-shirt. He pulled it up, and then he bent, rimming the hardened nipple with his tongue.

She made some involuntarily noise low in her throat. Hearing it, he raised his head, allowing the cold air to touch the wetness his lips had left on her skin. A flickering sensation, like summer lightning, shimmered through her body, to be followed by another release of moisture.

She wanted more. More of him. More of this. More reminders of what it felt like to be a woman and to be wanted by a man.

Her hands pushed at his chest, just as she had in the attic last night. His body went still, but when she pushed again, more strongly this time, he released her. He stepped back, allowing her T-shirt to fall into place.

She was light-headed with need, her bones molten with desire, so that she almost staggered at the loss of his supporting hand. She was unable to compose a coherent explanation that hadn't been what she'd wanted.

Instead, she crossed her arms, her fingers fastening over the hem of her shirt. She peeled it over her head, bringing the light fleece jacket and the tangled bra with it. She dropped them on the floor and took the single step that would put her in contact with his body, the tips of her breasts brushing against the tightly woven cotton of his sweatshirt.

Again she stood on tiptoe, reaching up to put her arms around his neck. Her tongue teased his mouth, as his had rimmed her nipple.

Caught by surprise, it took him a heartbeat to respond. Then he crushed her to him. His hands found the curve of her hips, lifting so that they were pulled up hard and close against the bulge of his erection. His lips fastened over hers, putting an end to her teasing.

Frantic now, her hands slipped under his sweatshirt to locate the buttons of the dress shirt. As she began to slip the first one through its buttonhole, he lifted his mouth from hers far enough to whisper, "Wait."

He stripped the sweatshirt off over his head, dropping it to the floor beside her shirt and jacket. Then he pulled the tail of the oxford cloth free from the waist of his pants. Without bothering to unbutton it, he reached behind his back and, grasping a handful of fabric, jerked it and his undershirt off over his head.

A button popped, pinging away into the darkness after it bounced off the wooden floor. Without looking, he tossed the garments he'd removed to one side. They landed on the edge of the coffee table and then slid onto the floor.

For a moment they stood facing one another, unmoving. The fire painted the flat planes and angled bones of his torso with red. An arrow of dark hair trailed down the channel between his ribs to disappear into the waistband of his trousers.

There wasn't an ounce of spare flesh on his body. His chest was long, muscled like a swimmer's. Lean and hard and fit, he was even more impressive *without* clothing.

Looking at him, she took another deep breath. Her nipples, still hardened by desire and the growing chill of the room, lifted.

His eyes fell, watching their movement. With the fingers of one hand he reached out and touched the curve beneath her left breast, the caress far different from before.

There was no urgency. No demand. The contact of his fingertips was almost reverent.

"You are *so* beautiful," he whispered.

The firelight would mask the imperfections she was too aware of. At what was in his voice, she relaxed, willing to believe he saw her that way.

It was a gift, especially now. The first exposure. The first lovemaking. Considering the circumstances under which her body had been bared the last time—

She fought the power of that hated image, determined not to allow any of it—any of who or what she was—to interfere with what was happening now.

"So are you," she said.

Only when the words were in the air between them, did she realize how that would sound to a man so blatantly masculine. A slow upward tilt disturbed the stern line of his lips, indicating he wasn't offended by the ridiculousness of her statement.

"Thank you."

"Thank *you*," she whispered back.

She had found there was something enormously erotic about what they were doing. Facing one another in the firelight. Taking time to learn one another visually.

Perhaps only to someone like her would that seem important. She shivered, relishing the gentleness with which he touched her.

"Still cold?"

This time he didn't offer her jacket. Instead he held out the hand that had touched her breast, its palm up.

She hesitated only a second before she placed her fingers into his. As he drew her to him, her anticipation was so great that she was mindless with it. Mindless with wanting him.

A sound from behind her halted her forward motion. The creak of a door? Or of bedsprings?

She had realized almost immediately that it was neither, but rather a log shifting in the fire. Still, she pulled her fingers from Matt's grasp, glancing over her shoulder.

Thankfully, she saw that Taylor was *not* standing in the hall that led to the bedrooms. The door to the room where she had put him down appeared to be in the same position she'd left it in.

She couldn't believe that she had never even thought about that open door. Or of the possibility that, despite appearances, Taylor might not have been as sound asleep as she'd thought.

She took an unsteady breath before she turned to face Matt. Instinctively, she had crossed her hands over her breasts, very conscious now of her nudity.

He was bending over to retrieve her clothing. He straightened, holding the bundle out to her.

As she took them, she shook her head. "I'm sorry. I thought— I thought that was Taylor."

"I know."

Fumbling with the garments he'd handed her, she managed to extricate her T-shirt. Holding the jacket and bra in one hand, she struggled to pull the shirt over her head. She took time to smooth it down, a deliberate delay, before she looked up at him again.

"I don't think this is a very good idea." She sounded as if she were sixteen and in the back seat of someone's car. "He could wake up at any time."

Matt had made no move to gather his scattered clothing, his arms still relaxed at his sides. She could read nothing from his face.

"I really am sorry," she continued. "I feel as if…"

His right hand moved, approaching her face. Instinctively she flinched, jerking her head to the side and raising her arm, her shoulder hunched defensively.

"What the hell?" he said softly.

With his tone, she realized the magnitude of her mistake. Slowly she turned to look at him. His hand hesitated in midair, the fingers still outstretched.

"You didn't think…?" He laughed, a breath of sound that contained no hint of amusement. "I've never hit a woman in my life."

She swallowed the thickness in her throat. "I'm sorry."

"Stop *saying* that. You don't have anything to be sorry for. Your son's asleep in the next room. It isn't as if I don't understand."

"I shouldn't have started this."

"I don't believe you did."

"I meant tonight."

"It didn't *start* tonight. And it isn't going to end tonight either. But…right now we both have things to see to that are more important than this."

She nodded, fighting the sting of tears. Seeing them, he put his hand on the back of her neck, drawing her to him again.

This time he simply held her, her cheek against his chest. She could feel the still-frantic beating of his heart.

After a moment, he bent, pressing a kiss against her hair. As suddenly as he had reached out for her, he released her, turning away to find his clothing.

"I don't want to go back into the darkness."

He couldn't possibly understand what that word encompassed, and she couldn't possibly explain. Not tonight.

He understood enough, however. "Then stay here. Sleep on the couch."

"Maybe it would be better—"

"I'll check on him. And I'll leave the door open so you can see into the room."

Matt moved into the hallway and eased open the door she had partially closed. To test what he'd said, she walked over to the couch and sat down.

He was right. She could see straight into the bedroom. She watched as he bent over the boy to adjust the covers. Her throat closed again, hard and tight.

For a moment he disappeared. When he emerged from the hallway, she saw that he was carrying a blanket in his hands.

"Lie down," he directed.

"Do you think—"

"What I think is that you should lie down." He spread

the blanket over her and then handed her one of the loose cushions from the other end of the couch.

He had already begun to turn away, when she reached out and caught his forearm. "I really am sorry."

His smile was visible, even in the low light. "For what it's worth, it's not the first time something like that has happened. Anyone who's ever had a child—"

The words were cut off abruptly.

"Matt…"

"Go to sleep," he said, putting his hand over hers. After a moment he lifted it, folding her fingers into the palm. "And stop worrying. There's nothing for you to worry about tonight."

Even as she nodded agreement, she knew that was a luxury she couldn't possibly afford.

THE MOVEMENT, seen only peripherally, was masked by the shadows around the door that led to the hall. Not the direction from which he had expected a threat to come.

The sudden flood of adrenaline was so powerful it was literally sickening. Matt lifted the weapon he'd held all night, training it on the area. He watched the shadows, holding his breath while the slow seconds ticked off.

Nothing happened. No sound. No motion.

What he thought he'd seen had been subtle enough that he began to wonder if it could have been a trick of firelight. Caused by an uneven burning of damp wood perhaps.

Or a trick of the mind. A phenomenon that anyone who had ever been on a stakeout or who had waited for the order that would send him into an unknown situation would recognize. A phantom movement that was nothing more than the brain over-stimulated by tension. The eye expects to see something, and suddenly it does.

Just as he had decided that, whatever was in the shadows moved again. The semi-automatic, which had begun to droop as he'd relaxed, lifted again.

And then it was as quickly raised so that the muzzle pointed toward the ceiling. An unmistakable shape materialized from the darkness of the hall. Color and size made Matt's identification instantaneous.

Taylor. Undoubtedly looking for his mother.

Matt's eyes tracked to the couch where Robin lay. The depth of her sleep was evidenced by the slow, regular rise and fall of her breasts beneath the surface of the blanket he'd covered her with.

When he looked back toward the boy, Taylor had advanced far enough into the room to be completely revealed by the firelight. With one hand he rubbed at his eyes as he walked, bare feet making no sound on the wooden floor.

Matt considered cautioning him to let his mom sleep, but he doubted Robin would appreciate that. The kid was obviously frightened or he wouldn't be up in the middle of the night.

After all he'd been through, he had a right to that fear. And a right to have it comforted.

Instead of heading toward the couch, however, Taylor walked straight toward the chair in which Matt was sitting. He watched as the boy crossed the small room and came to a stop right in front of him.

"What's wrong, big guy?"

Despite his whisper, Robin didn't stir. When Matt glanced back at the child, Taylor was again rubbing his eyes.

"You okay?"

The question elicited a nod, but no answer.

"You need to go to the bathroom?"

A more vigorous shake of his head, bangs swinging slightly from side to side.

"Bad dream?"

It took the little boy a second or two to decide about that one, but when he had, the motion of his head was again positive.

"Want me to come and tuck you in again?"

"I don't want to go back in there."

Again Matt glanced toward the couch, but not even the sound of her son's voice had awakened Robin. The loss of sleep during the last forty-eight hours had finally caught up with her, and he didn't have the heart to disturb her.

Besides, he was already committed to staying awake. It didn't make sense that both of them should.

"You don't have to. Come on."

Despite the weapon he held, Matt reached down for the boy. Maybe he could hold the kid for a few minutes until he went to sleep and then ease him back to bed.

He expected Taylor to shrink back, leery of being picked up by someone he didn't know very well. Instead, the boy put both arms around his neck, allowing Matt to settle him onto his lap.

An unforgotten instinct prompted him to wrap both arms around the small, warm body, cradling it against his chest. Just as he'd done in the attic last night, Taylor responded by putting his face against Matt's neck.

The smell of baby shampoo cruelly thrust him backward in time. Carrying Josh in from the car. Or to bed after he'd fallen asleep on the couch or the floor. Getting him out of his crib in the morning, warm and sweet and helpless, so that Karen could steal a few more minutes of sleep.

The sudden rush of tenderness he felt for Taylor Holt

was exactly the same. It washed over him in a wave of longing so great his eyes burned with its force.

He blinked, controlling the emotion that had literally blindsided him. He had vowed to protect this child. That was his job. What he hadn't expected was the way he would come to feel about him.

"Can I stay with you all night?"

The boy's question represented a danger as great as taking Robin in his arms had been. And it drew him as surely—as strongly—as the vastly different emotions that had drawn him to her last night.

Unable to speak for the knot in his throat, Matt nodded, the roughness of his unshaven stubble catching in the boy's baby-fine hair. With a sigh of contentment, Taylor settled into a more comfortable position.

One of his arms eventually slid free of the grip they'd taken around Matt's neck. The hand came to rest against his chest. After a moment it lifted two or three times to pat his shoulder.

Approval or comfort? Matt wondered. In any case, it was clearly a gesture that indicated the boy intended to stay right where he was.

And despite the painful emotions holding Taylor had evoked, that was something that Matt knew he, too, now wanted. It was too late to guard himself against the dangers of letting another child into his heart.

WHEN SHE OPENED her eyes to the faint light of dawn, Robin was surprised to find that she'd slept. Just as she'd feared, as soon as she'd lain down, the nightmare images had begun to play through her mind in spite of everything she could do to make them go away.

At some time during that struggle, however, she had apparently fallen into a restless sleep, punctuated by dreams that bore the taint of the last few days. She had forced herself awake now in an attempt to escape from one of them.

She'd been running, but she couldn't remember from what. A nameless fear that had been terrifying enough to pull her out of a much-needed sleep.

It took her a few seconds to remember where she was. Another few to understand why she was again lying on the couch in the central room of the cabin rather than in bed with Taylor as she'd planned.

The dying embers of the fire glowed in the grate. Despite the wind she could hear howling outside, she was warm under the blanket Matt had spread over her.

That memory prompted her to lift her head, her eyes searching the still-darkened room for the man who had promised to watch over them all night. He was exactly where she had expected to find him—in the armchair he had placed in front of the outside door. And he was no longer alone.

Held securely on his lap was her son, the small fair head and the dark one touching. Taylor's arm was against Matt's chest, the pale cotton knit of his pajamas a contrast to the black sweatshirt.

Although the little boy's face was relaxed in sleep, the man who held him seemed to contemplate the dying fire, unaware that she was awake. Unaware that she was watching him, savoring the picture the two of them made.

She tried to imagine what scenario had led to the scene before her. If Taylor had called out to her, she hadn't heard him. For once the mother instinct that usually brought her awake at his first outcry had given way to exhaustion.

Or maybe he had come to find her and, rather than allowing him to disturb her sleep, Matt had offered to play surrogate parent. *Parent.* She wondered how he felt to be holding a little boy again, one who looked to him for comfort and reassurance.

Did the soft, regular breathing of a sleeping child bring back memories that were painful or merely bittersweet? Whatever feeling it evoked, either was an emotion she could share.

She had known that only a man like this could teach Taylor the necessary lesson of masculine gentleness. One he would never have learned from his own father.

Matt turned his head, his eyes widening slightly as he realized she was awake. He glanced down at the boy as if to reassure himself that all was well.

When he looked up at her again, a small, almost secret smile hovered around his lips. Without any conscious decision to do so, she answered it.

The pale morning light that seeped into the room gilded both the fair hair of the boy and the hard angles of the man's face. His eyes were pools of darkness, the skin around them bruised with tiredness. The lean cheeks were shadowed by a two-day-old beard, while lines of exhaustion bracketed his mouth. To her he had never been more attractive.

She pushed up against the loose cushion of the couch she had been using as a pillow. Holding out her arms, she pantomimed an offer to take her son. Matt glanced down at the sleeping boy again, and then slowly he shook his head.

His movement must have disturbed Taylor, who stirred a little before settling once more against the shoulder that supported him. Robin smiled again and leaned back against the arm of the sofa, pushing the cushion into place behind her. She pulled the blanket over her bare arms, preparing to watch the two of them.

As he watched her.

Their eyes held for a long time, until the growing heaviness of hers caused them to close. Startled by the realization that she was falling asleep, she opened them quickly.

The vision before her was still the same. Her son in the arms of the man who had promised to protect them both. Still safe. Still secure.

When her eyelids slowly drifted downward again, she was no longer aware of their movement. No longer aware of anything but the unfamiliar sensation of letting someone else, if only for a little while, share the burden she had carried alone for so many years.

CHAPTER EIGHTEEN

"WE GOT a problem."

A dozen scenarios that could qualify as problems flashed through Matt's head. Some of them terrifying.

"What kind?" He was pleased with the tone of the question, given his anxiety.

"Well, we got a couple of 'em, actually," Hank Dawkins qualified.

Which sounded even less promising.

"We *are* still secure here, aren't we?"

His worst nightmare would be that their location had been compromised. Since he and the chief of police were supposed to be the only two in the department who knew where the Holts were, he didn't see how that could have happened. Not without Hank's complicity.

"It ain't anything like that. You remember putting through an inquiry about Ms. Holt the morning after the kidnapping?"

It had been a routine background check that he'd keyed into the Criminal Justice Information Service's database after he'd visited Parnell. The information on the employment record he'd been given had been sketchy, but he'd fed what he had into the state's computer system, which was tied into the national databases.

"Something turn up?"

As he asked the question, a coldness settled in Matt's

stomach. What the hell could have turned up that Dawkins would classify as "a problem"? He couldn't believe there could be anything criminal in Robin's past.

Maybe it was something like an unpaid speeding ticket. That kind of stuff could trail a person for years. Even things that had been resolved sometimes showed up in the databases.

Although the length of time they'd spent together had been brief, it had been in circumstances that, if they did nothing else, revealed character. He *knew* the kind of person she was.

He had to acknowledge, however, that he was no longer completely objective when it came to Robin Holt. More troubling was the possibility that he was no longer objective about the case.

"She ain't who she says she is."

He waited, but Dawkins didn't seem inclined to expand on that cryptic pronouncement. "What the hell does that mean?"

"The person her social security number belongs to is dead."

"Maybe I typed it in wrong."

It wouldn't be the first time he had done something like that. Considering what else had been going on the morning he'd keyed it in, he wouldn't be surprised if he'd made a mistake.

"That's what I thought at first, but I checked it against your copy of her employment record. That's the number she gave Parnell, all right."

"It's got to be some kind of mix-up," Matt said, refusing to accept what Hank seemed to be suggesting. There were a dozen explanations for that discrepancy.

"That ain't all, Matt. Some of the stuff she gave the school has been doctored."

Matt's gut tightened. "Doctored how?"

"Kid's name has been changed on the birth certificate. The one the school gets is supposed to be an official copy. The one she provided isn't. It's a good fake, but they tell me those are readily available if you've got the money to buy 'em."

"And you've checked all this out since that report came through?"

There was pause before Dawkins answered. "Actually, the Bureau did most of the checking. They're the ones who thought about asking to see the boy's records."

"So what do *they* think this means?"

He reminded himself that the crew from Atlanta had been wrong about almost everything else. The validity of Taylor's story. The significance of the off-duty cop's sighting of Lisa.

"Look, all I'm telling you is that there are some problems with the Holts' paperwork. In a situation like this, that puts up red flags for everybody."

In a situation like this... A kidnapping that had now become a murder. Two dead cops. An unidentified corpse.

"Except whoever killed the Evans girl has also targeted the Holts," Matt said. "Common sense tells you that whatever's going on with their 'paperwork,' it doesn't mean she had anything to do with anything that's happened."

"Common sense ain't never had much to do with the *law*, and you know it. We got a material witness who's been playing fast and loose with the truth. It kinda naturally makes everybody wonder what else she's been lying about."

Just as she'd lied about the doctor's appointment.

"Everybody being the Bureau."

"They want to ask her some questions," Dawkins admitted.

"You told them where she is?"

That had been more accusation than question. No matter what the GBI had suggested, Matt couldn't believe Hank would break their agreement.

"If I'd done that, I wouldn't be calling you up to tell you all 'a this. I'd be hightailing it up there with the two of them in tow."

"I'm not turning the Holts over to somebody else on the basis of what might be a clerical error." *Or two.* "You saw what happened the last time we went along with what those two wanted."

"Then you get me an explanation. One that checks out. And you do it soon."

"That sounds like an ultimatum."

"I got three people dead down here, Matt. One of them a fourteen-year-old girl and the other two cops. Everybody in this part of the state is screaming for us to get somebody charged. Shit rolls downhill. You want my cooperation, you give me yours. Bring Ms. Holt in *or* get the answers we need from her. And in either case, you damn well better do it now."

It was more of a concession than he'd expected. Hank was probably tired of being jerked around like a puppet by the Bureau. The chief was affable by nature, but if pushed too hard, he could become as stubborn as a mule.

"I'll get back to you," Matt said, grateful for the opportunity to question Robin himself. "Anything yet on the guy I got last night?"

"We got a match on his prints this morning. He seems to be associated with some elements of the Russian mob."

Russian organized crime was into everything from money laundering to credit-card fraud to drug dealing. Was that what the murder in the woods had been about? The execution of someone who hadn't played by their rules and had gotten caught.

Supposedly, the Russian mafia was as ruthless as their better-known counterparts. What someone associated with ROC had been doing in Mallory, however...

"You got a name?"

He heard the rustle of papers as Hank referred to the report he'd been given.

"Mikhail Skuratov."

"Anything I should know about him?"

"Age thirty-eight. Born in Moscow. No outstanding warrants, but several priors, which is why we had his prints. A couple of those were for assault. That ole boy musta had him some pretty good lawyers, considering he's still here."

The Russians could certainly afford the best legal representation. The fact that they had expended it on the behalf of the man he'd killed might mean he was someone of importance to them.

"Still nothing on the guy in the woods? There's got to be a connection."

He tried to think about the face that had been pressed against the frostbitten grass. Dark hair and eyes, but nothing about the man's features had made him think Eastern European or Asian. Of course, they had been discolored by death and so distorted by whatever had been done to him before death came that his nationality would have been difficult to discern.

"We're checking. That's something else the Bureau wants to take a look at."

"The connection to Russia?"

"Whether or not the woman calling herself Robin Holt has any ties to the area. And they need her name for that. Her real name. I have to tell you, Matt, they're getting mighty impatient with me for putting 'em off."

The woman calling herself Robin Holt...

"So what have you told them?"

"That you'll have some information for them before noon. Don't you make me out no liar now, you hear?"

"I'll call you," Matt said, breaking the connection without giving his supervisor time to protest.

He walked up the slope until he could again see the cabin in the clearing. Smoke from the stone chimney drifted up like mist into the November air. Surrounded by the snow that had fallen during the night, the place appeared as peaceful as a Norman Rockwell print.

He slipped his cell phone into the pocket of his jeans and picked up the firewood he'd come outside to chop. The anxiety in his stomach had turned to anger, which grew stronger with every step he took on his way back to the house.

Anger at Robin for whatever deception she'd tried to get away with. Anger at himself for having been taken in. A cold fury that he had let himself again care about something or someone. The emotional numbness of the last five years was preferable to what he was feeling now.

He had no time to gather control or think through what Hank had told him. No time to consider the best approach for getting at the truth. Dawkins had imposed a hard deadline that demanded he have an immediate confrontation with Robin. And if she didn't tell him what he needed to know—

Except she would. If there was one thing he still believed

about the image he'd created, it was that Robin Holt would do anything to protect her child.

That was the threat they were both under. She would tell him the truth and do it soon, or Dawkins would unleash the goons from the Bureau. He wouldn't have a choice.

And neither did he.

"IT'S ME."

It was only after Matt called out his identification that she realized she hadn't even glanced up when she'd heard the creak of the front door. She'd grown complacent in the time they'd spent here.

Despite Matt's confidence in their security, anything could have happened to him during the half hour he'd had been outside. He'd gone out to replenish their supply of firewood and to check the perimeter of the cabin. Instead of being alert to the possibility that something might have gone wrong, she had spent those minutes thinking about the two nights they'd spent here. Dreaming about things that would never come to pass.

She heard him drop the load of wood into the box beside the hearth. Since she had just poured three nearly perfect circles of pancake batter into the smoking skillet, she stayed where she was. He would come into the kitchen when he got through.

"Did you reach him?" she called.

That was the other thing he'd gone outside to do, she remembered. To try to reach the chief of police on his cell phone. Matt had thought that by walking a little way down the Mallory side of the mountain, he might be able to connect with one of the area's service towers.

"I got him."

She glanced up from the stove to find him standing in

the doorway, again watching her. Something had obviously changed. His eyes were cold and hard, as she had rarely seen them.

"What is it? What's wrong?"

Of all the possible disasters that immediately flashed through her mind, she was unprepared for his answer. That showed how far she'd strayed from reality into that fantasy world she'd been so busy creating.

"Chuck Parnell didn't ask many questions when he hired you, but he had to have a Social Security number."

She waited for him to go on, a growing coldness in the pit of her stomach. "And?" she prompted when she could stand the tension no longer.

"The one you gave him doesn't seem to belong to you."

He was working at controlling his anger, but she could hear it in the bitten-off syllables of that accusation. And she had no answer for it. Despite knowing that someone, someday, would surely ask these questions, she was unprepared to answer them.

"I don't know what you're talking about."

Stupid, stupid, stupid. B-grade movie crap.

"I'm talking about the fact that that number you gave Parnell belongs to a dead woman."

She should have told him everything days ago. He was a policeman, for God's sake. Did she think he wouldn't check on her? Did she think he was as stupid as she had been?

"That's ridiculous," she said, trying to keep her voice steady, despite this impending disaster. She had lied to him, and he knew it. She was still lying, and he probably knew that, too. "He must have copied it down wrong. Chuck isn't very good with details."

"Maybe you stole her mail," he went on inexorably,

ignoring what she'd said. "Or maybe you bought the number on the black market. I don't know, and I don't really care, but unless you start telling me the truth, you're going to be explaining to someone who'll be a lot less sympathetic than I am."

"You *know* who I am," she said.

"No, I know the name you gave Parnell and the utility companies and your landlord and me."

"My name is Robin Holt," she said, meeting his eyes unflinchingly in an effort to convince him she was telling the truth.

"And son Taylor."

At the quiet sarcasm, a tremor of alarm went through her. This was not just about the social security number, then. She might have been able to bluff her way through if it were only that...

"That's right," she said, refusing to react to the jibe.

"Son Taylor, whose birth certificate has been doctored."

Her hesitation before responding was too long. That would undoubtedly be very revealing to someone used to grilling suspects.

Suspect. The word had terrified her before. She didn't like it any better now.

"I wanted to change his name after the divorce. And I didn't want to go through the courts to do it."

"Why not?"

"Because his father would have objected." To gather control she turned back to the stove and flipped the pancakes. Then, realizing the futility of pretending that they were going to sit down and eat breakfast together when this was all over, she turned off the burner beneath them. "He objected to most things I did."

She turned her head in time to see the impact of what

she'd just said in his eyes. Maybe he had put it together with the fact that she'd thought he intended to hit her last night.

For that fraction of a second she had. But it felt like a betrayal to use his reaction this way.

I've never hit a woman in my life. She could believe that, despite the cold rage in his voice now.

"And *your* name? Or did you change that, too?"

"I told you. Chuck probably typed the number in wrong. Or one of the temps he's always hiring to catch up on the clerical did. This is *not* a big deal."

"It is when it turns up in the middle of a multiple homicide investigation."

"You know I didn't have anything to do with *any* of that. *You* know it. The *GBI* knows it. What does it matter if there's a typo in my employment record? And in case you've forgotten, while you all are wasting time investigating me, somebody is still trying to kill my son."

"As you said yourself, people around you seem to have an unfortunate habit of getting killed. You're a material witness in a triple homicide, and now we're finding out that you've also falsified records."

"I didn't *falsify* records. I changed my son's name to my maiden name to keep him from having to answer questions from the other kids at school. That isn't a crime. A million other women have done the same thing after a messy divorce. I probably could have just marked through the name that's on his birth certificate and explained to the school that that's what I was doing. No one would have thought anything about it. Because I didn't—"

"So why didn't you?" he interrupted.

"What?"

"Why didn't you explain it to the school?"

"Because I couldn't see what business it was of anybody there," she said, her voice rising at the end. "Of course, at the time I had no idea Taylor was going to see some murderers out in the woods or that my babysitter would be abducted and killed. I told you. I'm not omniscient."

She could tell by the subtle relaxation of his tension that he was beginning to believe her. The brown eyes, while not yet warm, were at least no longer openly hostile.

"Robin Holt is your maiden name?"

"And I wanted to use it again. I'll straighten out whatever Chuck put down with Social Security. All it will take is a phone call."

"And one to Dawkins. With the right number this time."

Which meant he planned to run it again through whatever database he'd used the first time. She was only delaying the inevitable. And in the process she was destroying whatever trust had been between them.

That, too, had been inevitable. The idea that what had been happening between them had anywhere to go was the product of her imagination.

"Robin? I have to get back to him. He's got Donovan and Burke breathing down his neck."

He was waiting for her to give him the number. As soon as he called it in to the police department, the clock would start on the truth coming out.

"After breakfast," she suggested, glancing back at the pancakes which had finished cooking from the residual heat of the pan and the stove eye. "Surely the GBI can wait long enough for you to eat."

She could tell that appealed to him. She wasn't sure if it was hunger or a desire to make the agents wait, but he had tacitly agreed to the delay.

And she wasn't sure what she'd accomplished by it. Another hour or two. If she were very lucky, another day or two before the house of cards she'd built came tumbling down around her.

"And would you call Taylor, please?" she asked, using the metal spatula to remove the pancakes from the pan. She turned the gas on again, setting the black iron skillet back on the burner. "There's no butter, but with enough syrup…"

June Cleaver at her best. As far from reality as she could imagine.

"As soon as breakfast is over."

"My purse is in the bedroom. As soon as we eat, I'll get the number for you. In the meantime, these are getting cold."

She set the two plates she'd just filled on the table, turning back for the bottle of syrup, which she placed between them. She had already picked up the bowl of batter when she heard Matt's footsteps cross the central room.

"Taylor? Come to breakfast."

She bent her head, closing her eyes against the wave of regret. A few more hours at the most.

And she intended to make the best of them.

CHAPTER NINETEEN

THE PHONE in the chief's office was on its fourth ring before someone finally picked up. Matt had decided that for all Hank's bluster, he hadn't exactly been waiting for the information he'd demanded with bated breath, a conclusion quickly verified by the voice on the other end of the line.

"Mallory Police Department. Sommerville."

"Matt Ridge. I need to talk to the chief."

"He left about an hour, hour and a half ago, Matt. You can try to reach him on his radio. Or I can take a message if you want."

Dawkins refused to carry a cell phone, preferring to rely on his car's radio equipment when he wasn't in the office. The chief's old-fashioned prejudice was something Matt hadn't considered when he'd set up this arrangement. His failure to do so was coming back to haunt him.

"He say where he was going?"

"Not to me. 'Course that don't mean nothing," the cop said with a laugh. "As you well know."

Glenn Sommerville had been with the department a couple of years, but he wasn't on anybody's fast track to promotion. He was hotheaded and not particularly bright.

"Want me to ask around?" Glenn went on. "See if he told somebody else where he was headed?"

"The guys from the GBI still there?"

"Making themselves at home."

Which meant that whatever Hank was doing, it wasn't bringing the agents up here. At least not yet.

Matt debated the wisdom of leaving a message, and then decided he didn't have a choice. "Would you call him on the radio and tell him something for me? I've got a couple of things going on right now."

Since he'd brought the SUV rather than the cruiser, he couldn't access the department's radio system. He was probably out of range up here, anyway.

"Okay. Shoot."

"Tell him I have the information he wanted. Tell him to call me at this number, and I'll give it to him." As he reeled off the number of his cell phone, he wondered if Dawkins would be able to reach him at the cabin. And what the chief would do if he couldn't. "Tell him I said everything is okay. That there's nothing to worry about."

"You're the only one who's thinking that today," Sommerville responded.

"He'll know what I mean."

"I'll pass it along."

"Thanks."

Matt had already taken the phone away from his ear when the cop's voice stopped him.

"By the way, that guy from the Marshals Service called again. Said it was important that he talk to you today."

The guy from the Marshals Service... For a moment the phrase meant nothing.

"U.S. Marshals?" What the hell did someone from the Marshals want with him? And why hadn't he been told that they'd called before?

"Evan Rippetoe. Ring a bell?"

It did. It was the name Hank had given him on the phone the night they'd found Lisa's body. He hadn't mentioned

Rippetoe's affiliation with the Marshals Service, however. Matt knew he would have remembered that. Disconnected from that vital piece of information, the call had slipped his mind. Hardly surprising in light of subsequent events.

"You got a number?"

Even as he asked, he realized that his notebook and pen were back at the cabin. He concentrated on remembering the ten-digit number as Sommerville read it off.

"Did he say what the call was in reference to?"

"Not this time. There's a note here on the chief's desk with that same number though. Want me to read it to you?"

Matt had a mental image of Glenn with his boots on the boss's desk, reading, between taking down the occasional phone message, whatever was written on the papers Dawkins had left exposed. He could only hope the directions to the cabin weren't on one of them.

"Go ahead."

"It's got the number I just gave you and then it says 'in reference to the Evans case.'"

"That's all?"

"That's it. Somebody connected with your case must be a fugitive from justice. Or maybe they're in witness protection."

The last suggestion was clearly intended to be humorous. To most people that was the most well-known of the duties the Marshals were responsible for—putting federal witnesses under protection after they'd testified. Former mobsters, their family members—

Just that she ain't who she says she is...

Hank's words had implied that Robin had stolen someone else's identity. And that if she had, it had been done for some nefarious purpose. To hide a criminal past.

But what if she had been *given* that identity instead? To hide her and Taylor?

Was it possible that the witnesses he was protecting had already been under the Witness Security Program run by the Marshals? Maybe Rippetoe had seen the same news clip the cops in Marietta had watched. Maybe that was why Robin had been reluctant to meet him at the school that morning. Because she knew the media would be there in force.

The ideas that had been sparked by the knowledge that someone from the Marshals Service was trying to reach him connected like the links of a chain. Everything fit. Even the timing of that phone call from Rippetoe.

If he was right about this, why hadn't Robin told him the truth? Why the charade about Parnell's typos and changing the kid's name after a divorce?

Because whoever she'd been hiding from before this started still represented as great a danger to her and Taylor as the men the boy had seen in the woods? Or because she had learned the hard way not to trust anyone with her secret?

Not even a man she had almost made love to.

As bitter as that revelation was, the theory he'd just formulated explained many things he hadn't been able to understand. His instincts, both personal and professional, had told him that Robin couldn't be involved in anything criminal. This seemed a confirmation that he'd been right.

It was also a complication to a situation that had already been threatening enough. The thought that there were dangers to her and the boy that he hadn't known about was unacceptable. That was the bottom line.

If he were going to be able to protect Taylor, then Robin had to level with him. And she had to do it now.

WHEN HE OPENED the door to the cabin this time, he again called out an identification. Robin and Taylor were sitting on the couch, their heads close together. A children's book was spread out across her lap, one of those she'd found in the bookcase in the bedroom.

She looked up at his entrance, her eyes questioning. Taylor, still enthralled in the pictures, didn't even glance at him.

"Everything okay?" Robin asked, her tone too cheerful.

"We need to talk."

The smile she'd greeted him with faded, but she nodded. He tilted his head toward the kitchen, and then, without waiting to see if she'd follow, he walked across the central room and into the next. When he reached the sink, he turned and leaned against the counter, watching her.

She had risen from the couch. She leaned down to whisper something to the boy, ruffling his hair as she did. He ducked away from her hand, using his own to smooth it down again.

"You read the next page by yourself," she said aloud. "I'll be right back."

Matt held her eyes as she walked toward him. She seemed apprehensive, but that wasn't surprising considering what was going on.

He felt a prickle of guilt that he hadn't told her up-front what he wanted to talk about, but he resented the hell out of the fact that she hadn't trusted him enough to tell him about this. If she didn't trust him now, who did she trust?

"What is it?" she asked, her voice low enough not to carry into the central room.

"Rippetoe called and left a message. You want to tell me what's going on?"

He would have sworn the confusion in her eyes was genuine. Either that or she should be on the stage somewhere.

"Rippetoe?"

"From the U.S. Marshals Service. Is he the one responsible for you and Taylor?"

"I don't understand."

Disappointment surged. He had been so sure that if he opened the door, revealed what he knew, she'd be eager to tell him everything. *So sure and so wrong.*

"Don't you think it's about time you leveled with me?"

Her lips parted, but after a moment they closed again. She shook her head. "I don't know anyone named Rippetoe. I don't have any idea what you're talking about."

"We've got enough trouble that I do know about. If there's something else—"

The unmistakable sound of tires crunching over the chert in the turnaround interrupted not only what he'd been about to say, but any other thought. His fear was immediate and powerful.

With his thumb he unsnapped the leather holster and slipped the semi-automatic out. He felt marginally better with the weapon in his hand. More in control, although he knew that was an illusion.

With as many unknowns as there were in this situation, there *was* no control. He motioned for Robin to get down and started toward the kitchen windows.

"Taylor," she said.

He reached for her, but she evaded his hand to run into the central room. She scooped Taylor up from the couch, the book they'd been reading falling to the floor as she did. As she ran back toward Matt, her eyes were questioning, obviously expecting him to give her some direction.

Unlike those in the central room, the windows in the

kitchen were covered only by blinds. If they were struck, glass would fly everywhere. He needed to get them into some semi-protected location until he could figure out who was outside. His eyes fell on the solid oak trestle, which had been built by Karen's grandfather.

"Under the table," he ordered.

Robin set the boy down on the floor. Together they scrambled beneath the trestle as Matt took the two long strides that would bring him to the row of narrow windows over the sink. Standing to one side of them, he eased back one of the blinds, expecting the panes to shatter under a rain of shots as he did.

There was no reaction from whoever was outside. The only thing visible from his vantage point was a portion of the front end of a big black Mercedes. One headlight, the left fender and an identifiable part of the grille.

A car door slammed, followed by a second. There were at least two of them, then. Since this particular automobile could easily hold five people, there was the possibility that there were several more.

"Who is it?" Robin asked. "Who's out there?"

He put his hand up, palm turned toward her, cautioning her to silence. He was straining to hear what was going on outside.

There seemed to be no conversation, which could mean they were waiting for something. Or someone. For a second car? The GBI agents, maybe?

Of course, the silence might just as well indicate they had no need for any discussion about what they intended to do. That was a scenario he liked even less than the first.

They had arrived openly, however, which seemed to suggest they weren't here for the reasons he'd initially ascribed to them. Or that they were so confident they saw no need for stealth. As he considered the options, it was becoming increasingly obvious that none of those questions could be answered from in here.

"Stay put."

He whispered the order as he eased out of the kitchen, his back against the wall, leading with the Sig Sauer. He held the 9mm in both hands and at chest level.

When he reached the first of the windows in the front room, he used the muzzle to lift the edge of the quilt and the curtain under it so he could see outside. This view was more revealing of the vehicle, but whoever had exited the Mercedes only seconds before was nowhere to be found. And from this angle it was clear there was no second car.

Whoever this was, they weren't here under police escort. And they had chosen not to knock on the door. Those actions seemed as ominous as his first instinct had warned him they could be.

The walls and the exterior doors of the cabin had been hewn from solid logs, which meant any attack would concentrate on the windows. The quilts he'd hung over the ones in this room would protect the occupants from flying glass far better than the blinds in the others would. For that reason if for no other it would be better to make his stand here.

Still alert for any sound from outside, he hurried across to close the doors to the bedrooms. If he retreated with Robin and Taylor into one of those, he would have had only one entrance to guard. But like the attic where Robin had hidden, there would also be fewer options if that single entrance were breached.

He turned back toward the kitchen and realized Robin had been following his movements. She was holding Taylor close as they huddled under the table.

He motioned for her to join him. By the time he returned to the couch in the middle of the room, they had met him there.

"Stay down," he warned again.

With a gesture he directed them around to the front of the couch, a location which would put the fireplace at their backs and the hallway to the bedrooms on their right. Since he had no idea from which direction an attack might come, he was gambling this would be a viable defensive position, with their lives as the stakes.

"Who's *out* there?" Robin asked again.

"Nobody I know."

He could tell by the sudden widening of her eyes that she understood the significance.

"Is it those men?" The tone of Taylor's question verged on the edge of hysteria.

"Shh," Robin comforted, putting her hand on his temple to pull his head against her breasts. He was visibly trembling.

Her eyes hadn't left Matt's face. She was waiting for him to do something. To save them. To keep all those promises he'd made.

Nothing's going to happen...

"Keep your heads down," he ordered again because he couldn't think of anything else to tell them.

He tried the window on the other side of the front door, following the procedure he'd used before. More of the car was visible from here, but in the snow-dappled landscape beyond it nothing moved.

The sun had begun to melt the accumulation off the roof. There was a drip line of depressions in the snow below the eaves. Beyond it he could see footprints, but not well enough to determine the number of people who'd made them.

Keeping low, he moved to the other side of the window and again lifted the double layer of fabric over it. There was nothing new to be seen from that position.

He started back to where Robin and the boy crouched in front of the sofa. If he turned it over, he could put the two of them under it and still use it as a barricade to fire from behind.

He stooped beside them, motioning for her to move the boy back a few feet, pantomiming what he intended to do. She nodded her understanding, taking Taylor's arm to draw him away.

Matt had reached for the top of the sofa when one of the windows in the kitchen exploded inward, sending glass flying across the room despite the blind that had covered it. He hadn't heard the gunshot, but there was no doubt about its effects. With his free hand, he pushed Robin flat, throwing himself down so he lay over the lower part of her body and almost on top of the boy.

"I know you're in there."

The shout came from the direction of the kitchen. Another in the row of narrow mullioned windows over the sink shattered. This time it was obvious that it had not been hit by a bullet. Rocks? Or something being wielded by the man who was yelling.

"Rachel? You answer me, goddamn it."

Cautiously Matt raised his head. The high back of the sofa blocked his view into the kitchen.

He had begun to climb up onto its seat when he felt Robin move as if she intended to sit up. He reached down to push her to the floor again. Instead, she grabbed his wrist.

Surprised at the strength of her grip, he looked down.
The pupils of her eyes were so widely dilated that the blue
of the irises had virtually disappeared.

"Don't," she whispered.

"I have to see what's going on."

He tried to free his arm, but her fingers bit into his flesh,
squeezing so hard he could feel the imprint of his nails
despite the thickness of the sweatshirt he wore. He could
probably wrench his wrist away by force, but he was afraid
he'd hurt her in the process.

As he hesitated, the man outside shouted again. "God-
dammit, Rachel, get your ass out here. I'm tired of this
shit."

Robin closed her eyes. She had rolled her lips inward,
her teeth pressing them so tightly they were bloodless. Beneath him, Matt could feel Taylor's body vibrating as if he
were in the throes of a convulsion.

"Ra*chel*."

Her name this time was a scream. Another window shattered, showering more glass across the kitchen floor.

With the sound, it was as if whatever barrier had kept
him from understanding was shattered, too. *The woman
calling herself Robin Holt...*

Hank had been right. She *wasn't* Robin Holt. She was
someone named Rachel and whoever was out there...

"Who the hell is that?" he demanded.

At his tone, her eyes opened. Slowly her lips parted. Her
mouth moved as if she intended to speak, but no words
came out.

"Answer me, damn it. Who *is* that?"

For a heartbeat her eyes pleaded with him. And then,
seeing the implacable demand in his, she whispered, "My
husband."

CHAPTER TWENTY

SHE HAD ALWAYS KNOWN Danny would find them. What was happening now had been the culminating scene of every nightmare she had had over the last four years.

All the hiding, all her precautions, which had become such an ingrained part of their existence that they were now routine, all the lies she had told—none of them had made any difference in the outcome. The moment she had always known would come was finally here.

"Your *husband?*"

She hadn't even realized what she'd said until she heard Matt repeat it. "Ex-husband," she corrected. "Taylor's father."

As she watched him try to assimilate that, Danny broke another window, shouting more obscenities.

"What does he want?"

It was a good question. Surprisingly good for someone who knew nothing about the situation.

And it was one for which she'd never been able to formulate a satisfactory answer. She knew what he *said* he wanted, of course, but she also knew that his desire to have custody of Taylor, which he had expressed to anyone who would listen, was far from the reality.

He wanted revenge. Or to be able to say he'd won. Or maybe he just wanted what he had always wanted—absolute and total control of their lives. The one thing she was very sure of, however, was that he had as little interest in Taylor as he'd had from the day the boy was born.

She shook her head, unwilling to say anything that would further traumatize her son. She had never been sure how much Taylor remembered about what their life had been like before she'd taken him. Given his age at the time, probably nothing consciously.

She had always prayed that was the case. There were times, however, when he would say something or ask a question about the role of fathers that made her wonder.

"Robin?" Matt prodded as glass continued to shatter.

"He's insane," she said instead of trying to explain the man she had married.

She had long ago come to believe that was true, although not in any sense of the word as it was recognized by the courts. When he wanted to, Danny could control the madness that had ruled her life for five years.

He had done that throughout all the hearings and the psychological evaluations, conducted by the professionals his parents had hired. He had succeeded so well that finally she'd been left with no choice. No option but to take her son and flee.

Matt's eyes broke contact to look back toward the kitchen. Danny's assault had taken on a new dimension.

He had now started on the wooden mullions that once held the panes of glass he'd already destroyed. The sound of their splintering was somehow more disturbing than the glass had been. Despite her determination not to let him terrify her again, she flinched with the sound of each blow.

"Don't let them in," Taylor begged, his voice muffled.

When the first window had been broken, he had burrowed his head into her side. He hadn't moved since.

She reached down, putting her arm around his trembling

shoulders. "It's okay. He's not going to get in. We won't let him in."

"There are two of them," Matt said, apparently reminded of that by the pronoun she'd used. "Who would he have brought with him?"

She shook her head, trying to think. "His lawyer maybe. Maybe his father."

"Nice guys."

Matt was starting to get his equilibrium back. She knew that when the destruction in the kitchen had started, he had been anticipating another kind of danger. Her identification of their assailant as her ex-husband had thrown him.

She should have told him long before now. She had been afraid that something like this would happen when he'd told her their pictures had been on a cable news network.

It hadn't been fair to let him walk into this situation without giving him the facts. It had been such a long time since she'd been able to bring herself to trust anyone, however, that she had hesitated too long.

Besides, with his assurances that no one could find them up here, she had put this particular anxiety out of her mind. It was painfully obvious now that she shouldn't have.

"How did he find us?" she asked.

"He couldn't have on his own. Somebody told them."

It was evident from his bitterness that the betrayal was hard to accept. She wasn't surprised it had happened, however, no matter who was to blame.

Danny would have arrived in Mallory with reams of legal documentation in hand. After all, he had the weight of the entire justice system behind him. As far as it was concerned, she was the guilty party, her ex-husband the one who had been injured.

While she was dealing with her own bitterness over that

injustice, Matt's head lifted. His attention had shifted to the kitchen.

She realized belatedly that the noise of windows being destroyed had stopped. Maybe there was nothing left to break, or maybe Danny had grown tired of hitting things.

She'd be surprised if that were the case. Especially this soon. He'd always had a very high tolerance for that particular exercise.

"Son of a *bitch,*" Matt said.

She didn't have any idea what had prompted that until she, too, got a whiff of smoke. Although she had just claimed that Danny was insane, she couldn't believe he would try to burn the cabin down. Not with his own son inside. The son he claimed to want to nurture and take care of.

"Wait here."

Matt's instruction was hardly necessary. There was nowhere else to go. *Nowhere to run.*

"Armed?" He paused long enough to throw the question at her.

"What?"

"Will he be armed?"

Would he? Firearms had never been a part of the violence she'd experienced at his hands, but then they hadn't been necessary to achieve what he'd wanted back then. That didn't mean he wouldn't think they weren't necessary now.

"I don't know," she said truthfully.

The terror she had felt on hearing her ex-husband's voice was a conditioned response. Now she had accepted that what she had dreaded for so long had finally come to pass. And she would no longer have to lie to Matt, a relief he would probably never understand.

With his question, the tension that had begun to ease again tightened her chest. Matt's weapon was in his hand. She had already seen what it was capable of.

She had welcomed his willingness to use it against the intruder in her home. If he used it now…

"Wait," she said, knowing that there was one more thing she had to confess. One more thing he had to know.

The smell of smoke, carried inside through the empty windows, seemed even stronger now. There was no time to procrastinate. No time to formulate words that would spare her the responsibility of what she'd done. His eyes were focused on her, although she could read the impatience in them.

"They gave him custody of Taylor," she said. "They said he had a legal right to keep me from ever seeing him. None of the things they said about me during those hearings were true, but the judge believed them—" She stopped because his eyes had narrowed.

"*He* has custody?"

She nodded, watching the impact of her confession in his face. "They lied about me. And about him."

As she repeated her explanation, she knew, just as she had known then, that it didn't matter. Nothing mattered except what was on the papers they had given Danny.

"So you took him. You just took him and ran."

His mental processing of the information was almost visible. Her confession made sense of all the things he had asked her about this morning. The doctored birth certificate. The stolen social security number.

"If after this, you can't understand why…" She looked in the direction of the devastated kitchen.

Maybe he couldn't. Like Eph Stokes, the law was his life. His calling. And she had broken it.

"Stay here," he ordered again. "And stay down."

"Matt." Her hand closed over his arm, this time its touch tentative. "Be careful. He really is insane, even if they didn't recognize it."

He nodded once. Then he broke her hold, vaulting over the back of the couch to disappear behind it.

HIS FEET CRUNCHED on the debris that covered the floor with every step he took. The kitchen looked like a war zone. A few splinters of wood hung in the frames, all that was left of the mullions. There was not one unshattered pane of glass.

He approached what had been the windows above the sink with no attempt at stealth. There was nowhere inside this part of the cabin where he could have walked quietly. He didn't even try.

He held the semi-automatic out in front of him, just as he had before he'd understood the nature of this threat. Robin's warning, however, made his using it unlikely.

Rachel's warning, he amended.

Rachel, who had lied from the first. Who had literally lived a lie since she'd been in Mallory.

Which didn't mean she wasn't entitled to his protection. Not that he had a choice about offering it. Despite what she had just told him, his feelings for her hadn't changed. Or for Taylor, who had been abducted just as illegally as Lisa Evans.

The fantasies he'd allowed himself as he'd held the boy last night were mocked by that single, unpalatable truth. Taylor had a father. A father who wanted him. And more importantly, one who had a legal right to take him. A right that he, as an officer of the law, was sworn to protect.

He's insane. The words haunted him because, as evidenced by the destruction before him, he thought the man might really be.

Even if he were, he was still Taylor's custodial parent. And Robin was not.

Rachel.

Rachel, who had been threatened with losing her son to a madman. And who had reacted to that threat in the only way she believed she could.

He knew what it meant to lose a child. Would he have broken the law to keep Josh?

Any law on the books, including that against murder.

The admission created an unexpected sting of tears, which he fought to control. No one who knew the pain of that loss as he did could judge what Robin Holt had done. Not judge and condemn her.

He reached the opening over the sink, the cold, moisture-laden wind blowing through it as if he were standing outside. The Mercedes was still parked where he'd first seen it. Beyond it, perhaps fifty yards from the cabin, two men stood engaged in an animated conversation.

They were too far away for any of what they were saying to be audible, but their postures told him most of what he needed to know. The first and most important revelation was that neither seemed to be armed, although what looked like some kind of mallet lay halfway between their position and the cabin. The weapon that had been used on the windows?

The taller and heavier of the two, who appeared to be at least a couple of decades older than his companion, was holding the forearms of the other. He was talking earnestly, his face very near that of the second man, who had turned away, refusing to look at him.

Matt found that he wanted very badly to see that man's

features. He had thought from the first night that there was nothing of his father in Taylor. For some reason, he needed to verify that impression.

What he *could* see was chestnut hair, stylishly cut, although a little long by the small-town standards of Mallory. It shone with health and vitality in the morning sun.

He wore a black, double-breasted overcoat, which looked expensive. Dark slacks and a pair of dress shoes, both unsuitable for the conditions on the mountain this morning, were visible below the hem of the coat.

Neither man was paying attention to the cabin. Nor did they appear to be conscious that they were being observed.

On the ground around their feet were several blackened pieces of what appeared to be charred rags or paper. The snow they lay on had put a quick end to the fire. Matt wondered if the larger man had physically taken them away from the slighter one and thrown them down there.

He's insane, she had said.

If he isn't, Matt thought, *he's missing a good bet.*

At that moment, the man who was a captive audience turned his head to spit invective at the other. His profile revealed an arrogant nose and a strong chin. The color in his cheeks was high, probably from anger or his recent exertions in destroying the windows.

The flush overlay a smooth, dark tan. The kind you got from playing a lot of tennis or golf. Or polo, Matt realized, looking back at the mallet that lay between them with a new understanding. At this time of year, whatever activity he'd engaged in, it would have had to be in some fairly tropical location to get that deep a tan.

It fit with the Mercedes. With what he was wearing. Even with Robin's suggestions that the witnesses had lied.

Had they been paid to lie? The son of a bitch looked as if he could afford that.

The sounds of a car engine straining up the slope caught his attention. The men he'd been observing became aware of the noise at the same time.

The older one said something to his companion before he released his hands and turned to face the oncoming car. That the new arrival was the police cruiser Matt had expected earlier was verified even before the vehicle pulled into view by a couple of short wails of its siren.

A little late, Matt thought caustically, but at least whoever was driving had sense enough to issue that warning. Not to have done so when approaching a safe house was an invitation to have a round put through your windshield.

The car pulled up to the two men rather than alongside the vehicle parked in the turnaround. Henry Dawkins had dragged his two hundred and fifty pounds out of the passenger-side door almost before the forward motion of the Crown Vic halted.

His face was beet-colored. In contrast to the interrupted conversation of the men he was addressing, Matt was able to understand a few words of what Hank was shouting.

The fact that his supervisor was so visibly furious mitigated some of Matt's anger. Whatever the chief had intended when he'd provided those men with information about this location, it clearly wasn't what had just happened.

The older man appeared to be conciliatory. The movement of his hands, outstretched and chest high, was expansive. His face had been arranged in a more congenial expression than that he'd displayed when talking to his companion.

Despite the demonstration, Hank's anger didn't appear

to be abating. He gestured toward the cabin, looking in its direction for the first time.

When he spotted the damage to the windows, he stopped talking, although his mouth remained open, as if frozen in midmotion. After his first shock, it was clear that he had also spotted Matt standing in the damaged kitchen, his weapon still pointed in the direction of the group.

Hank shouted something, the wind whipping away all but the last words.

"...all right?"

Matt nodded without lowering the semi-automatic.

The chief turned back to say something to the man who had been trying to sooth him, pointing at the destruction. More conciliation, which appeared to have no more effect than his earlier efforts. His round, florid face reflecting his disgust, Hank looked at Matt again, motioning for him to come outside.

He would have to, Matt realized, although he wasn't looking forward to meeting the man who had fathered Taylor. The term might be biologically correct, but it was wrong on so many levels that there ought to be some other word to use in a case like this.

When he turned around to find Robin watching him over the back of the couch, he knew what that word was. The one he'd used a few minutes ago.

Her arms were crossed over her chest, hands resting on the top of their opposite shoulders. The posture was defensive. As if she expected a body blow.

And her face had literally drained of blood. In the sunlight coming through the open space behind him, he could see the tracks of the tears that stained her cheeks.

As he looked at her, she lowered her head, wiping moisture on the back of her hand. Her mouth opened, as if she wanted to tell him something. Then, apparently realizing the futility of anything she might say at this point, she closed it again, her lips tightening into a line. Another tear slipped over the curve of her cheek.

There was nothing he could do to comfort or reassure her. She had gambled against the system, and she had lost. She knew it. So did he.

The bastard standing out in the snow had won. All because her son had walked into the woods one day and stumbled on something no one was supposed to see.

It was one of the tricks life played on the unsuspecting. *Just when everything seems to be going your way...*

"Wait here," he said.

She nodded, bending her head to wipe the corner of her mouth against her wrist. She sniffed, gathering control.

Knowing her as he now did, he guessed that she wouldn't want to give her former husband the satisfaction of seeing her cry. He fought the urge to walk across the room and pull her into his arms. To cradle her head against his chest as she had cradled Taylor's.

He didn't, because he knew how this was going to play out. He'd walk out into the snow. Hank would explain all the good and proper reasons he'd brought the two men up here. He would be shown the documentation the chief had already seen. The papers that had granted custody to the man outside. The court orders enforcing it.

And after that he would have to walk back inside and arrest the woman who had called herself Robin Holt for kidnapping.

CHAPTER TWENTY-ONE

IT BECAME OBVIOUS to Matt as he listened that Hank Dawkins's heart wasn't in arguing the merits of Danny Akin's claim. The chief of police was in over his head, and he knew it.

The lawyer who had come with Robin's ex-husband was too smooth, his manner as polished as his moisture-stained wingtips had once been. To give him credit, he had waited, with unconcealed impatience, through Hank's explanation to Matt of why the two had arrived at the cabin unannounced before him.

According to Dawkins, he had repeatedly tried to reach Matt on the cell phone after Akin and his lawyer had arrived at the courthouse this morning. They'd demanded immediate access to the boy. And they'd had the papers to prove Akin's legal custody.

"Then I had a flat on the way up here," Hank went on apologetically. "First one I can ever remember having on police business. I pulled onto the shoulder and waved these two over. Mr. Akin pulled around me going like a bat out of hell. I was afraid you'd shoot 'em before I could get up here. Wouldn't have blamed you if you had."

"Luckily Detective Ridge isn't as impulsive as you feared," the lawyer, who had been introduced as Max Carpenter, broke in.

"Damn straight," Hank said under his breath. "What I

don't understand is why you two were in such a fool hurry to get up here.''

''Because Mr. Akin very much wants to see his son, who was unlawfully stolen from him four years ago,'' Carpenter said. ''We've come to take him back home. It's as simple as that.''

''Not quite,'' Matt said. His tone challenged the assumption that had just been made that they could waltz into town, load Taylor into the Mercedes and drive away with him. ''Mr. Akin's son is a material witness to crimes currently under investigation in this jurisdiction.''

''I understood that there had been some unpleasantness, however—''

''Four homicides is not what we call *unpleasantness* in Georgia.''

The reminder of their location wasn't intended to be subtle. This *wasn't* wherever Mr. Max Carpenter was accustomed to practicing law.

''No, of course not,'' the lawyer agreed, sounding properly apologetic. ''However, Taylor was certainly not involved in all of those. And according to your chief here…'' A nod in Hank's direction. ''…you already have his testimony on tape. I'm sure that the details about his future cooperation can be worked out between us. In the meantime—''

''Someone's trying to kill him. You *do* understand that, don't you?''

The lawyer had the grace to look embarrassed, but he soldiered on with the line he'd adopted. The one he was being paid to deliver, Matt reminded himself. And it was becoming increasingly obvious that man who was paying him was interested in only one thing.

''I assure you the boy will be adequately protected. Removing him physically from the situation would seem to me to be highly desirous for us as well as for the police. I understood that was your thinking in bringing him up here, Detective Ridge. While the idea was admirable, I believe we can do even better by getting him out of the state and back to his home.''

Taylor's father had said almost nothing. His dark, handsome face was sullen, his cheeks still stained with the flush of his previous exertions.

After their eyes had met for the first time, Matt deliberately avoided looking in his direction. The temptation to see how good the bastard would be at hitting something other than wood or glass or a woman was almost biblical. He had to force his mind away from the memory of Robin flinching from his hand last night.

Rachel. Not Robin. Rachel, who had lied to him from the beginning.

''I'm afraid I can't agree, Mr. Carpenter. The child is a material witness in several unsolved homicides. In *this* jurisdiction.''

The lawyer smiled. It looked almost genuine.

''My client has legal custody of his son, who was criminally abducted four years ago. He wants to take the boy home. We have the necessary court orders to do just that. I can assure you the boy will be protected.''

''And you promise us he'll be available when we bring the murderer or murderers to trial?'' Hank asked.

''Why don't we cross that bridge when we come to it. It's my understanding that you haven't yet made arrests in any of these cases.'' Although Carpenter paused expectantly, neither Matt nor Hank confirmed the accuracy of his statement. ''Who knows how long it might be until you have someone to bring to trial? In the meantime…'' The lawyer raised one salt-and-pepper brow.

''Detective Ridge,'' Hank said, jerking his head backward to indicate he wanted to talk somewhere away from the other two. ''Gentlemen, if you'll excuse us.''

Whatever Hank wanted to say, Matt suspected he wasn't going to like hearing it. He hesitated, his eyes considering Danny Akin again.

''Matt?''

At the chief's prompting, he turned and walked a few feet toward the cabin. Dawkins followed. When they stopped, Hank kept his back to the others.

''That guy gives me the creeps,'' he said.

''Carpenter?''

''The other one. He's a real piece of work. What set him off?'' Hank glanced toward the opening in the side of the cabin that had once held the kitchen windows.

''She didn't come outside when he told her to. The next thing I know, he's pounding on the windows with a polo mallet. After they were all broken, he started playing around with the idea of burning us out.''

''Jesus.''

''The other guy, the lawyer, had to pull him away. I think he told him that what he was doing wasn't going to strengthen his case.''

''The thing of it is, he's got some good points. The lawyer, I mean. Getting the kid out of the area might be safer for him.''

''The guy they sent to kill him came here all the way from Russia. What makes you think they won't send somebody to wherever those two want to take him? The people Taylor saw in those woods aren't going to give up looking for him just because we send him home with his daddy.''

The last word had been rich with sarcasm. If there had ever been anyone in the history of the world that term seemed inappropriate for, it was Danny Akin.

And somewhere in the back of Matt's mind, where he kept the memories he could bear to take out and examine only infrequently, he heard Josh's voice.

Look at this, Daddy.

Watch me, Daddy.

I love you, Daddy.

"He's got custody, Matt. *Legal* custody. And he's got a court order that allows him to take the kid."

"Then we get a judge to override it. Get a restraining order to prevent him from taking the boy anywhere. At least until this case is solved."

"You know a judge around here that's gonna do that?" Even as Hank asked the question, he realized the answer. "Hell," he said softly. "You think he'll do it?"

Karen's father had retired from the bench a couple of years ago, but due to a shortage of qualified judges, he'd remained on supernumerary status. Matt thought that once he'd explained that the situation was about protecting a child, Lloyd Stoddard would go along with it. And if he didn't—

As Max Carpenter had said, he'd cross that bridge when the time came.

DESPITE Akin's handiwork, the cabin felt warm, almost inviting after the cold outside. He opened the front door to find Robin on the couch with Taylor in her lap.

The last of the logs he'd brought in before breakfast had been added to the fire. As a consequence it had roared to life, the heat it produced fighting with the draft from the open wall in the kitchen.

Robin had appeared to be watching the blaze when he entered, but she turned her head immediately. All trace of her tears had been erased, although her eyes were red.

"Now?" she asked.

Her hand lifted to brush Taylor's bangs away from his forehead. Just as Matt had seen her do a dozen times.

There wasn't much good news he could offer her. Taylor's immediate whereabouts would be her primary concern.

"We're going to try to get a judge in town to issue a restraining order."

A heartbeat's hesitation. "What does that mean?"

"An order to keep them from taking him out of the state."

"But...? I don't understand. He *has* custody. Do you think—"

"I don't know. We're going to ask a judge to leave Taylor with you for the time being because of the trauma of what's been going on. Giving him back to a father he hasn't seen in years would not only be cruel, it would put him in more danger. And then maybe, if you want to pursue it, on the additional grounds that you intend to challenge the original custody arrangement."

He couldn't ever remember asking Karen's father for a favor as long as he'd known him. Certainly not one of this magnitude. Seeing what was in Robin's eyes at the possibility they might be able to keep Akin from taking Taylor was enough to ensure that he would.

"Do you think that will do any good?"

"It might slow things down."

"I meant challenging the agreement."

Matt's gaze lifted to survey the destruction in the adjoining room. "I don't know, but I suspect the judge we're going to approach won't feel that's exactly the behavior of a normal father." Nor of anyone who might be considered normal. "We will have to go back to town to do this, however."

She nodded. Obviously she'd been expecting to hand Taylor over to Akin immediately. Despite his reservations about what might happen, this must seem a reprieve to her.

"I'll get our things."

"Are you coming, too?" Taylor asked.

"Every step of the way," Matt assured him. "You want to stay here with me while your mom gathers up your stuff?"

The little boy looked questioningly at his mother, who nodded. Matt reached down to take him from her, knowing, even as he did, that he was setting himself up for more heartache.

There didn't seem to be anything he could do despite that knowledge. This was one temptation he couldn't find the strength to resist.

As he lifted the small, solid body, Taylor put his arms around his neck, pressing his face against his shoulder. Automatically Matt's arms tightened, hugging him to his chest.

He wanted to make promises, if only to himself, but he knew he might not be able to keep them. Instead, he put his face against the silk of the child's hair and swallowed the ache in the back of his throat.

"Hey, buddy," he whispered. "It's gonna be okay. Don't you worry. You leave the worrying to your mama and me. Okay?"

The head under his cheek moved up and down.

"You want to ride in a police car?"

Taylor straightened, looking into his eyes for confirmation. "With a siren?"

There wasn't much in the way of promises he could make about how this all would turn out, but that one he could handle. "And flashing lights."

The sirens and lightbar wouldn't make any difference up here. Hank could give the boy a ride with the full effects for a quarter of a mile or so after they left the cabin.

"Cool," Taylor said, his voice awed.

Matt laughed, squeezing him close. When he raised his head, he saw that Robin was standing in the doorway to the hall watching them. She held the small bag she'd brought from the house last night.

"I'm ready."

She hadn't questioned what would happen if he couldn't get the restraining order he'd told her about. It was as if she didn't want to think about it.

Or maybe she had thought about this day for so many years that she was simply living from one moment to the next. There was not much point in trying to plan for eventualities when you had no control over any of them.

"What about the things you brought up here?" she asked. "Do you want me to—"

"I'll get them later."

After this is all over.

She nodded, but she didn't move.

"We have to go. I'm not sure how long Chief Dawkins can manage to keep—" he almost said *your husband,* but she didn't deserve that "—those two at bay."

"I was eighteen. He had money, a lot of it, and he didn't mind spending it. Not even spending it on me. I thought all my dreams had come true."

Matt didn't want to hear this, but apparently she needed

to say it. Taylor had settled back down against his shoulder, his breath warm against Matt's neck.

"We all make mistakes," he said. "Most of the time we don't have to live with them for the rest of our lives."

"I had to take Taylor. I couldn't take a chance. What he'd done to me..." Her eyes considered her son a moment before they rose to his. "It was already starting to happen. That's why I'd filed for divorce. I thought I could protect him. And now..."

No promises, Matt told himself. He didn't know if he could keep them, which meant he had no right to make them.

"I'll do the best I can to see that doesn't happen."

"I wanted you to know that last night... That *was* my dream come true. All of it, but...especially your holding Taylor. I didn't know what to say to you before about your son's death, but seeing you with Taylor... I know your little boy was happy. He had to be. He would have known how much he was loved. They both would have known. That's the greatest gift you can give anyone. Knowing they're loved. But especially a child."

There seemed no words with which to respond to that. Even if he had known what they were, he wouldn't have been able to push them past the knot in his throat.

Watch me, Daddy. I love you.

"Maybe if I'd been older. Or wiser," she added, smiling at him through her own tears. "Maybe I would have known what to look for. Thank you for showing me. I'll never forget that. And I'll never forget you. No matter what happens to us, I wanted you to know that."

Still unable to speak, he nodded.

Then, without waiting for him to precede her, she walked

across the room and opened the door. She paused for a moment in the opening.

The sun off the snow added light to the fair hair. She glanced back at him, holding his eyes for a heartbeat before she lifted her chin and stepped outside.

CHAPTER TWENTY-TWO

SHE REMEMBERED Max Carpenter from the custody hearings. He was a friend of Danny's father, someone who had known him all his life. Someone who knew the truth about him, if anyone did. And because of that, she should have realized he'd be the one Danny would bring with him.

As she walked across the snow to where the police cruiser was parked, she hoped that she wouldn't be expected to interact with either of them. It should be enough that they'd won.

Of course, knowing her ex-husband as she did, she should have realized that he wouldn't be able to resist taunting her with his victory. He came charging toward her as soon as he saw her.

"You stupid bitch," he yelled as Carpenter grabbed his arm. "I *told* you that you couldn't get away from me."

She ignored him, determined not to let him see that his screaming bothered her. The sooner she got into the police car the better it would be. She might still be able to hear Danny's ravings, but at least he wouldn't be able to get to her physically.

And it was clear he wanted to. Max had his arms hooked through Danny's, holding him by the elbows as he strained forward. The obscenities grew more colorful the closer to them she came.

She didn't look back, but she was very conscious of the

man who was behind her, carrying her son. She was ashamed to have either of them witness another such display. Ashamed to have Matt know that she had once been so foolish as to think she loved the man who was now straining against the hold of his father's lawyer.

Chief Dawkins had opened the door of the cruiser long before she reached it. She bent, sliding gratefully onto the back seat. It was not until she looked up and saw the grill separating it from the front that she understood the significance of him putting her into the back.

No one had arrested her. Not yet. Maybe that's what Matt was supposed to have done when he'd come back inside.

It didn't matter that he hadn't. She had understood the consequences of what she'd done from the moment she'd decided to take Taylor.

And she had gotten to spend four years with him that she wouldn't have otherwise had. Well worth any price she would have to pay now.

She turned her head, watching Matt close the front door of the cabin. He had taken time to wrap one of the blankets he'd brought around Taylor, who again had his face nestled between Matt's neck and shoulder.

Once she'd been put inside the police car, Danny's anger had seemed to evaporate. Max had released his arms as they, too, watched Matt's approach.

It was clear from their waiting postures that they expected him to bring the boy to them. When it became apparent he was heading toward the cruiser instead, Danny's volatile temper flared again.

"Where the hell do you think you're going with my son?" he shouted, starting across the snow.

Max grabbed his arm, clinging to it almost desperately.

When she glanced back at Matt, she realized that his forward progress had slowed at the sound of Danny's screams.

Don't stop, she urged. *Don't let him near Taylor.*

"What do you think you're doing?" Danny screamed again. "Where do you think you're taking him? He's coming with me."

Taylor raised his head from Matt's shoulder, staring at his father. She knew in her heart that he could have no idea who the shouting, red-faced man was. He'd been too young when they'd left. Too young to remember other scenes like this. The look in his eyes, however, was one of absolute terror.

Suddenly Danny broke from Carpenter's hold, sprinting across the snow toward Matt and the boy. As he did, Taylor began to scream, the noise high-pitched and piercing, clearly hysterical. He began to struggle, flailing around in Matt's arms like some wild creature.

Seeking to comfort and then to control the panicked child, Matt's attention had shifted from Danny to the boy. Neither she nor Dawkins moved quickly enough during those critical seconds, watching the scene unfold before them as if mesmerized.

It was only when Danny bent and grabbed the mallet he'd used on the kitchen windows that the spell which held her was broken. As unbelievable as it seemed, she knew him too well to doubt he'd use it.

Her warning cry was lost amid the child's shrieks and Danny's obscenities. She scrambled out of the car, but she seemed to be moving in slow motion while everything else was happening too fast.

She watched as Danny swung the long, flexible mallet with the expertise of long practice. Matt's attention was still distracted by the hysterical child, but at the last second he seemed to sense what was about to happen. He threw his arm up in a belated and unsuccessful attempt to avoid the coming blow.

The head of the mallet caught him squarely on the temple. He staggered and then went down on one knee, putting the hand he'd raised to ward off the mallet on the ground to keep from falling over. The snow around him was suddenly sprinkled with bright red splatters of blood that quickly changed to pink in the slush.

As he swayed, attempting to hold himself upright, Taylor lunged from his arms and fell out onto the snow. For a second or two he remained tangled in the blanket. Then somehow, incredibly, he managed to free himself. Getting to his feet, he darted past his father, who made an unsuccessful grab at him as he went by and then turned to give chase.

She could hear Dawkins shouting something behind her, but she couldn't make sense of the words. She was too focused on reaching Taylor before his father could.

Despite the boy's terror, Danny was gaining on him with every step. There was no way she could overcome the advantage her ex-husband's head start and physical size had given him.

Still she ran, the cold air burning her lungs as she sucked it in. The black cashmere overcoat flapped in front of her as she followed Danny. Seeing it, she finally realized why Taylor had reacted to him as he had.

He hadn't recognized his father. He couldn't have. He had lifted his head from Matt's shoulder to see two men in black overcoats, one of them raising a mallet to strike at the man he had learned to trust.

And he had been thrown back into *his* nightmare. *Don't*

let them in, he had begged, but neither she nor Matt had understood the significance of that plea.

"Danny, stop," she begged. "You're frightening him."

The wind whipped her words away, as useless now as they had ever been against his anger. She thought she could hear someone running behind her, but she didn't take the time to look back. Dawkins or Max Carpenter. Or Matt.

Please God, let it be Matt. Let him be all right.

Taylor had made it nearly to the edge of the woods. Danny was right behind him, so close it seemed he could reach out and touch the boy.

She couldn't imagine the horror her son must feel, believing that he was running from the men who had taken Lisa. How much more terrified would he be when his father's hand closed over his shoulder?

"It's all right, Taylor," she screamed. She had realized the futility of trying to stop Danny. All she could do was to try to mitigate her son's fear when it happened. "He's not one of the men in the woods."

He's your father.

As reassuring as those words might have been, even now she couldn't bring herself to utter them. Not after what Taylor had just seen him do to Matt.

At the sound of her voice, Taylor glanced back, his face anguished. As he did, he stumbled and almost fell. Although he righted himself, Danny took advantage of the hesitation in his stride.

He threw himself forward in a football-style tackle, bringing the child down with him. At the same instant, there was a crack of sound from the woods to their right. The noise echoed into the sudden stillness, but still she didn't understand what it was.

She continued to run, wondering why Danny didn't get

up. Why didn't he pick Taylor up and turn to taunt her with his possession of the boy?

It was only with the sound of the second shot that she knew what had happened. That one came so close that she literally sensed the bullet go by a fraction of a second before she heard the crack of the rifle.

She threw herself to the ground, crawling across the few feet that separated her from Taylor as shots rang out behind her. Those were different in tone. Definitely not the clear, sharp cracks she'd heard before. Apparently someone— Chief Dawkins perhaps—was firing back at the sniper.

That wasn't her concern, however. Her concern was Taylor, and her terror grew as she closed the distance between them.

Danny was lying prone, the overcoat spread out around him like dark wings because he'd been reaching for Taylor when he fell. Beneath one edge of the coat, she could see a small bare foot and part of a leg covered in beige knit.

There had been no doubt in her mind that her ex-husband was dead, even before she saw the blood on the snow. There had been something about the boneless sprawl and the absolute stillness with which he lay. Danny had never been still or quiet during all the years she had known him. Now, in death, he was both.

"Taylor?"

She began to push at Danny's shoulder, trying to lift his weight off the child. A bullet struck the ground next to her. Instinctively she ducked, allowing Danny's body to shield her as it had shielded his son.

"Mama."

Her heart lifted, and she took a sobbing breath at the realization that Taylor was alive.

"Be still," she warned. "Don't try to move."

"Get him off me."

The hysteria that had fueled his flight was also in that plea. And there was nothing she could do about it. Nothing she *should* do. Sheltered under his father's body was as safe a place as Taylor could be right now, given their exposed location.

"I will," she promised, reaching out to put her fingers around his bare foot. "Just be still a few more minutes, baby, and then I promise I'll get you out."

She glanced to her right and realized her assumption had been correct. Dawkins, along with Max Carpenter, had taken refuge behind the police cruiser. As she watched, the chief squeezed off a shot, aiming into the woods from where the cracks of sound had come.

She searched the area beyond the car, looking for Matt. There was enough of an incline to the terrain that she couldn't see the place where he'd fallen after Danny had hit him. Either he had found something to hide behind or he was still lying on the bloodstained snow.

She didn't dare lift her eyes far enough to search for the shooter. She could literally do nothing but stay down and try to keep Taylor calm.

Just as she decided that, a flurry of gunfire rang out. Dawkins was moving toward the back of the automobile. He appeared to be deliberately challenging the sniper, who was responding. She wondered if they had only sent one man as they had before, or if there were several of them hidden in the shrouded woods.

"Mama."

The cry was plaintive. Demanding. In answer, she squeezed his foot.

"Shh," she whispered. "Shh, baby. Just stay put. Just don't move."

"Get him off," he said, trying to wiggle free of the body. "I don't want him on me."

"Pretend it's a game. Hide and seek. You've got a good hiding place. You just have to stay here and be still so they won't find you."

Hide and seek. A game she had been playing for the last four years. Today all the hunters had closed in.

"Son of a bitch!"

Dawkins's expletive was loud enough to carry despite the wind. She glanced back at him and saw that he was holding his right arm, just above the elbow. Although he still gripped the handgun he'd been using, he was no longer firing it. And if he couldn't...

Driven by necessity, she lifted her head enough to look into the area from where the shots had come. As inexperienced at this as she was, even she had been able to pinpoint the location by their sound alone. Dawkins obviously had a more exact idea of where the sniper was located.

She could see nothing, however. Wherever he was, he was apparently well camouflaged.

Her gaze traced along the tree line, looking for any anomaly. If Dawkins were no longer able to provide protection for them—

At the outside edge of her vision, something moved. She focused on the area, waiting for whatever it was to move again.

She wasn't disappointed. Someone darted from behind the trunk of one of the huge pines to the next. The movement had been so quick, she might have missed it had she not been concentrating with every fiber of her being.

Another of the hunters, coming to join the sniper who'd killed Danny? Or was it possible that someone was stalking the stalker?

Her eyes flicked back to the patrol car, searching for Dawkins. There was no sign of the chief. No sign of Max Carpenter either.

Her sudden terror was mindless. *Don't leave us,* she begged, although she knew there was only one way to end this standoff. And that wasn't to maintain the status quo.

There was also danger to Taylor in his prolonged exposure to the cold dampness of the ground he was lying on. She knew something dangerous would have to be done in order to extricate them. She understood that, but the only thing she could think were the words she had thought before.

Don't leave us. Please, God, don't let them leave us.

CHAPTER TWENTY-THREE

MATT HAD WORKED his way close enough that he could see the bastard. The barrel of a high-powered rifle was propped on top of a rock in front of him and he was sighting through the scope, unaware that he was also in the crosshairs.

Except Matt didn't have a scope. And even if he had, he would still be at a disadvantage. One he couldn't do anything about.

His vision was badly blurred from the effects of the blow to the head he'd taken. He knew that probably indicated a concussion, but at least his sight had become a little clearer than when he'd heard the first shot.

He had been able to tell that someone had gone down, but he couldn't distinguish which of the running figures had been struck. Those seconds until he could focus well enough to locate Robin had been the longest of his lifetime.

Safely hidden for the moment behind a tall pine, he opened his eyes wide, blinking a few times in an attempt to make them work together.

The scene in the clearing again swam into focus. Robin was lying in the exact same spot she'd been in the last time he'd looked for her. He held onto the fact that he had watched her crawl toward Taylor and Akin.

She's okay, he told himself, forcing his mind away from the danger she and the boy were in and back to his job. *She has to be okay.*

Every tangled emotion he'd felt had crystallized. All the things he'd been confused about had, in a single heartbeat, become unforgivably clear.

Allowing himself to love someone as much as he had loved Karen and Josh meant risking that nearly unbearable pain of loss. But choosing not to love Robin and Taylor had become even more unbearable.

It was up to him to see to it that both he and Robin had a second chance. He hadn't had an opportunity to save his family, but this time…

Another shot rang out, snapping his wandering attention back to the sniper. His position hadn't changed. Thank God for Hank Dawkins, who was keeping him pinned down. The shooter would also still be concentrating on his original target, hoping Robin would panic and try to run with the boy.

Keep down, he urged her mentally.

The same demand he'd made before he had understood that, although her ex-husband represented a threat, it was not the one he'd been expecting. In the aftermath of Akin's madness and Robin's confession, he had let down his guard.

That wouldn't happen again, he promised himself grimly. And all he had to do to make up for that near-fatal mistake was to get in close enough to take a shot at the assassin.

He slipped forward to the safety of the next tree, thankful for the cushion of snow that lessened the possibility a crackling twig might give him away. Securely sheltered behind the massive pine, he leaned to the side, venturing another look at his target.

The attention of the sniper was focused on Dawkins, who would keep him from coming out of the woods after his prey. Years of hunting experience had allowed Hank to locate the sniper, just as Matt had.

And Matt had an added advantage. He knew these particular woods as well as he knew the face in his mirror.

Which would also be blurred right now.

He widened his eyes again, blinking in another attempt to improve his vision. With the back of his hand, he wiped at blood that was still seeping from the gash the mallet had opened in the thin skin beside his left eye. The numbness of the initial shock to the nerves was wearing off, and the place hurt like hell.

That was the least of his worries right now, he acknowledged. *One chance.* That's all he'd have. If he didn't manage to take the bastard out with the first shot...

Discarding the possibility as defeatist, he moved forward again, slipping into place behind the next tree before he reevaluated his position. Under ordinary circumstances, he would be close enough here to risk a shot, even with a handgun. These were hardly ordinary circumstances, however. Not given the handicap of his damaged vision.

And yet, despite the cushion of the snow, if he tried to get closer, he risked being heard. Or sensed. The sniper's instincts would be working overtime. Every faculty alert to danger. Every nerve attuned to the very atmosphere around him.

All Matt could do was hope that Dawkins could keep the shooter busy a little longer. Time enough for him to manage to move a few feet nearer his target.

He closed his eyes, squeezing the lids tightly in the hope that when he opened them there would be some further improvement. There wasn't. He was out of options. And out of time.

He eased around the trunk of the tree, the Sig Sauer

stretched out in front of him. The scene before him was distorted, as if he were looking through heat waves rising off a summer pavement.

From this angle, the only chance he had to take the sniper out instantly would be with a head shot. And he couldn't be sure he could make it. Not at this distance. If he missed, all he would accomplish was to warn the shooter that he himself was being stalked.

Matt edged forward again, starting toward the next tree large enough to hide him. The noise he made crossing the snow-shrouded ground seemed no louder than that of his previous moves, but something—sound or motion—finally attracted the sniper's attention.

The barrel of the rifle began to track away from its previous target. Matt didn't wait for the gun to complete the arc.

No longer in profile, the sniper presented a far larger target. Matt aimed for the broadest part of his chest, just as if he were firing at the paper silhouette on the qualifying range.

As his finger tightened over the trigger, time seemed to stand still. Unable to rely on the evidence of his eyes for confirmation of their effect, he didn't stop squeezing off rounds until he had emptied the gun.

Long after the crack of the rifle that had answered his first shot. Long after its barrel had swung upward, the scope and sight useless. Long after he knew that at least one of his bullets had struck home.

He'd kept firing because he couldn't afford to take any chances. Not given the stakes.

As the echoes of his shots faded away across the mountain, an eerie stillness settled around him. Slowly, hearing nothing but the wind in the tops of the trees, he straightened from the shooter's crouch he'd assumed.

Before he did anything else, he replaced the clip in his weapon. Then, alert for any sign of life, he walked over to the man he'd shot.

He lay on his back, the rifle a foot or so from the outstretched hand that had held it. Matt could tell from the location and amount of blood on the front of the camouflage jacket he wore that the sniper was dead. Or if he weren't yet, he would be in a matter of minutes.

He thought briefly about trying to get information about who had paid him. Something that might lead them back to whoever wanted to keep Taylor from testifying.

That impulse quickly gave way to reality. A man who would shoot a seven-year-old in cold blood was unlikely to have enough conscience to talk, even if he knew he was dying.

"Matt?"

Hank's voice. It didn't seem as if the chief had had time to reach him, but Dawkins's call sounded as if he were very near.

"Over here."

As he gave the directive, Matt leaned back against the trunk of the nearest tree. The pain in his head had grown to staggering proportions in the last few seconds. Or maybe it was that for the first time he had an opportunity to be aware of it.

"You okay?"

Squinting to protect his eyes from the dazzle of sunlight reflected off the snow, he looked up to find the chief staring down at him in concern. For some reason he was now sitting on the ground, his back against the tree he'd leaned against only seconds before. Although Dawkins still held his weapon in his right hand, he was supporting that arm, its sleeve soaked with blood, with his left.

"I'm all right," Matt lied. He nodded toward the older man's wound. "We need to get that tied up."

His voice sounded strange in his own ears. Breathless and strained. And the effort to form those few words had almost been beyond him.

"I'm too old and ornery to bleed to death. Besides, the lawyer used his tie as a tourniquet." Hank turned, allowing him to see the striped silk rep incongruously tied around the stained khaki. "First time I've ever known a lawyer to be of any use. Anybody you know?" Hank asked, nodding toward the body.

Matt tried to focus on the sniper's features. Like those of the man they'd found in the woods, they seemed distorted by the violence of his death. More a mask than a face.

"I don't think so."

"Son of a bitch," Hank said feelingly. Cradling his injured arm against his body, he stooped down, performing an efficient one-handed search of the man's pockets. "No ID."

"You expect one?"

Whoever was behind this, they weren't amateurs.

"Hell, everybody makes mistakes."

Mistakes. The word reverberated unpleasantly in Matt's brain. It had been his mistake in concentrating on Akin that had led them to this point. And now...

"The Holts," Matt said, struggling to get to his feet.

As soon as he had, a sickening wave of vertigo washed over him. He staggered and might have fallen had it not been for Dawkins's quick support.

"They're all right," Hank said, looking toward the clearing. He waved at someone, and then turned back to Matt to explain. "I gave Carpenter the shotgun out of the cruiser."

"Does he know how to use it?" Matt asked, straightening away from Hank's supporting arm.

The nausea had passed, and the pain was manageable if he didn't move his head.

"Hell, all he's gotta do is pull the trigger. Even a lawyer ought to be able to handle that."

"It's over, Rachel. They got him."

She looked up over the protection of Danny's body to find Max Carpenter running awkwardly toward them, carrying what looked like a shotgun. Her first impulse was to ask him to be careful with it. In the midst of the chaos that surrounded her, however, the request seemed out of place. She should be glad he was armed. Glad he was coming to help them.

"Are you sure?" She didn't dare raise her head too far, despite his assurance.

"Chief Dawkins waved to me from the woods. What about Danny?"

Carpenter stooped, laying the shotgun down in the snow beside him. He put his hand on Danny's face and then felt for a pulse in the artery in his neck.

"I think he's dead," Rachel said flatly. She supposed she should feel something about her ex-husband's death, but she didn't. Not even relief. "Help me roll him over."

Max looked up, his eyes wide with shock. She wasn't sure if that was because he had realized she was right about Danny or because he thought her request to move his body callous.

"Taylor's pinned under him," she explained.

Tentatively, as if he were reluctant to disturb the corpse, Max helped her lift Danny's shoulders enough that the boy could scramble free. As soon as he had, they reached for one another, Taylor burying his face against her breasts.

She could feel the cold, wet material of his pajamas through her jacket and shirt. She held him close, trying to warm his trembling body. When the sobs began, she rocked him from side-to-side, just as she had when he was a baby.

"Is he all right?" Max asked.

He was alive. That's all she knew right now. And it was really all that mattered.

She nodded, unable to speak. Danny was dead. And Taylor, who had been the sniper's target, was alive.

How many times had she prayed that Danny wouldn't find them? When he did, she had thought it was the end of the world. Her small, perfect world.

Instead, his insane quest to take his son away from her had saved Taylor's life. Even Danny's fearful temper had played a role in what had happened. If he hadn't run after Taylor...

"Let's get him inside," Max suggested. "He must be freezing."

No matter what happened next, it was obvious Taylor would not now be going home with his father. Anything was better than that, she thought. Almost anything, she amended, remembering her terror as she'd realized the sniper was firing at him.

"Come on, son," Carpenter said. As he reached down to take the boy, Taylor shrank back, burrowing closer against her body.

"I'll carry him."

She tried to stand up, but in this position Taylor was too heavy to lift. And as much as she hated to let him go, she knew Max was right. They needed to get him warm and dry before hypothermia set in.

"Come on, Taylor," Carpenter said again, holding out his hand. "There's nothing to be afraid of. I'm a friend...of your mother's," he finished.

"It's okay," Rachel whispered. She bent, putting her lips against the crown of Taylor's head as her hand cupped his cheek. "You go with Mr. Carpenter. I'll be right behind you."

She pushed him away from her body, despite his determination to cling to her. "Go on, baby. I'm coming, I promise."

Carpenter reached out and grasped an arm, pulling Taylor off her lap. The boy began to whimper.

"We'll wait right here for your mama. Then we'll all go inside together—"

The reassuring words had changed into a croak of shock. Rachel looked up to find Max standing stock-still with his arms around Taylor, looking into the woods where the boy had been headed when his father had overtaken him.

Rachel's eyes followed his. A man was emerging from the woods, the gun in his hand pointed toward the child.

"Get down," she screamed.

She turned, trying to verify that Max had obeyed. Lying between them at Danny's feet was the shotgun Carpenter had been carrying.

She threw herself forward, reaching for it. As she lifted the weapon from the snow, she was surprised by its weight. Parroting what she'd seen other people do, she put the stock against her shoulder, swinging its double barrels in the direction of the approaching man.

Just like pointing your finger, Matt had told her. She had

no idea if that advice would apply to this weapon, too. And no time to worry about it.

Because of its weight, the muzzle wavered wildly as she tried to focus it on her moving target. Before she had, her finger tightened over the trigger.

She had expected a recoil, but she hadn't had time to brace for it. The shotgun's kick threw her back, off balance, but she quickly righted herself.

Desperately, she again began the process of trying to line the muzzle up on the man coming toward them. She heard him shoot before her finger found the second trigger.

Not too soon. Not like before.

One last chance, and all she had to do was get close. The shotgun's spread would do the rest.

Somewhere close, she told herself again, fighting to align the weapon. At that instant, incredibly, the double barrels seemed to steady, the deadly payload focused on the running man. She pulled the second trigger and knew instantly, despite the recoil, that at least some of the shot had hit him.

There was a hesitation in his forward motion, but then he seemed to gather himself, to begin moving forward again. Knowing there was nothing else she could do, she glanced toward Taylor.

Max Carpenter had gathered the boy into his arms, his dark head bent over the fair one. He had turned his back on the approaching man so that his own body was between the second assassin and the boy. Waiting, tensed for the impact of the bullets he expected at any moment.

There must be something else, Rachel thought frantically. Something...

As the thought formed, she realized that the empty shotgun could be used as a club. She scrambled to her feet, shifting the weapon so that the barrels were in her hand, the wooden stock poised to strike. Then her eyes returned to the solitary figure silhouetted against the snowy backdrop of the woods.

He was no longer moving forward. As she watched, he dropped onto his knees, his gun still pointing toward Max's back. Then, as if in slow motion and without any attempt to break his fall, he fell face downward in the snow.

Unable to believe that he was dead, she still held on to the shotgun, ready for him to threaten her child again. It was not until Chief Dawkins took the weapon from her hands that she understood it was over.

She had already turned, intending to go to Taylor, when she saw Matt. He was walking slowly across the expanse of snow. He looked dazed. Almost disoriented.

She glanced again toward Taylor to reassure herself that he was safe. Carpenter had set the boy on his feet, and he had already started toward the man who had, in only a few days, become more of a father to him than any he had ever known before.

Taylor threw himself into Matt's legs, causing him to stagger slightly before he righted himself. He stopped, putting his hand on Taylor's head to pull it close against his body.

His eyes, narrowed against the glare of the sunlight off the snow, lifted to hers. She took one step and then another before she began to run.

Even before she had reached them, Matt's free arm had opened, making a place for her against his heart.

CHAPTER TWENTY-FOUR

"KRUCHIN HAD ALREADY given the prosecutors quite a bit of information regarding Nemtsov's operations. Bank and credit card fraud. Money laundering. If your witness can identify any of Nemtsov's associates as the men he saw in the woods, then they're back in business with conspiracy to commit murder charges."

"My witness is seven years old, Mr. Rippetoe. I don't know how much good his testimony would do you. *If*, of course, he can make such an identification."

"All I'm asking is that you let him take a look at these," the U.S. Marshal said, holding up a manila folder he'd brought into the conference room. "What harm could it do?"

How much harm *could* it do? Matt wondered. As an officer of the law he was sympathetic to the plight of those attempting to make the case against a particularly vicious criminal. As someone who cared very much about a child who had already been traumatized beyond belief by the results of an act he'd accidentally witnessed, he was reluctant to subject Taylor to anything else.

"I don't think—"

"He and his mother will be protected. I assure you of that."

Matt refrained from reminding him of the fate of the last

witness against Grigory Nemtsov they had provided security for. His skepticism must have been evident in his eyes.

"Anatoly Kruchin had some peculiar habits that he refused to give up. Believe me, he was repeatedly warned of their possible consequences. The warning didn't result in a change in his behavior. Witnesses who refuse to cooperate are almost impossible to protect."

"You're saying that he brought about his own death."

"Some addictions are even more powerful than the desire for self-preservation. Kruchin's particular addiction involved underage girls engaging in certain...sexual perversions. To that end, he stalked teen chat rooms. He could disguise his identity, but he couldn't disguise his peculiar fascinations. And Nemtsov had people watching for anyone who might express an interest in those. It was only a matter of time until Kruchin got an offer he couldn't refuse."

An assignation that was to have taken place in a wooded area behind a school? Another piece of the puzzle fell into place.

"I'd been thinking of him as some poor bastard who couldn't possibly have deserved what was done to him. It's hard to imagine that anyone could."

"Kruchin was almost as unsavory as Nemtsov himself. The difference was he got caught. And he was willing to talk about Nemtsov in exchange for his freedom. Too bad he couldn't keep his mouth shut about anything else."

There was a small silence as Matt digested the information he'd been given, weighing his options.

"You understand that I'd have to talk to the boy's mother before we could go any further with this."

"Of course. From what your chief told me, she's managed to keep her son hidden from an abusive ex-husband for several years. If she could do that on her own, she'd be the perfect candidate for Witness Security. Nobody needs to worry about the same thing happening to this boy that happened to Kruchin.''

''I'll tell her that.''

Without making any further commitment, Matt stood, offering his hand. The marshal rose and took it, his handshake firm as he held out the folder containing the pictures he wanted Taylor to examine.

''You might remind her that even if the boy *doesn't* agree to testify, they aren't going to let this go. He'll always represent a threat to them. They don't know how much he saw, so they'll assume, as they have up to now, that it was enough to be dangerous. You tell her that without our support, she's always going to be on the run. And if *they* find her... Suffice it to say that the consequences will be a lot more serious than those she was running from before.''

Rippetoe was right. The Russian mobsters had tracked them to the cabin by putting a homing device on the chief of police's car. Anyone that determined wouldn't give up.

It would be better for Rachel and the boy if Taylor *could* identify the men in the woods. That way they would be provided with protection for as long as they needed it. Even after the trial, if necessary.

Reluctantly Matt took the folder. ''Videotaped testimony?''

''At his age, it's a possibility. The Service couldn't guarantee it, of course. That would be up to the judge. After what the kid's been through, I doubt many would want to force him to face those people.''

''I'll get back to you,'' Matt promised.

''For his sake, you should do that sooner rather than later.''

"Do *YOU* THINK he should look at them?"

Rachel might have been asking him as the detective in charge of the case, simply as a matter of information. They both knew she wasn't. She wanted his opinion as to how much harm he thought letting Taylor see those pictures might do.

"If he can identify any of those men, and *if* you're willing to let him testify against them, the U.S. Marshals Service will immediately put him under protection. As much as we might hate to have Taylor confront that memory…" He hesitated, and then told her the absolute truth. "They're after him anyway, Rachel. This can only help."

"Will they let me stay with him?"

Her question surprised him. He thought she had understood. Not even Max Carpenter seemed inclined to pursue the abduction charge.

Danny Akin's mother had died in the years since Rachel had taken Taylor. Without the driving force of his wife and his son's quest for revenge, the lawyer didn't believe Akin's father would want custody. Carpenter had already left the state, flying home with Danny's body.

"Of course," Matt said.

"In spite of what I did?"

"I don't think anyone's interested in pursuing what you did. If the New York authorities want you, your best option would be to try to work out a deal with the Marshals Service."

"What kind of deal?"

"Taylor's testimony in exchange for a suspended sentence. To be served under the supervision of the marshal assigned to his case."

"Would they do that?"

Seeing hope flare in her eyes, Matt shrugged, praying he

wasn't promising more than Rippetoe could deliver. "They make deals all the time— With people guilty of far more serious crimes than what you're accused of."

"Stealing a child? *Is* there a more serious crime?"

In normal circumstances Matt might have agreed. Having seen Akin in action, he knew Rachel's circumstances were far from normal.

"Your situation should warrant a second look from the courts. Chief Dawkins and I would be willing to sign an affidavit to that effect. I suspect Carpenter would, too, if you asked him. Since he was your husband's attorney in the original custody hearings, that would go a long way in your favor."

"Ex-husband," she corrected softly. "So...you're saying it would be to my advantage if Taylor can identify someone in those photographs as one of the men he saw in the woods?"

"To his as well. They aren't going to let this go. And I don't think you can protect him on your own."

The question was in her eyes, but she didn't ask it. Unwilling to risk influencing her against making a decision he believed was in Taylor's best interest, he didn't offer to answer it.

After a moment she looked down at the folder he'd laid on the conference table between them. "May I look at them?"

He pushed it toward her. Despite her request, she hesitated before she opened it. When she had, she fanned the photographs it contained.

Matt hadn't even bothered to look at the pictures after Rippetoe handed over the folder. He did now, evaluating those faces of the members of Grigory Nemtsov's inner cadre upside down.

"What if he's wrong?" Rachel asked. "What if he points to one of these men and says he was there when he wasn't. He's just a little boy."

"He hasn't been wrong about anything so far. He told us exactly what he saw that day. That's all we're asking him to do now. To tell us if any of these are the men he saw with the body. I think we have to ask him, Rachel. As much for his sake as because it's the right thing to do."

She made no indication she'd even heard him. For a long time, she didn't look up from the pictures.

Finally, she stacked them together and closed the top of the folder over them. Then she pushed it back across the table.

"Ask him."

THEY HAD SPREAD the photographs out before they brought Taylor into the conference room. Matt had asked both Dawkins and Rippetoe to be present, but he had also asked them to let him explain to the boy what they wanted.

As much as it would be to Rachel's advantage to have Taylor identify one of those men, he wanted this to be as fair a test as he could arrange. He hoped that the presence of the others would make Taylor take things more seriously than he might if only Matt and his mother were watching.

He seemed subdued when Rachel led him into the conference room, eyeing the marshal anxiously. When Matt held out his hand, however, Taylor readily put his into it, following him over to the end of the long conference table.

"We've got some pictures we want you to take a look at, Taylor. Did your mom explain that to you?"

The boy nodded, his eyes seeking confirmation from his mother before they came back to Matt's.

"I want you to tell me if you've ever seen any of these

people before. And if you have, I need you to tell me where it was. That's all there is to it. Just tell me if you've seen any one of these men before and where. You understand?''

The child nodded again, looking toward the photographs lined up along the side of the table. He wouldn't be able to see the faces from this angle.

''Take your time and be absolutely sure before you say anything. Okay?''

Another nod.

Matt looked at Rippetoe, raising his brows. The marshal shrugged.

He would undoubtedly have preferred that the photographs be put into some perspective for the child, but Matt felt that even mentioning the scene in the woods would prejudice Taylor's identification. In light of Rachel's concerns, this was the best he could come up with to keep it unsullied.

''Ready?''

Taylor nodded again, turning once more to look at Rachel. She smiled encouragingly at him.

''Okay, take a look and tell me if you've seen any of these people before.''

Matt put his hand on the little boy's back, directing him to the side of the table. Taylor moved slowly down its length, from one picture to the next.

When he reached the last one, the blue eyes lifted to Matt's. He hadn't said a word.

They had known all along it was a long shot, Matt acknowledged, fighting his disappointment. Even if this hadn't worked out as they'd hoped, it had been worth the chance.

''Anybody look familiar?'' he asked, more as a matter of course than in hopes that he'd get an affirmative answer.

The child reached out and touched the bottom edge of the last picture with his forefinger. He pushed it a little so that it slid out of line with the others. Behind him, Matt felt someone stir, either Rippetoe or the chief, leaning forward to see which one the boy had indicated.

"That one look familiar?" Matt prodded, controlling his elation.

The boy nodded, his eyes once more focused on the face in the photograph.

"Are you sure?"

Another nod.

"Taylor, do you remember *where* you saw that man?"

There was a long silence. It seemed that no one in the room breathed as they waited for the child's answer.

"He's the one who picked up the red thing," Taylor said. "He was still holding it when Lisa started yelling."

At the scene and next to that mutilated body.

"And you're sure that's the same man?"

"I saw his face real good when he turned around to look for Lisa. He's one of the men who were in the woods behind the school that day."

Matt's eyes rose to meet Rippetoe's. The marshal nodded once, the motion abrupt, his expression triumphant.

"THEY'LL HANDLE everything," Matt said. "You don't have to worry about a thing. They'll pack up the house and see to it that your personal items follow you to the placement."

"And they decide that, too?"

"If you have a preference for a particular geographic area, you can probably—"

"No, it isn't that," Rachel said quickly. "I was just... curious, I guess."

"All they ask is that you don't contact anyone. If you feel that you must stay in touch with family members, then they ask you to do it through them."

"That won't be a problem. I don't have family," she said. "My father didn't hang around long enough for us to get acquainted. My mother died when I was seventeen."

Shortly before she'd married Akin. He wondered how big a role loneliness had played in that decision.

"What about maintaining contact with an old friend?" she asked. "Or isn't that allowed either?"

The smile that had accompanied the question was slightly tremulous. He knew that she must feel this was all happening too fast. He did. He hadn't been prepared for the speed with which Rippetoe was making the arrangements.

He appreciated the fact that the marshal had gone out of his way to allow him some time alone with Rachel. Rippetoe had taken Taylor to the chief's office with the promise of ice cream and cake.

They had cause for celebration, he supposed, only it didn't feel that way to him. It felt like loss. And grief. The kind he was already too familiar with.

"Actually, they discourage any contact with your past life."

It was the truth, but that didn't make his saying it more palatable. He could see the hurt in her eyes, but she nodded.

"I knew as much, but I thought I should ask. Taylor's going to miss you. I think he was beginning to imagine…" She stopped, taking a breath. "He's always had a vivid imagination."

"He'll be fine. He's a good kid. You've done a good job with him."

Without a father. Without any help at all.

There were a dozen other homilies he could have tacked onto his praise. None of them represented what he really wanted to say.

But then, what he really wanted to say seemed ridiculous. His life was here. He had a job he loved. One he was good at. Or he had thought so until Lisa Evans had disappeared.

He also had friends. In-laws he still cared about. And memories that were infinitely precious.

Throwing all of that away wasn't something you did on the spur of the moment. At least not something he did. His life had consisted of reasoned decisions, meticulously planned and then carried out.

Except for falling in love with Karen. Staying in Mallory. Neither of those had been in his plans. Even Josh had been an accident, he thought, smiling a little at the memory.

Rachel smiled back at him, not realizing that he was remembering another time. Another woman. Another child.

"Thank you," she said. "He is good. I just hope that all this…" She stopped again, letting the sentence trail.

"I could come with you."

The words hadn't even been in his consciousness before they'd been in his mouth. Unplanned, as almost nothing else in his life had ever been.

Except the very best parts of it. As he knew this would be.

"I don't understand," she said, but her eyes said that she did. She just wanted him to put it into words.

She deserved that. She deserved so much more than that.

"If you want me to," he said, "I could come with you."

There was a long silence, their eyes holding.

"As what?" she asked finally.

As whatever you'll let me be.

Once he'd made the offer out loud, everything had

shifted into perspective. His view of his life. The future. Their future.

"Do you mean like…a bodyguard or something?" she asked.

"That wasn't exactly what I had in mind."

"Then…what *did* you have in mind? Exactly."

"I thought that maybe—" He hesitated, wondering if she might accept his idea better if he appealed to her on her son's behalf. "Taylor needs a father. Boys his age do."

Look at me, Daddy. I love you, Daddy.

"Boys of *any* age do," she said. "But if that's the only reason…" She stopped, shaking her head. "No, that's not right. Even if that *is* the only reason—"

"It isn't. You know that. It was just the easiest to get out."

Her lips tilted. "Why was that the easiest?"

"Because we've known each other…I don't know. A few days. Less than a week. It's not the way things are supposed to happen."

"And because of that, you're not sure."

"Are you?" He laughed at the absurdity of being sure of anything on such short acquaintance.

"Of course," she said, her eyes very serious. "Of course, I am."

In the face of that kind of courage, he couldn't let her believe that her son was the only reason he'd made that offer.

"It isn't just Taylor."

"I know."

"They're going to think—" He gestured vaguely toward the rest of the building.

"They're going to think you've lost your mind," she finished for him. "Do you care?"

There was only one thing he cared about, he realized, and it was within his grasp. All he had to do—

All he had to do was reach out and claim it. Claim them. A child who needed him. A woman who wanted him.

He shook his head, the movement slow and deliberate.

"Then come with us. They need good cops everywhere."

He waited. He needed to hear *her* say it, too.

"And we need you. Maybe me more than Taylor. We can start over. We can leave all the bad that's happened to both of us behind and start over together."

"It wasn't all bad."

"I know. And we'll take those memories with us. The good ones. The ones you want to keep. I won't mind them, I promise."

Karen wouldn't mind either. She would *want* him to take care of them. To love them, just the way he had loved her and Josh. As much as he could. For as long as he was able.

"We need to do it right," he said.

"What does that mean?" she asked, but she knew. He could see the knowledge in her eyes.

"Marry me," he said simply. "You and Taylor. You need a new name anyway," he added, smiling at her.

"Yes," she said. "And yes."

"One for you and one for Taylor? You didn't ask him."

"I don't have to. Anyone could see that."

"This isn't just for Taylor," he said quickly, needing to be sure she understood.

"I know," she said softly.

And once more he could tell by her eyes that she really did.

EPILOGUE

"NIGHTMARE?" Matt asked as she took off her robe and slipped into bed beside him.

"Anticipation, I think."

Taylor had been invited to a friend's birthday party and sleepover after school tomorrow. That he felt confident enough to agree to go had been a turning point. One they had all celebrated.

Once he'd made up his mind, the little boy had talked of nothing else all week. Rachel had helped him pack his backpack tonight, and his building excitement had made it difficult for him to settle down. This was the second time she'd gotten up, but this time she'd stayed with him until he had fallen asleep.

Matt put his arms around her, cradling her shivering body against the warmth of his. The renovated ranch house was sturdy and well insulated, but they were predicting several more inches of snow before dawn tomorrow, and the damp chill that preceded them was in the air.

"Is he asleep?" he asked, his breath feathering against the back of her neck.

"Finally."

The warmth of breath became solid, his lips caressing the top of her shoulder.

"Hmm…" She settled more closely against his body, feeling the first stirrings of his erection.

"You like that?"

"Not really," she lied. "I'm just indulging you."

"Then turn around and indulge me some more."

Obligingly she turned over until she was facing him. Despite the weather forecast, the moonlight was bright enough that she could make out his features in the darkness.

"You always wear too many clothes to bed," he said, slipping his hand under the hem of her nightshirt to push it upward.

The sensual abrasion of callused palm moving over her thigh caused another shiver, one that had nothing to do with the cold.

"I'm an old married woman. What do you expect?"

"Silk. Scanty. Seductive."

"You should have thought of that before we ended up in Montana in the winter."

"I like Montana in the winter. All the better for snuggling."

His hand continued its exploration, fingers spread to cover the curve of her hip.

"You think he'll be all right?" she asked, unable to control that niggling anxiety.

"I think he'll be fine. I think you will be, too."

"Was that supposed to be a double entendre?" she asked, smiling.

"It was *supposed* to be reassuring, but you can take it any way you want."

"Then I'll have it missionary style, please."

His hand hesitated. "Missionary style?"

Since she had never before expressed a preference for any of the ways he chose to make love to her, she could understand his surprise.

"It's supposed to be safer," she explained, her pulse

beginning to race at the enormity of what she was about to say.

"*Safer?* For what?"

"For babies," she said softly.

She had thought a long time about how and when to tell him, now that she was sure. For some reason, maybe the hopeful signs of Taylor's progress, tonight just seemed right.

"For *making* babies?" His tone was still puzzled.

"For protecting one."

She waited through the long, breathless silence, praying that his reaction would be the same excitement she had felt.

"A *baby?*"

She could read too little in his repetition of the word. Shock, of course, but none of the important things. Like whether or not he was pleased. She so wanted him to be.

She had known he would be apprehensive. There was no way he couldn't be, having lost a child.

But she was healthy as a horse. Even the doctor she'd seen almost as soon as she suspected had agreed with that assessment. There was no reason for Matt to worry about her *or* the baby. No reason to anticipate that they wouldn't have another perfect son.

Or a daughter, she thought, cherishing that still-secret longing in her heart.

"Well, say something," she prodded.

She put her hand on his chest. Beneath the hair-roughened skin she could feel his increased heartbeat. She allowed her fingers to slide across until they encountered his nipple. Slowly her thumb circled it, causing the small nub to tighten.

"A *baby?*" he said again.

"Cries, eats, sleeps. You remember."

She knew immediately that it had been the wrong thing to say. His body stiffened almost enough to move away physically from hers. To counter that unconscious withdrawal, she leaned forward, putting her face very close to his.

"You could *pretend* to be pleased."

"Are you sure?"

"Given this reaction," she said, smiling at him again to lessen the sting of what must sound like criticism, "do you think I would have told you if I weren't?"

He took a breath, but at the same time his hand came up to shape her face. He drew his thumb across the fullness of her bottom lip, obviously an attempt to rectify the mistake of his less-than-enthusiastic response.

She leaned forward and took his finger into her mouth, holding it gently for a second. When she released it, she placed a small kiss on top of the knuckle.

"It's going to be all right. I promise."

"I know. It was just…a shock."

"It shouldn't have been."

After less than four months of marriage they were, for all intents and purposes, still on their honeymoon. And before she'd had time to find a doctor after the move and get some permanent form of birth control, there had been enough unplanned lovemaking that neither of them should have been surprised at the result.

"A *baby*," he said again, the inflection this time softer. Considering. "Do you know what it is?"

"Not yet. I'm not sure I want to. Do you?"

"I don't know."

They were silent for a moment.

"We don't have to decide that tonight," she said. "I

will be a few weeks before they could tell us, *if* we decide we want to know.''

"You have a preference?''

"Healthy. Perfect.''

"That goes without saying. Nothing beyond that?''

"It doesn't really matter to me. Do you?''

His mouth pursed a little. "Not really.'' And then, "I've never had a daughter.''

That *would* be better, she thought. A new start. New memories to be made.

"I can't guarantee a daughter, of course, but if not this time...we could work on it for the future.''

"I take it you're planning a big family?''

His tension had eased. His voice was again gently teasing. She had always loved the sound of that, especially when she eavesdropped on him with Taylor.

"I never had much family,'' she said. "Not until now. Until us. I just think adding to ours occasionally would be smart. Keep us young,'' she said, smiling at him.

"Are you implying that I'm old?''

She had never been conscious of the nearly nine years that separated them. She hadn't realized at first that the gap between their ages was that wide. And after she had, it seemed perfect to her.

"Hmm. Not exactly *old*...'' Her smile widened.

He leaned forward, finding her lips with his. Then he lifted his mouth only far enough to ask, "Was that some kind of challenge, by any chance?''

"I know better than that,'' she said, laughing.

"Because it sounded like one to me.''

"If you want to take it that way...''

"Or maybe this way...''

He moved suddenly, wrapping his arm around her in

order to carry her with him. She ended up on her back, looking up into his eyes. In the moonlit darkness, they were almost black. Unfathomable. Until he smiled at her.

"Missionary. As requested."

"Not yet, it isn't."

"So damned demanding," he said with a theatrical sigh.

He lowered his head, his mouth closing over hers. The same jolt of sensation she had experienced the first time he kissed her surged through her body again. The reaction to his touch had never lessened in intensity.

Perhaps that was because every day they lived together, what she felt for him grew, nourished by the small unthinking things he did to let her know how much she was loved.

Taking her hand when they were out in public. The reassuring feel of his palm against the small of her back when they walked.

The morning kiss. His genuine interest in her paintings. His encouragement of it. His endless patience with Taylor. *This.*

His body had slipped slightly to the side of hers, his left hip and leg resting on the mattress beside her, his right lying across her thighs. He bent his head, his tongue rimming the nipple of her breast, which was cupped in his right hand.

She laid her cheek against his hair, the now-familiar fragrance of the shampoo he used almost an aphrodisiac, evoking memories of his touch. His kiss. His body moving over hers in the darkness.

It also evoked all the other feelings she associated with him. Safety. Security. Being loved and protected. For someone like her, those were perhaps as important as the way he could make her feel.

His lips trailed lower as his hand continued to caress her

breast. They traced down the center of her rib cage, following the small, concave channel to her navel. His tongue explored it, sending a flood of heat through her veins. Making her bones molten. Weightless.

Her eyes closed, anticipation building as he again changed position. His mouth trailed lower still, as with his tongue and teeth and lips he began to prepare her body for the entry of his.

Her breathing quickened, small gasps and inhalations audible as he touched her. Her reaching fingers found the solid strength of his shoulder, her nails biting into the muscle as his mouth continued to tantalize with the promise of what was to come.

Taking her to the edge of the abyss. And then relentlessly forcing her away from it, only to slowly, so slowly carry her back there once more.

Again and again he brought her almost to climax, seeming to know exactly when to stop. Relieving, for endless moments, the pressure of the demands he made on her senses. Letting her breathing ease. Allowing the clamor of sensitized nerve endings to still and grow quiet.

And then, just as she believed the momentum was forever lost, he would touch her again. Beginning that unhurried progression, which they both knew would ultimately lead to the loss of control she sought above all things.

It happened more quickly now. Almost as soon as his tongue flicked against the most sensitive part of her body, she was at the point of no return. Her fingers tightened convulsively over his arm as she cried out. The involuntary tremors had already begun deep inside, but before they could reach cataclysm, Matt shifted his body over hers.

Face to face. Chest to chest. Hip to hip.

His mouth closed over hers as he entered her, the first

downward stroke sure and powerful. Her hips arched, straining to meet it.

The air thinned around her, thought spiraling away into the darkness to be replaced by pure sensation. On some level she was aware of his movements, aware even when he joined her, his body convulsing above hers. She watched as he threw back his head, the tendons in his neck tight, his mouth open.

The sound that came from deep in his throat was hoarse. Guttural. Primitive.

And it echoed the cry of her heart.

Joyful. Triumphant. Fulfilled.

His body collapsed onto hers, his chest heaving with the depth of his breathing. She welcomed the solid weight of it. The feel of its sweat-dampened skin, subtly masculine, moving against hers.

She put her arms around him, holding him close, their bodies still joined, until gradually the shuddering ecstasy that had gripped them began to ease. Strained muscles quivered and relaxed. Nerve endings flickered slowly into stillness.

After a long time he raised his head. Then he lifted his torso, propping on his elbows above her. Again looking down into her eyes.

"That's hard to believe, isn't it?"

"What?" she asked, willing to be teased.

"That it gets better and better."

"It's not hard for me to believe."

Smiling down at her, he dropped a light kiss on her nose. And then he moved so that his hip was beside hers again. He bent, placing another light kiss on her stomach.

"Hello, baby," he said softly. "Welcome home."

When he straightened to look down on her face again, his features were blurred by her tears.

"Happy crying?" he asked, the note of concern clear.

"The happiest," she assured him, knowing that in all her life, it really was.

* * * * *

I hope you enjoyed IN PLAIN SIGHT. If so, please look for the other Gayle Wilson stories coming in the near future. Harlequin Intrigue will publish two more PHOENIX BROTHERHOOD titles this year, SIGHT UNSEEN in July and the other in October. Then, in early 2005, I'll have another single title romantic suspense on the shelves from Harlequin's new imprint HQN. Until then, happy reading!

Gayle

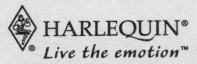

Forrester Square

LEGACIES . LIES . LOVE .

Coming in April 2004...
a brand-new Forrester Square tale!

ILLEGALLY YOURS

by favorite
Harlequin American Romance® author

JACQUELINE DIAMOND

Determined to stay in America despite an
expired visa, pregnant Kara Tamaki turned to
attorney Daniel Adler for help. Daniel wasn't an
immigration lawyer, but he knew how to help
Kara stay in America—marry her!

Forrester Square...Legacies. Lies. Love.

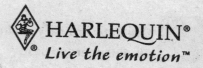

HARLEQUIN®
Live the emotion™

Coming in April 2004
to Silhouette Books

Gideon Faulkner had lived a life in captivity, kidnapped and brainwashed years ago by the Coalition. But he had found a way to sneak into the outside world, and finally had a chance to find his real family...and true love!

Five extraordinary siblings.

One dangerous past.

Unlimited potential.

If you enjoyed what you just read,
then we've got an offer you can't resist!

Take 2 bestselling novels FREE!
Plus get a FREE surprise gift!

Clip this page and mail it to The Best of the Best™

IN U.S.A.
3010 Walden Ave.
P.O. Box 1867
Buffalo, N.Y. 14240-1867

IN CANADA
P.O. Box 609
Fort Erie, Ontario
L2A 5X3

YES! Please send me 2 free Best of the Best™ novels and my free surprise gift. After receiving them, if I don't wish to receive anymore, I can return the shipping statement marked cancel. If I don't cancel, I will receive 4 brand-new novels every month, before they're available in stores! In the U.S.A., bill me at the bargain price of $4.74 plus 25¢ shipping and handling per book and applicable sales tax, if any*. In Canada, bill me at the bargain price of $5.24 plus 25¢ shipping and handling per book and applicable taxes**. That's the complete price and a savings of over 20% off the cover prices—what a great deal! I understand that accepting the 2 free books and gift places me under no obligation ever to buy any books. I can always return a shipment and cancel at any time. Even if I never buy another The Best of the Best™ book, the 2 free books and gift are mine to keep forever.

185 MDN DNWF
385 MDN DNWG

Name	(PLEASE PRINT)
Address	Apt.#
City	State/Prov. Zip/Postal Code

* Terms and prices subject to change without notice. Sales tax applicable in N.Y.
** Canadian residents will be charged applicable provincial taxes and GST.
  All orders subject to approval. Offer limited to one per household and not valid to
  current The Best of the Best™ subscribers.
  ® are registered trademarks of Harlequin Enterprises Limited.

BOB02-R   ©1998 Harlequin Enterprises Limited